"I don[...]
at the [...]

Raine said.

"Ah, yes, I remember now. I can try again in five years."

"You've got it."

Trevor laughed, a truly unrestrained, amused sound, holding no rancor. "You've got to be kidding."

"There are other things in life besides sex."
Oh, God, she thought, *I sound like a repressed maiden aunt.*

"I couldn't agree more," he said smoothly. "However, making love is a nice, pleasant diversion from lofty, cerebral pursuits, and a natural enough activity for normal, healthy people."

"So is swimming."

"But not nearly so satisfying."

She smiled sweetly. "I'm sorry I can't be your partner in your quest for satisfying exercise."

Dear Reader,

Welcome to Silhouette **Special Edition** . . . welcome to romance. Each month Silhouette **Special Edition** publishes six novels with you in mind—stories of love and life, tales that you can identify with—as well as dream about.

And this December brings six wonderful tales of love! Sherryl Woods's warm, tender series, VOWS, concludes with Brandon Halloran's romance— *Cherish*. Brandon finally meets up again with his first love, beautiful Elizabeth Forsythe. Yes, Virginia, as long as there is life and love, dreams *do* come true!

Heralding in the Christmas spirit this month is *It Must Have Been the Mistletoe* by Nikki Benjamin. This winsome, poignant story will bring a tear to your eye and a smile to your lips!

Rounding out this month of holiday cheer are books from other favorite writers: Trisha Alexander, Ruth Wind, Patricia Coughlin and Mona van Wieren.

I hope that you enjoy this book and all the stories to come. Happy holidays from all of us at Silhouette Books!

Sincerely,

Tara Gavin
Senior Editor
Silhouette Books

P.S.—We've got an extra special surprise next month to start off the New Year right. I'll give you a hint—it begins with a wonderful book by Ginna Gray called *Building Dreams!*

MONA VAN WIEREN

A PRINCE AMONG MEN

SPECIAL EDITION®

Published by Silhouette Books New York
America's Publisher of Contemporary Romance

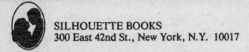

I want to thank Jopie Huisman for the enjoyment
I have received from his wonderful paintings,
especially the painting of the two dolls,
Vriendschap (Friendship),
a reproduction of which I have hanging in my home.

SILHOUETTE BOOKS
300 East 42nd St., New York, N.Y. 10017

A PRINCE AMONG MEN

ISBN: 0-373-09783-2

First Silhouette Books printing December 1992

Printed in the U.S.A.

Books by Mona van Wieren

Silhouette Special Edition
A Prince Among Men #783

Silhouette Romance
Rhapsody in Bloom #630

MONA VAN WIEREN

was born in Holland, where she started writing short stories in Dutch. She met her American husband in Amsterdam and later married him in Kenya, where he was a Peace Corps volunteer. Her husband's work as a development economist has also given them opportunity to spend several years in Ghana and Indonesia.

"Writing in English was a challenge at first, but with the encouragement of my husband I kept going and finally made it into print." Mona now lives in Virginia with her husband and three children. She has also published books under the pseudonym Karen van der Zee. Her first Silhouette Romance novel, *Rhapsody in Bloom,* won the Romance Writers of America's RITA Award for Best Traditional Romance in 1989.

North Sea

Sneek

The Farmhouse

Amsterdam

Utrecht

Den Haag

Rotterdam

THE NETHERLANDS

GERMANY

BELGIUM

N

All underlined places are fictitious.

Prologue

The girl in the photo looked at him with crystalline green eyes. There was a haunting quality about that face, that red hair, those melancholy eyes. It stirred something deep inside him, a feeling, a memory. Strange for a photograph to have such an impact on him.

He returned his gaze to the woman behind the desk. An elegant lady, her gray eyes cool, her makeup immaculate, her clothes fashionable. He hadn't seen her in years, but she was aging beautifully. Maybe it was the health food that did it. It made him smile. Who'd ever have thought that this spoiled, rich Chicago woman would have it in her to start her own health food company and make a big success of it?

He glanced back at the photo of the red-haired girl and tapped the glass. "Your niece."

"Yes."

"I remember her. All that red hair, those eyes. I met her once, at a party, about ten years ago, I think." She'd been a young kid then, fourteen or something, and she'd just moved into Wanda's glass-and-chrome apartment. He remembered her—wounded, withdrawn, sitting on the fringes of the party, her eyes as desolate as any he had ever seen, a sparrow among the birds of paradise. Wanda's parties were always glamorous affairs.

"Yes." Wanda's perfectly chiseled mouth curved. "And before you ask—no, I have no idea where she is."

"You have no idea where she is," he repeated, raising his brows in surprise.

"She simply vanished several months ago. She was working for me at the time. I wanted her to take over for me eventually." She glanced down at her lap, stroking the little gray cat that lay there, purring contentedly. "Then one day she told me she was leaving. She just walked out of here."

He glanced at the picture. "Why?"

A slight pause. He noticed the almost imperceptible twitch of muscles on the beautiful face. The cool gray eyes blinked.

"I don't know," said Wanda.

She's lying, he thought. *She knows why. She's not prepared to tell me. And why should she?*

Once Wanda had been married to an English uncle of his and he would see her on occasion at family get-togethers. Later, after the divorce, he'd seen her only once or twice. And now he was here to see if they could do some business together. No bosom buddies, for sure.

Yet he was oddly curious, as he had been curious ten years ago when he'd first seen the girl, Raine. To think that this cool, emotionless woman had taken in the skinny waif in braces had surprised him. Wanda was not the nurturing type, and looking at the freckled teenager with the sorrowful eyes, it was clear that a lot of nurturing would be in order. He had left the country soon after the party for a long-term assignment in Guatemala and he had forgotten Wanda and the girl.

Only now the memories of that night surfaced again with surprising clarity.

"Have you tried to find her?" he asked.

Wanda went on stroking the cat. "I hired an investigator. He couldn't find her." Her voice was low and husky, a sexy voice, he imagined, were it not for her businesslike tone.

"I'm sorry," he said, wondering where a girl like Raine would flee. Flee. What made him think she had fled? And she was no longer a girl now, but a grown woman of twenty-four or -five who could go wherever she pleased.

Wanda shifted in her chair and the little cat leapt to the floor. "Anyway," she said, dismissing the subject of Raine, "let's get back to business."

So they did. But it was difficult for him to keep his mind on tropical fruit juices and his eyes off the photo.

"Come for dinner," Wanda said as he got up to leave to go to another meeting. "Stay the night."

"I was planning to stay at a hotel," he said.

She waved his words away with a hand sparkling with rings and shiny with nail gloss. "There's no need to. I have a perfectly good guest room. Besides, I'd like to catch up, talk about that island of yours. What about the rain forests? Are they doing anything with them?"

His first inclination was to decline her invitation, but her interest surprised him, and something in her eyes, her voice, made him accept.

At seven sharp, a taxi dropped him off at Wanda's luxurious apartment building, the same place where he had met Raine at the party so many years ago.

A maid let him in and preceded him to the living room. The place was much as he remembered it, all gleaming glass and shiny chrome. White rugs, white walls. Black leather sofa and chairs. A huge marble coffee table. Everything was cold and sleek except for a couple of surprising touches—a crystal bowl of crimson roses on the table and a huge modern abstract on one wall, all white and black with a violent streak of passionate red, like a scream across the middle.

Dressed in loose black silk pants and a white tunic, Wanda was sitting on the floor, a cardboard box next to her, papers in front of her, a highball glass in one hand. There was a wild, excited look in her eyes.

He stared at her in astonishment. Was this the same woman he had seen at her imposing desk in her sumptuous office this afternoon?

"Look at this!" She held out a stack of paper and he took it from her, glancing at them. They were college newspapers and there was nothing unusual that he could see. Wanda's eyes glittered.

"She wrote for them," she said in a low voice. "Every week there's something of hers in there."

He leafed through the papers, finding Raine's byline, reading the headlines, overwhelmed by curiosity.

"She won a short story contest," Wanda went on. "Look, it's written up in this article. I didn't know. I never knew she wrote."

"Didn't she tell you?"

"She didn't tell me much when she was in college." Wanda took out more papers, notebooks, textbooks, spreading everything around her on the floor, a harvest of secrets, a treasure of information. "I found it in her closet when I looked for some blankets. She must have overlooked it when she left." She raked a hand through her hair, which looked less than immaculate. "I'm a terrible hostess. I do apologize. Let me get you a drink. What would you like?"

There was a wet bar in the corner of the room. "I'll have a Scotch. I'll get it myself." He crossed the room, helping himself to a drink, trying to make sense of the strange scene.

He glanced around the room again, wondering about the fourteen-year-old girl with the coppery hair and desolate eyes growing up in these beautiful, cold surroundings. It seemed wrong, somehow. Very wrong.

Wanda's attention was back on the papers. "I want to find her," she said, her voice frantic. "I've got to find her."

"Maybe she'll come back of her own accord," he said, taking a healthy draft of his whiskey. "You're her only family, aren't you?" Another small fact that had lodged itself in his memory.

He saw her body tense, her knuckles turn white. "She won't come back. I know she'll never come back."

He saw fear in her eyes, and something else he could not identify. She was hiding something, but he didn't have the heart to ask her what.

Wanda was not a woman who inspired pity, but as he watched her sitting there on the floor, surrounded by paper, he could only feel sorry for her.

The face had haunted him again all night. The clear green eyes, the heavy mass of copper hair, the warm, sensuous mouth, smiling faintly. Months since he'd seen her picture and still her image intruded in his sleep.

He threw off the sheet in exasperation. The trade wind breeze blew in through the open window, cooling his damp body. He heard the rustling of the palm fronds outside, the cacophony of chirping and shrieking of crickets and other nocturnal creatures. He was not the only one awake. He stood in front of the window and looked out over the placid waters of the Caribbean, glimmering darkly in the silver light of a ripe moon.

He was going crazy.

What was it about her that wouldn't leave him alone? Was it the photo? The words she had written that kept echoing in his mind? The things Wanda had told him about her? But all of that had been months ago...

It had been the strangest night of his life, sitting in Wanda's apartment, reading Raine's articles, looking at photographs Wanda had dug up from a drawer, listening to Wanda's stories.

He dragged his hands through his hair and sighed. He could not go on losing sleep over a woman he didn't even know, a woman he'd last seen when she was just a girl. He was thirty-five years old, not a romantic teenager with an overactive imagination. He liked a woman in the flesh, not an elusive image on paper, an image he'd created from memory, photos, stories, written words.

There were other things too, other images, another face. The cool gray eyes of another woman. Words, spoken calmly, without emotion. *I have no idea where she is. She has simply vanished.*

And again that same woman, her eyes wild. *I have to find her. I've got to find her.*

And the question still lingered in his mind: What was it that Wanda wasn't telling him? What was it that made him feel sorry for her?

And then yesterday her phone call. One of several over the past few months, mostly dealing with business, but always, always with some small, cool, offhand mention of Raine.

But this time no reference to business.

"I know where she is," Wanda had said, her voice cool.

There'd been no need to ask who, so he'd asked where.

"Holland."

Holland. His stomach tightened. His ticket to Amsterdam lay in the top drawer of his desk along with his passport in preparation for contract negotiations for a project in the Netherlands Antilles, small islands off the coast of Venezuela. And Wanda was aware of his trip.

"I see," he said carefully.

"I'd like you to go see her."

Silence quivered over the phone wires. He did not know what to say.

"Please," said Wanda. "Just find out how she is doing. You're going to be there anyway."

Which, undeniably, was true. And, undeniably, the request was a reasonable one.

"I'll have to think about it," he'd said, feeling ambivalent, and not sure why.

Thinking back to that conversation, he let out a groan of frustration and turned away from the window. Taking a towel from the bathroom, he walked naked across the cool tile floors of the villa, out the back door and down the narrow path leading to the beach. Maybe a swim would do him good. Some exercise to calm down the restlessness stirring inside him, to make him tired enough to fall asleep again.

Swimming had helped after Suzanna had left. That, and long hikes in the rain forest in the mountains. Suzanna had never wanted to go on these hikes. She didn't like bugs, she'd said, nor snakes and creeping greenery. Suzanna liked working out in nice clean health clubs. No bugs. Air-conditioning.

He had loved her, beautiful Suzanna with her dark hair, her brown eyes, her infectious laugh. She was a dynamo of energy, always on the go. She was intelligent and independent and sexy. Yet her intensity had begun to grate on him, more so after he had moved to the island.

Suzanna hadn't liked much of anything about the island. She grew restless and bored after two days. "How can you stand it?" she'd asked. "The place is stagnant! Nothing happens here! You can't even see a decent movie! What possessed you to leave civilization and move here?"

He stepped carefully along the dark, rocky path, hearing small creatures rustle around in the undergrowth. He took in a deep breath, inhaling the clean, salty air, feeling the breeze caressing his body. This was why he was here: the peacefulness, the clean air, the sea. He could step out of his house onto his own small beach and swim any time of day or night. He no longer felt like a caged rat in his high-rise apartment in New York.

It was the rat race that had driven him here, the polluted air, the craziness of rushing in and out of airports all the time, of coming home to a place where he felt trapped.

His work as an agricultural economist had initially taken him all over the world. After he'd become an independent consultant he'd concentrated on work in the Caribbean and Central America, sometimes spending weeks at a time in the islands. Coming home to New York had become increasingly unpleasant.

The sand was powder-soft under his feet. He dropped the towel and waded out into the warm water. It was shallow for some time, but when he hit depth, he struck out and began to swim with even rhythmic butterfly strokes.

At first his body slipped effortlessly through the water, then his muscles began to feel the strain. The exertion felt good, exorcising the tension that had taken possession of his body like an alien force.

He turned on his back and floated on the calm water, relaxing his tired muscles. The sky was alive with stars. He liked looking at the stars, wondering about galaxies far away, about possible life on other planets.

He grimaced. Life on this planet took energy enough. Working in the islands wasn't always easy. The poverty was depressing, the solutions few. So many tiny islands with so little economic potential. Yet people deserved a decent life. Children deserved good food and education and health care. It was an obscenity that there were hunger and poverty in the world at all, with so much money, so much food, so many resources to go around.

Only they weren't going around very efficiently.

Most of the world's food and wealth were stuck in a few special places. Ending hunger and poverty was not a priority in everyone's life, nor was it a priority on the political and economic agenda of every nation.

In his own way he did what he did best. He worked with governments, companies, agencies and businessmen to find solutions, to increase agricultural output, improve livestock quality, find new crops for export, plan strategies, find new resources. It was work that gave much satisfaction, despite its many frustrations. Coming to St. Barlow to live had been good for him.

He turned over. It was time to go back, see if he could catch some more sleep before the sun would chase the night away.

By the time he reached the beach, he felt thoroughly relaxed. He rubbed his hair and face with the towel and slowly made his way up the narrow path. The house lay silent and dark in the shadows. It was a small, simple house, with a tiled terrace surrounded by flowering hibiscus. He had not wanted an opulent villa, though there had been two for sale on the island when he'd come looking. The luxury of them had seemed obscene on this small, poor island where people barely scraped by growing bananas or herding a few goats.

Inside, he dried himself more thoroughly and lay back down on the bed, pulling the sheet up to his chest. His limbs relaxed against the mattress, heavy and still. He closed his eyes. Yet fate was not kind. Deep sleep eluded him, and all he managed was to doze fitfully, tossing and turning.

And all the time he saw in his mind the woman with the red hair and the green eyes. And he could hear Wanda's frantic voice on the fringes of his consciousness. *I have to find her... I know she won't come back. She'll never come back.*

Green, melancholy eyes, smiling at him.

At five he gave in and sat up. He covered his face, as if trying to force the image out. It stayed right there where it had been for the past several months.

He hadn't seen her in ten years. Maybe this was what happened to men living alone on tropical islands. They started suffering from delusions. They turned eccentric, like General Meecham, the old bald Brit who was writing the history of the island. Obsessed and absorbed, all he could talk about was pirates and wars. He'd lost all sense of the present time and escaped into the past, which was full of romance. And blood and gore.

Obsession.

That's what it was. The craziness inside him was turning into an obsession. And it was getting worse as time went by. He listened to the rustling of palms outside his window, the soft swishing of the water splashing onto the beach. Whisperings in the dark. Messages hidden in code.

There was only one thing he could do to help himself.

He had to find her.

Chapter One

It was a true *eyes-met-across-a-crowded-room* moment. Raine stood frozen as her eyes met the dark penetrating black ones. The noise of the party around her stilled—no more voices speaking in four or five languages, no more tinkling of ice in glasses, no more laughter.

For a moment there was nothing but those eyes looking at her.

The tray with canapés trembled precariously in her hands. She tore away her gaze and forced herself to walk calmly from the room, feeling his eyes boring holes in her back.

In the kitchen she put the tray down and let out a deep sigh. Kim was bending over, taking a sheet of tiny pastries from the oven. Her face was flushed as she straightened. Her big brown eyes settled on Raine's face and she frowned. "What's the matter?"

Raine lifted the heavy weight of her hair away from her neck. "There's a man out there," she said.

Kim cocked an eyebrow. "No kidding," she said dryly. "I thought there were at least fifty. Of every available European make and a few others."

Raine sat down on a stool. "He was looking at me."

"I'll be darned. What a shock."

"Oh, stop it, Kim!" Raine laughed. "He was looking straight through me. He has the blackest eyes I've ever seen. It was weird. He gave me the creeps."

"What did he look like?"

"Like the devil." She saw him in her mind's eye—the mop of black curly hair, the ruggedly featured face with its deep tan.

Kim grinned, her eyes gleaming. "Oh, goodie!" She transferred the hors d'oeuvres onto a serving platter. They were pieces of art, each and everyone, handcrafted by the two of them. "Let's get back in there and have a look at him. Is he Dutch?"

"How do I know? I didn't hear him speak. He was all the way on the other end of the room. I only saw his eyes, and his face."

"It's getting fascinatinger and fascinatinger," Kim said. She frowned in concentration. "Maybe it's love at first sight. He's wild about tall redheads and the moment he saw you he decided you were the one for him and he couldn't tear his eyes away."

Raine groaned. "Oh, please spare me your fantasies."

"You should have your own. No, you shouldn't. You should have a real-life, wild and passionate love affair."

"Dutch men don't strike me as the wild and passionate type."

Kim grinned and winked. "You'd be surprised."

Kim had married a Dutch engineer right after both she and Raine had finished their master's in Chicago. Kim was her best friend, and Raine hadn't been happy to see her depart for foreign shores, though she had certainly been happy for Kim. Kim had managed to catch herself a prince among men. Next to her golden boy, Kim had said, all men, foreign or domestic, were mere toads.

"Great," Raine had said, "where does that leave me?"

"I may be exaggerating," Kim admitted. "Surely there is a prince for you, too." So far, however, none had materialized.

Kim's departure had left a great hole of emptiness in Raine's life. Secretly Raine had felt abandoned, a sentiment she had never verbalized of course, because it was unfair and unreasonable, but there it was nonetheless.

And then, on that nightmarish day six months ago, Kim's letter had arrived from Holland. It had been a day when Raine had thought she had no one left to turn to and what she needed more than anything was a friend, a little salvation, a little good fortune. The letter had presented her everything.

Kim had written that her friends Kees and Femke Beintema were leaving for Morocco for a year and needed someone to stay in their remodeled yuppie farmhouse and take care of their assortment of farm animals. "This is your chance!" she'd written. "Come and write that torrid novel you've been dying to do. Dump Wicked Wanda. Come to Holland and LIVE!" It had sounded like an advertisement slogan. Kim was good with words. So was Raine. In college they'd worked on the college newspaper together. Raine had won prizes in short story competitions. There was an editor in New York who'd seen her novel proposal and was interested in it.

Raine had called the instant she'd received the letter, giving no thought to time and distance, and had caught Kim sleeping the sleep of the innocent at twelve midnight.

"It sounds perfect," Raine had said to a very groggy Kim, "especially the sheep and goats. I'm not sure I'll know one from the other."

So she had left for Holland, leaving Wanda, leaving a job and a life she could no longer tolerate.

She was happy here in the peaceful serenity of the Dutch countryside. She was happy to have Kim back in her life. But she was very busy and preoccupied and there was no time for men, at least not now, not for a while.

After the Michael fiasco she'd not been very serious about her relationships with men. Most of them bored her. She hadn't felt any raging passion for any of the men who had crossed her path, maybe because she hadn't wanted to. Then again, it was hard to feel very serious about a man who valued his collection of obscene oriental carvings, or a man who still slept with his raggedy boyhood teddy bear.

"Good God, Raine!" Kim had exclaimed more than once. "Where do you find these nuts?"

They'd been amusing, and that was about it. No heartstoppers, but good for a laugh. Now she didn't want to bother. It was all just a waste of time, and time was precious.

"I have no time for men," she said to Kim. "I'm writing a book, you may recall." She spread her arms wide in a theatrical gesture. "I'm going to make something of myself!"

Kim groaned. "Oh, Lord, yes, the Five-Year Plan. Raine, you're out of your mind. You can't plan life. You can't force fate."

"Watch me."

In five years Raine intended to be a writer earning an income with which she could support herself. By all accounts, this was an ambitious goal, if not an impossible one. Marriage and kids would come after that. She wanted to get married and have a family, but not yet. If she didn't get herself established first, she'd never make it.

Kim rolled her eyes, picked up the serving platter and swung out of the large kitchen. "You're out of your mind, Raine."

Out of her mind or not, Raine had never felt happier and more at peace. She knew why. For the first time, she felt in control. For the first time in years she was doing what she wanted to do. It was as if some heavy weight of duty and guilt had been lifted from her.

Raine followed Kim out with her own tray. Kim was small and slim, with short dark hair. Both of them were wearing long black harem pants of soft flowing material and white silky blouses.

Kim had talked her into helping her cater the party at the sailing school, just for the fun of it, for old times' sake. They'd done it in college in Chicago to make money. They didn't need the money now. Besides, it was probably illegal for Americans to work in Holland without a work permit, but for this once it was fun and they were doing Max a favor. Max was Kim's brother-in-law and he owned the sailing school. Every spring and summer groups of students and young people would come from all over Europe and learn to sail. He also owned a modest fleet of cabin cruisers, which were rented out during the summer months.

The sound of voices and laughter enveloped her as they entered the large room. Normally this was the dining room, but most of the tables and chairs had been put away.

The man was still there. Raine was aware of him without even seeing him, felt a prickling sensation travel down her spine.

"Who is it?" Kim whispered.

Raine glanced around. "The tall one by the glass doors, talking to Max." They could only see his back and the wild, black hair.

Kim gave a low whistle. "He's gorgeous. Look at those shoulders, that physique!"

"Watch your mouth, you're married!"

Kim laughed. "A girl can look, can't she? Besides, I'm not looking for myself. I'm doing it for you."

"I can do my own looking, thank you very much."

"No, you can't. Your track record is abysmal. All toads, every one of them. Now, let's get over there and offer the man some goodies."

They weaved their way through the crowd of guests, offering canapés, smiling, Raine not understanding more than the odd word of all the Dutch and German and French floating around them.

It was a cosmopolitan party of sailing aficionados and boating enthusiasts who gathered every year in the northern province of Friesland where they spent time on the lakes sailing and cruising on their yachts or checking out the facilities for schools and sports clubs.

They'd reached the other end of the room. Beyond the large windows stretched the lake, glimmering peacefully under a full moon. Kim held out her tray and smiled at Max and the dark stranger. He was wearing casual khaki slacks and an exotically flowered shirt in muted browns and greens. They were speaking English. "Would you care for one of these?" Kim asked, smiling pleasantly.

The men each took one of the hot tidbits, smiling back at Kim. Raine braced herself as the stranger's dark gaze slid away from Kim and settled on her face. "May I try one of these?" he asked politely, taking a cheese puff from Raine's tray. He was American, no doubt about it. His voice was deep and a bit gravelly and it fitted his looks perfectly.

She smiled politely. The black eyes held hers, much too long for normal courtesy, and she felt the heat race through her body.

"You're staring at me," she said tightly.

An odd expression flitted across his face. "It's your hair. You've got the most beautiful coppery hair I've ever seen."

She almost dropped the platter in her hands. *He's wild about tall redheads.* Kim's words were still fresh in her mind and the uncanny coincidence momentarily threw her off balance. Quickly she gathered her composure and gave him a cool look. She didn't know what to say, so she turned and walked off without a word.

She circulated among the guests until her tray was nearly empty, all the while aware of the man's intense gaze following her around the room. She tried to avoid looking in his direction, but as if a magnet drew her, she couldn't help meeting up with his eyes. He was mingling as she was and when he appeared in front of her suddenly, it startled her. She knocked a glass out of a guest's hand, splashing wine onto the floor, but luckily missing the woman's dress.

She made her apologies to the woman, threw the man a furious glance and marched out to the kitchen to find some paper towels to clean the floor. He was right behind her.

"I'm sorry I startled you," he said. "Let me clean it up. It was my fault."

She glared at him. "Just leave me alone! Stop looking at me!"

He was about to say something, then apparently changed his mind. She went into the kitchen and closed the door behind her. Damn that man!

"What's wrong?" Kim asked, giving her a puzzled look.

"He made me knock a glass out of somebody's hand. He keeps looking at me! What's the matter with him?" She found paper towels, stormed out, mopped up the wine and went back into the kitchen.

Kim was filling several small bowls with marinated mushrooms. "Listen to what I found out about him," she said, her voice full of barely contained excitement.

"I don't care to know anything about him," stated Raine bravely. This, of course, was not true and she knew it. Any woman with a beating heart who met a man the likes of the intriguing stranger would want to know more.

"I asked Max," Kim went on, ignoring Raine's statement. "His name is Trevor Lloyd. He's American but he lives on some obscure little island in the Caribbean and he's here on business. He's rented a cabin cruiser from Max and that's where he's living right now."

Raine wondered what kind of business an American living in the Caribbean was doing in the Netherlands, then pushed the thought away. She didn't care what he was doing here.

"I think he's fascinating," Kim went on. "Rugged and mysterious. I like his looks. A real pirate type, you know. All that's missing is a gold earring and a black patch over his eye."

Raine groaned. "Oh, please, do me a favor."

Kim laughed and put more trays of food in the oven. She closed the door and straightened, smiling at Raine. "Think of the possibilities here. You..." Kim's voice trailed and her smile faded. Her face turned ashen. She made an awkward gesture, reaching for the counter, but her hands slipped away and she slumped to the floor.

Raine thought her heart would stop. "Oh, my God," she whispered and sank down on her knees next to Kim, who lay out cold on the floor. In a panic Raine jumped up and ran for the door.

"Max!" she called out across the room, her voice touched with hysteria. "Max, come quick!" People looked at her strangely. The talking ceased instantly as if someone had turned a switch, the sudden silence eerie in the crowded room. Moments later Max was in the kitchen and so was the man named Trevor Lloyd.

"Kim..." Raine gulped for air. "She fainted."

Both men knelt down by her side.

"Open the outside door," the stranger ordered. "We need more air in here."

"How did it happen?" Max asked, gently straightening Kim's left arm.

Raine's heart was pounding, her legs shaking. It terrified her to see Raine lying on the floor, pale, unconscious. She swallowed hard. "She was putting something in the oven and then she straightened and she turned white and I saw her grab the counter and the next thing she was falling over. I couldn't even catch her, it all went so fast."

"Did she eat dinner?" the stranger asked.

"Dinner? Yes, eh, we had some take-out Chinese we brought with us."

Max came to his feet. "I'll call the doctor."

Kim began to stir.

"She'll be all right," the other man said.

Kim was coming to, blinking her eyes and looking dazed. Max lifted her up into a sitting position, resting her back against the wall.

"What's going on?" she muttered, looking disoriented. "Why are you all here? Why am I on the floor?"

"You fainted." Raine went down on her knees again. "Oh, Kim, what's the matter with you?"

"I fainted? I've never fainted in my life. It was the craziest feeling...." She closed her eyes and sighed, as if she were very tired.

Max moved to the door. "I'll call the doctor," he said again.

"No, no," Kim muttered. "I'll be fine. There's nothing wrong with me. It must have been the heat from the oven or something." She sighed again. "Just give me a drink, brandy or something. No, no, make that tea."

The dark man frowned. "You need a doctor, not a cup of tea. And you don't faint when nothing is wrong."

Raine watched in amazement as Kim began to smile. She folded her hands in her lap. "Nothing is wrong," she repeated slowly. "It's very, very right."

Raine felt concern rise. "Kim, what are you talking about?"

Kim's smile lit up her face. "I'm pregnant," she said. "I'm sure I am. I don't need a doctor just now, I shouldn't have alcohol, so I'll have tea."

Max rolled his eyes heavenward. "Pregnant women. I'm out of here." He opened the door and fled. "I'll call Menno," he tossed over his shoulder.

Raine laughed. "Some hero." Max's own wife had only recently delivered their first baby. Raine, on her knees, hugged Kim. "Oh, Kim, that's wonderful!"

Not long ago Kim had told her she'd been having trouble getting pregnant. Menno and she had been trying for four months, which she considered an eternity and no book or doctor was going to tell her otherwise. Raine looked at Kim's flushed face. "I'm so happy for you." She came to her feet again and filled a glass of water. "Here, drink some of this and then I'll make some tea."

She was suddenly aware of the stranger leaning casually against the counter, arms crossed in front of his chest, his black eyes gleaming with amusement. She was amazed she had actually forgotten about him in the heat of excitement.

"Perhaps you'd rather escape, too?" she suggested helpfully, wishing he would go.

"Not in the least." He pushed himself away from the counter, picked up the kettle and filled it with water. "How about if I make a cup of tea for the pregnant lady?"

"I can do it," said Raine. "No need for you to—"

"Raine! The oven! Those shrimp things!" Kim was trying to come to her feet and Raine grabbed hold of her. The man plunked the kettle down, opened the oven door and extracted the two trays. "They're fine," he said. "Didn't you set the timer?"

"I neglected to think of it as I passed out," Kim said dryly as she sat down in a chair at the kitchen table. "Not very efficient of me."

He smiled. "Sorry." He turned on the gas under the kettle.

Kim lowered her head on the table. "I feel limp like a wash rag."

"Fainting is hard work."

Kim lifted her head again. "Anyway, who are you? I think we should introduce ourselves." She waved her hand weakly. "You do it, Raine."

She had no choice. "That's Kim and I'm Raine," she said evenly. "We're the caterers."

"Trevor Lloyd." He pushed his hands in his pockets and leaned against the counter. "What are two American women doing catering a party in Holland?"

"This is not Holland," Kim said with the voice of a worn-out grade school teacher. "This is Friesland, which is part of the Netherlands. Don't tell Friesians they're from Holland. It's like telling the Scotch they're English."

His mouth curled. "I'll try to remember that."

Raine transferred the hot shrimp balls to a serving platter and Trevor took it from her. "I'll take these out. You take care of your friend. The water is about to boil." He opened the door and was gone with the tray. Raine looked at Kim, who shrugged.

"Max is back at the bar, the pirate is passing out the food—we might as well have a cup of tea." The kettle shrieked in agreement. Raine made the tea and put two more trays of hors d'oeuvres in the oven to heat. Other platters with cold snacks stood ready on the counter.

Fifteen minutes later, Trevor was back in the kitchen, followed by Menno, Kim's tall, handsome husband, the prince among toads. His usually relaxed features were tense and his deep blue eyes looked worried as his gaze fixed on Kim.

"Max shouldn't have called you," Kim said, smiling at him.

"Yes he should have." He moved over to her chair and touched her cheek. "Are you all right?"

Kim's eyes were shining. She looked young and girlish. "I'm fine, just fine."

"I'll take you home."

"I can't leave! I've got to finish—"

"I'll do it," Raine said. "I can handle it, don't worry about it. I'd feel better if you were home, Kim, really."

"I'll give you a hand," Trevor said, looking at Raine, his dark eyes determined.

Kim protested some more, but Menno was hearing none of it and moments later the two of them were gone and Raine was left alone with Trevor.

"What would you like me to do?" he asked.

Go away and leave me alone, she wanted to tell him, but didn't. "I can handle this by myself," she said, trying to be polite. "Really, everything is done except passing things around and the cleanup afterward. It's no problem."

"Why don't you let me serve the hungry masses out there?"

"I'm sure you have better things to do. You came to socialize or talk business, I assume, not help out in the kitchen." She turned away, dismissing him, and put the tea cups in the dishwasher, still avoiding his gaze.

He was not to be dismissed.

"I get bored real easy," he said casually. "Especially at social affairs like this. Do me a favor, put me to work."

She had the distinct feeling he wasn't going to give up. He didn't look like a man who gave up, which was not reassuring. What she wanted was for him to get out of the kitchen. One way to do that was to give him something to do in the party room.

She shrugged and indicated a tray full of hors d'oeuvres. "All right, if you insist. Take these." Then, turning away, she opened the refrigerator and scanned the contents. Behind her the door swung open and closed and she let out a sigh of relief. Maybe he wouldn't come back.

No such luck, of course, but hope springs eternal. He marched in just as she was taking the two large trays of hot appetizers out of the oven.

"Did you make all this stuff?" he asked.

"Kim and I did. We used to cater parties when we were in college." The previous days they'd spent hours in Kim's kitchen making bacon and liver roll-up, Greek cheese and spinach triangles, tiny quiches, stuffed dates and all kinds of other fancy doodads.

"Pretty enterprising."

"Kim's mother has her own catering business. Kim worked with her for years, so she knew what to do. I learned from Kim. It was better than washing dishes or flipping hamburgers and—" she stopped herself, biting her tongue and suppressing a sudden smile.

"And what?" he asked.

She looked at him levelly. "And a good way to meet men. At least Kim said so."

He raised one brow, clearly amused. "You don't agree?"

"I've never yet met an interesting man when I catered a party." She gave him a stony stare. He had to be deaf, dumb and stupid not to get the message.

His eyes held hers. "Ah, you must be very discriminating."

She smiled sweetly. "Very."

"What about Kim? Did she meet her husband at one of these affairs?"

"No. She met him at a meat counter in a supermarket in Chicago. He pretended to be a helpless foreigner in need of assistance. Kim took one look at him and obliged."

Trevor Lloyd gave a hearty laugh. Raine had to admit she liked the sound of it. It seemed to come from deep within him. The problem was, she had not intended to amuse him; it had just sort of happened. She was trying to get rid of him and making him laugh was not the way to do it. She turned away and busied herself, trying to ignore him.

"I'll take these," Trevor said, reaching for one of the platters and moving out again through the swinging door.

Raine stared out the kitchen window. It had a view of the narrow road winding through the fields, but in the dark she could only see the lights of a farmhouse farther down the road and the cluster of lights of a village on the horizon.

Kim was going to have a baby.

The joy she had felt for her was suddenly no longer there. A painful sorrow washed over her, unwanted, unexpected—sorrow for a lost dream, a shattered illusion. Once she'd made plans to be married, dreamed of having a home of her own, of having a baby. "Oh, damn," she muttered.

"Damn you, Michael. Damn me for being so naive and gullible. Damn me for believing you."

Michael wasn't the man she'd thought him to be and she didn't grieve over him. It was only now and then that the pain of a lost dream hit her, the feeling of betrayal.

She heard the door open and she turned automatically. Trevor came in and deposited an empty serving platter on the counter.

"It's all gone. They're wolfing it down as if they're starving. Is there anything else?"

"No, thank you." To her horror her voice sounded thick with tears.

There was a silence as his dark eyes scanned her face.

"What's the matter?"

"Nothing." She swallowed hard. "Stop staring at me!"

"You're upset," he said softly.

"I'm not!" It was a silly lie and she wasn't sure why she said it, except perhaps because she had some perverse need to contradict him, to fight him, to keep him at a safe distance.

He took a few steps toward her and she felt his hand on her arm. She jerked away as if his touch burned her.

"Don't touch me! Mind your own business!"

He turned sharply on his heels. "Right." He took another tray and marched out of the kitchen door.

She leaned against the counter, almost limp with relief. She was a fool to cry over what had happened in the past. It was all over. Taking a deep breath, she went back to work.

Trevor helped her for the rest of the evening; she could not stop him. She said as little as possible, avoiding his eyes, avoiding standing near him. He was the perfect gentleman, helpful, making no unnecessary comments. After the guests had left, he helped her clean up. When everything was washed and put away, she forced herself to look at him.

"Thank you for your help," she said.

He gave a crooked smile and his eyes sparked with humor. "It was my pleasure."

She picked up her purse and jacket. "Good night."

"Good night, Raine."

She fled. Out the kitchen door, into the dark parking area at the side of the building, into the Beintemas' little red Fiat. She sat in the driver's seat, leaned her head on the steering wheel and took a deep breath.

Who was this man? What did he want from her?

He could not sleep. He sat on a chair on the deck of his rented cruiser and stared at the sky. He'd pulled on a cotton sweater against the cool evening air and he sat slowly sipping a Scotch.

She was gorgeous. Tall and slim with masses of shimmering copper hair, like he'd seen in the picture. The translucent green of her eyes was brighter than on the photo. She walked with a confident stride, her body moving with regal grace.

He closed his eyes, smiling. Apart from her hair and eyes, she wasn't anything like what he had expected. He'd visualized her as small and delicate, and possibly a little shy or withdrawn. That's how she had been at the age of fourteen. He laughed softly at his own folly. It could be an interesting experience trying to get to know her.

He stared up at the stars. The sky looked different here, the stars more distant. Finding her had not been easy, and he certainly had not expected to end up here, in this Dutch village, sleeping on a cabin cruiser. At least it made him feel at home. He spent a lot of time on his own boat, sailing around the islands, sometimes alone, sometimes with friends.

He wasn't sure what he had expected, or hoped for, when he found her. Part of him wanted to be relieved of this craziness that had him chase this fantasy woman halfway around the world. He had hoped it would all have been solved easily—that she would be a disappointment one way or another. Just a woman with red hair. He could have gone back to the island and continued with his life, slept again at night without her image floating around in his dreams.

He tossed back the last of his Scotch. He was wide awake and it would be useless to try to sleep. But there was always work, and he'd brought plenty to keep him occupied in case he was staying for any length of time. He went inside and placed the portable computer on the table and took out his files. The World Bank to the rescue. He had two weeks to write up the report for the Barbados project he'd worked on last month. Maybe exotic fruits and vegetables would take his mind of the woman with the green eyes.

Fat chance.

Chapter Two

The prince was dead. Elizabeth ran, not along the path, but straight through the woods, holding her skirts so she wouldn't trip. They had killed him and she no longer was safe herself. The Gypsies would come and get her. But she didn't care so much about that. Nothing mattered now that the prince was dead. Everything was gone—her home, her dreams, her love. So why then was she running? She stopped, catching her breath, then sank down on the damp leaves, clutching the bag of gold coins in her hand. Let them catch her; she didn't care....

Raine lifted her fingers from the keyboard and leaned back in her chair. She frowned. Maybe Elizabeth should care. Who wanted to get caught by a bunch of Gypsy hoodlums set on revenge? They'd have their way with her right there in the woods. She should care about that.

Raine looked out the window at the countryside. It was a sunny day in May. Black-and-white cows grazed peacefully in the green fields; the blue sky above them was dotted with white clouds. Everything was flat. On the horizon she saw the small red-roofed houses and the steeple of the church in the village. It all looked just like the pictures she had seen— clean and green and fresh. There were even tulips growing just outside the window, a multicolored mass of blooms.

She smiled, leaning back in her chair. It was lovely here in the middle of all these peaceful green meadows. Almost too lovely. It was difficult to write about a gloomy winter night in a dark Hungarian forest when outside the sun was shining and the grass was dotted with the tiniest daisies she had ever seen. Maybe a coffee break was in order.

The kitchen window had a view of the narrow country road and as she busied herself with the coffeemaker, she noticed an unfamiliar car coming down the road. It slowed and turned into the long drive up to the house. It disappeared around the corner and she could not see who the driver was. A few moments later the bell rang.

Trevor Lloyd loomed in front of her as she opened the door. Instinctively she took a step back, holding on to the doorknob. The man was too big for comfort, his eyes too dark, his shoulders and chest too broad and imposing. He stood there on her doorstep like an impenetrable wall.

She stared at him. He was comfortably dressed in well-fitting jeans and a striped, short-sleeved shirt. It was impossible not to be impressed by his stark, masculine good looks.

"May I come in?" he asked. Even his voice affected her. It was deep and a bit rough. He spoke politely enough, though the hard, arrogant line of his jaw seemed to challenge her. Maybe she was imagining it. Maybe she imagined the intense look in his black eyes.

"What can I do for you?" she asked politely, anchoring her feet to the floor. She didn't want to see him, yet her heart raced at the sight of him. She clenched her jaws and willed her heart to calm down.

He raised a quizzical brow. "Are you angry with me?"

"I don't like pushy men."

"In general or me in particular?"

"In general *and* you in particular. How did you know where to find me?"

He shrugged. "I asked."

"What do you want from me?"

A small smile curved his mouth. "I want to talk to you. I had the uncomfortable feeling that I offended you last night. If I did, I'd like to apologize."

Apologize my foot, she thought.

"Don't believe me, do you?" he asked.

"Not for a minute."

He sighed, feigning defeat and looking dejected.

"What do you want?" she asked again, not impressed by his act.

"I want to see you again. Aren't you going to invite me in? I'm trying to be nice."

The phone rang. Raine sighed. "Oh, for heaven's sake, come on in then," she snapped, feeling uncertain. She crossed the entry hall and went into the living room and picked up the phone. He followed her in and stood by the window, his back toward her, hands in his pockets.

The caller was Max, thanking her for her help with the party the night before. She chatted absently with him for a few moments, watching Trevor's back, the long, lean line of hip and leg. She felt a tight knot in her stomach. Not one of fear or anger. Annoyed, she took a deep breath and fixed her gaze on a painting on the wall. Two old-fashioned cloth dolls with cracked faces and patched bodies sadly stared back at her. Old and discarded, no longer loved, they leaned against each other, looking for comfort. One doll's arm lay protectively around the shoulders of the other. It was a touching picture.

"Thanks again," Max said. "Maybe we can do this again later in the season."

Trevor turned away from the window as Raine replaced the receiver. He glanced around the room. "This is a great place."

It was. Spacious and comfortable, it was furnished with an interesting mixture of antique and contemporary furniture and decorated with intriguing foreign artifacts. Kees and Femke Beintema, who owned the place, had done a lot of traveling. She wouldn't at all mind owning this place herself. It had character and personality. Color and warmth.

"I enjoy living here," she said evenly.

He moved toward the piano and played a few bars, as if to test the sound of it. His hands were big and deeply tanned, she noticed, but his fingers moved over the keys with fluid grace. Good hands, strong and competent, yet capable of gentle touch. She swallowed and bit her lip hard. He turned to face her, his black eyes meeting hers. For a moment they looked at each other in silence, and apprehension rose in her again. She wished she hadn't asked him in.

"Are you afraid of me?" he asked.

She looked at him coolly. "Why would I be afraid of you?" There were plenty of reasons—she didn't know him and she was alone with him in the house, for one.

"I don't know. Why don't you tell me?"

"I'm *not* afraid of you," she said, trying not to raise her voice.

"You seem nervous and jumpy. Don't worry, you've got nothing to be afraid of. I may be pushy, but I'm not a rapist or an ax murderer."

She stared at him, seeing humor lurking in the dark depths of his eyes. She sighed and then she couldn't hold back a smile. She was overreacting. Bit city jitters. *Don't trust anybody. Be on guard always. Keep a can of mace in your purse.*

She gestured at a chair. "Well, in that case, have a seat. I was just taking a break. Would you like some coffee?"

"Thank you. Taking a break from what?"

"Working." Oh, damn, now she would have to explain. She didn't like to tell anybody she was writing a book. It sounded so presumptuous. After all, she didn't know if it was any good, if it would ever be published. Did anyone want to read an historical Gypsy romance?

"What kind of work?"

"I'm writing a novel," she said, her voice level. "How do you like your coffee? Sugar, cream?"

"What kind of coffee? American or Dutch?"

"Strictly American. Weak as dishwater as I'm told."

He grinned. "I'll have it black then, no sugar." He sat down on the big white-upholstered couch and Raine went into the kitchen to pour the coffee.

"So you came all the way out here just to see me?" she said as she returned with the tray.

"I was in the neighborhood. I'm on my way into Sneek. Tell me, what kind of novel are you writing?"

"It's historical, about Gypsies."

He looked impressed. "Must take a lot of research."

"Yes. I've read every book I could find in the entire city of Chicago. I did a paper on Gypsies in college."

"And why are you here, in the fairy-tale Dutch country-side? Tulips and cows and green grass..."

"Oh," she said, waving her hand casually. "I just wanted a change of scene, and Kim's here. She found this place for me to stay, complete with car. You can write books anywhere.''

Outside the side window, a sheep came into view. ''You have company,'' he said.

''They live here. There are two of them. And two goats and twelve geese and two wild chickens who seem to live in the trees. Oh, and the cat. One big arrogant tomcat. He's called Attila.''

He smiled. ''The Scourge of God.''

''At least the mice and moles seem to think so.''

She had to admit it had intimidated her in the beginning to take care of the odd assortment of livestock. Now it was a pleasant routine and she'd actually learned to like the individual sheep and goats, petting them and talking to them as they rushed up to her when she came with their feed.

He eyed her curiously. ''So, apart from being a writer, you're a farmer, too,'' he commented.

''Hardly. I'm just baby-sitting them for the people who own this place. They're in Morocco, doing research for a study on guest workers, something about their background, the villages and families they come from. There are thousands and thousands of guest workers here, you know. Moroccans and Turks and most of them are Muslim. Rather an interesting infusion of people in the culture here...but where was I? Oh, the animals. I think they just have the animals for fun. Back-to-nature illusions, I think. The sheep and the goats are meant to keep the grass short along the drive. The geese are for the freezer, I'm told.''

''You're very talented for a city girl from Chicago.''

''I know,'' she said, smiling sweetly. ''More coffee?''

He smiled back. ''Please. Tell me, how's your friend, Kim?''

''She's seeing the doctor this morning to confirm her pregnancy. She called me earlier on. She's fine, she said.''

"Why were you upset last night?" he asked.

The question came as a surprise. Her body tensed and her hands clasping the coffee cup shook. Carefully she put the cup on the table. "Why are you so interested in me? Why did you keep looking at me last night? Why were you so set on helping me out?"

"I asked you a question first," he said mildly.

"You're prying and you're being pushy. Why do you care?"

He didn't answer, just looked at her with a strange light in his eyes that made her heart race.

"It's going to sound odd," he said.

"I'll bet!"

He gave a crooked smile. "I have this feeling I know you very well."

"But you don't."

His eyes studied her face. "I suppose it's called attraction," he said slowly. "I'm very attracted to you."

She felt her heart skip a beat. Calm now, she admonished herself. Maybe he's perfectly honest. Maybe it was just as Kim had said: Love at first sight. She leaned back in her seat. "I see," she said as casually as he could manage. "A difficult affliction."

He nodded solemnly. "Quite. Especially if the object of my passion is not equally smitten."

"Passion? Smitten? Oh, come on, get real! You met me last night for the first time!"

His expression was blank. "Still, I feel I know you." He came to his feet, suddenly towering over her. "I also have the feeling I'd better leave now."

She came to her feet, too, uncomfortable with him looking down on her. "You've got good instincts."

For a long, tense moment he looked at her in silence. "I hope so," he said at last, his voice low. He opened the door and was gone, leaving her staring after him, puzzled and apprehensive.

Concentrating on her writing was a lost cause for the rest of the day. She kept seeing Trevor Lloyd's eyes as he looked at her. She kept hearing his voice, *I have the feeling I know you very well.* The words disturbed her, which was ridiculous. It was nothing but a come-on and she'd heard a whole lot better. She didn't like the way he had said *I hope so* when she'd told him he had good instincts. What exactly had he meant?

What did he want from her?

Use your imagination, her inner self said. *He says he's attracted to you, so what do you think he wants?*

In frustration she gave up trying to write and took herself outside to the terrace with some of her research material. The terrace was made of ancient small cobblestones, laid in a traditional spiral pattern. Attila the cat lay asleep on an old wooden school bench. The sun was warm and the sweet smell of hay drifted in the air. Bees buzzed around the flowers in the terra-cotta pots that ringed the terrace. Her body grew heavy with languor.

She dozed off; she simply had no resistance.

A voice startled her awake and she opened her eyes. Roses. A huge bunch of large pink roses. Dazed, she looked up. Trevor was holding the flowers in front of her face, and he was grinning.

"Sorry, didn't mean to scare you."

She let out a deep sigh and straightened in her chair. "Weren't you just here?"

"Ages ago, this morning. I had the urge to bring you these roses. Just a whim, but I couldn't help myself."

He was playing some sort of game with her, and she wasn't sure why. She took the roses from him and a heady perfume filled her nose. "They're beautiful," she said evenly.

"They know how to grow flowers in this country. Have you been to Lisse? Seen the bulb fields in bloom?"

"I was just there last week." It had been a magnificent sight—acres and acres of bright-colored blooms, like a fairytale fantasy. She came to her feet. "I'll find a vase. Have a seat." She waved at the weathered wooden chairs surrounding the old terrace table.

She went inside, found a large crystal vase and arranged the roses after trimming the stems. There were fourteen of them, she counted. A strange number. She frowned, counting again. Fourteen.

A memory floated up out of her subconscious. She saw another bouquet of roses, given to her by Michael. Not twelve, but thirteen—a mistake by the florist. It had bothered her, although she'd tried not to show it. Thirteen was not a good number. Thirteen roses—she'd hoped it wasn't a bad omen for their relationship. As it turned out, their relationship had been doomed from the beginning, but she hadn't known that at the time. Michael had not been a prince.

Raine looked at Trevor's roses. Maybe there was something in her karma that made florists count wrong. Maybe in the Netherlands roses didn't come by the dozen, but in bunches of fourteen.

Michael's roses, too, had been pink, not red. He had known she didn't like red. Red to her was raw and angry. Red made her think of the savage streak of carmine on the painting in Wanda's frigid living room. Red made her think of rage, of violence, of blood, of horrible car wrecks.

With one finger she gently stroked the petal of one of the pink roses. It was velvety soft, sweet and fragrant. Picking up the vase, she carried the flowers into the sitting room and put them on the big oak coffee table. Stepping back, she admired the roses. They were truly gorgeous.

Back on the terrace, she found Trevor reading one of the books she'd been trying to study. He looked up when she approached and put the book down.

"Interesting," he said.

She sat down. "I've always been interested in Gypsies, since I was a teenager. Their way of life seemed to me so free and romantic. No bonds, no ties. If they didn't like it someplace, they'd simply pack up and move on."

"And you liked that idea?"

She looked down into her glass. "Yes. When I was young I wanted to be a Gypsy and see the world. Leave Chicago."

Leave Wanda, she wanted to say. Leave the way of life that had made her unhappy, a life lived out of a sense of obligation, duty, and guilt. After all, Wanda had taken her in after her parents had died, given her a home. She'd been fourteen, a scrawny, shy orphan with no other place to go.

She looked up, meeting his eyes, seeing the questions in their depths. Now he would ask her why she'd wanted to leave Chicago.

He did not. He tapped the book. "And now that you've done all that research, do you still think it is? Free and romantic, I mean."

"In a way, maybe. But within their own groups they're well organized and have their own customs and rules they live by, very strictly, too." She looked down at the book cover. It featured the smiling face of a beautiful Indian Gypsy girl in bright-colored clothes and lots of jewelry. "They have a tragic history, though. Prejudice, slavery, persecution—you name it, they suffered it. All through the centuries they've been mistreated, condemned to death, hanged or mutilated. No wonder they stay aloof and keep moving on. It must be devastating to know you aren't welcome anywhere in the world.''

He nodded, his eyes intent on her face. ''The things people do to each other, even now in this enlightened age, are unimaginable.''

She rubbed the rough old wood of the chair's armrest. ''We are too ignorant of other people's lives. If people aren't like us, if they speak another language or eat strange food, we distrust them or fear them, or ridicule them. I think secretly we feel threatened.''

''Do you feel threatened living here?''

She gave him a look of surprise, then noticed the gleam of humor in his eyes. ''People here eat meat and potatoes and they watch 'Roseanne' on TV. How threatening can they be?'' She looked into his laughing eyes. ''You know what I mean.''

''I know what you mean, and you are right, of course, that we often feel threatened by what we don't understand.''

''Travel is a good remedy,'' she said. ''If you have an open mind, of course. I enjoy going to different places, learning a little about other cultures.''

''Where have you been?'' he asked.

''Around Europe and I've spent a few weeks here and there in Brazil and Mexico, vacation, mostly, but still, it gave me a glimpse of how other people live.''

These excursions into alien territory had been working vacations with Wanda. They'd stayed in five-star hotels and had been entertained by Wanda's well-do-do friends and business acquaintances. Despite the luxury of her surroundings, the poverty of the larger environment had not escaped her. Having a young boy sneak up to your table on a sidewalk restaurant and ask you if he could please eat the leftover food on your plate was the sort of scene that tended to stay with you. "And what about you?"

"I've been around. Asia, Africa, Latin America."

"Really? So tell me about yourself. Where do you live, what do you do—that sort of stuff." In spite of herself, interest and curiosity took over.

"I'm an agricultural economist and I work as an independent consultant, mostly in the Caribbean, but I used to work all over the world. I live on St. Barlow. It's a tiny island in the Caribbean."

"Then what are you doing here?"

"I'm on a working vacation. I need to oil up a few contacts in Geneva and Rome, but my main reason is that I'm part of a Dutch team designing an agricultural project in the Antilles, some Dutch islands off the coast of Venezuela. I thought I'd do some boating around here. Little old Sneek is supposed to be the sailing capital of Europe."

"I didn't know the Dutch had islands in the Caribbean."

"Oh, everybody and his brother at one time or other owned islands in the Caribbean. A lot are independent now, but not all."

She watched his face as he spoke, the way he moved his mouth, his eyes. It was not a handsome face—it was a little too rugged and unpolished for that, but with its strong chin and dark, compelling eyes, it certainly was very masculine. "Where are you from in the States?"

He was from New York, he said, and told her about his family—father, mother and a brother, all of them architects. "I'm the black sheep," he said, giving a half smile.

It was hard to see him as a black sheep. "You don't seem to mind much," she said.

"Neither does anyone else." He grinned. "They're aware they created their own monster."

She raised her brows. "Oh? How's that?"

He swiped at a fly that buzzed around his face. "Every summer we went on long vacations abroad to admire architectural works, to 'broaden our cultural education,' as my parents put it. Not only Europe, mind you, but they took us to Egypt and India and all over the Far East. We saw the pyramids and the Taj Mahal and umpteen Buddhist temples in Thailand and the Burubodor in Indonesia and my parents would explain how it all was put together and how it worked and about the people and their ways hundreds or thousands of years ago. We were learning not only about architecture, but about history and religion as well."

Raine sighed with awe and envy. "That sounds fantastic. What an education!" Then she frowned, trying to imagine what it would be like for a child to be dragged around the world to look at big heaps of old stones and to listen to a set of obsessed parents admiring their supposed glory. "I can't quite imagine it to be very interesting for kids, though. You must have been bored to death."

He laughed. "Well, sometimes, but my father knew how to make things interesting and it wasn't *all* we did. We'd get time in hotel pools, or on the beach, too."

He still hadn't explained why had hadn't followed in his parents' footsteps. "So why aren't you an architect creating glorious buildings for mankind to admire hundreds of years from now?"

"I found the people and their lives more interesting than the buildings built by their ancestors. I watched them walk by the road with huge loads on their heads or backs. I saw the children in their ragged clothes. I wanted to know why they were poor, why they lived in these shacks, why there were legless beggars on the street corners. They'd inherited all this ancient glory and I wondered if they cared at all, if they valued it."

"It doesn't seem very relevant if you have to worry about where your next meal is coming from."

"Right." He paused. "I had never seen poverty on such a grand scale. It made a great impression on me. There seemed to be something incredibly wrong about all these people struggling for survival in the shade of these great buildings. All these women bent over in the rice paddies, children carrying enormous burdens, men cultivating dried-out patches of land with hand-held hoes."

"I suppose seeing it on a TV documentary is not the same."

He gave a crooked smile. "No, not quite." He straightened in his chair, his expression lightening, indicating he did not intend to start a deep and serious discussion on the world's miseries. "So," he said, "I decided, when I was twelve or something, that the world had enough great buildings and would probably survive without my adding to the collection."

He stopped there. Raine waited for more, but it wasn't coming. She watched his face. "So instead you decided to become an agricultural economist and save all the poor people in the world." Her tone was light, but she could imagine the idealism of a twelve-year-old.

His mouth tilted at the corners as if amused at himself. "Something like that."

"Well, what's life without a dream?"

"Boring." His eyes held hers and she felt a tingling of excitement ripple through her. She couldn't help feeling interested in this man. The things he was telling her so casually seemed to hide a wealth of meaning. He was a man who took his work seriously, who had seen the world and found his place in it.

She felt an odd twinge of pain. It would be good to know your place in the world, to have a place to belong, to feel safe. She pushed the thought away.

"So, now that you're all grown up and old and wise, are you still an idealist?"

A smile tugged at the corners of his mouth. "I've had to tone it down with a liberal dose of realism, which is not to say there isn't room for dreams." He stretched out his legs. "But that's enough about me. Now it's your turn."

She swept her hair back over her shoulders. "I grew up in Chicago. After college I went to work for my aunt. She owns a health food company. I worked for her for six months." She made a face. "Health food didn't agree with me. Business wasn't my thing. You've got to wear suits and high heels every day of the week. Business suits give me headaches."

He laughed. "I know what you mean." His eyes narrowed and for a moment he studied her face. "So what is your dream?"

"Oh, I want to be rich and famous," she said lightly. *I want control over my own life. I want to make it as a writer. I want my own place in the world. In time I want a husband and children and a warm and colorful home.* Her dreams were too intimate to share, at least for now. It was easier to answer the question with humor than with seriousness.

"And what will you do when you're rich and famous?"

"I haven't decided yet. I'll let you know." She picked up the book from the table. The Gypsy girl smiled up at her. "I've really got to get back to work. I have a deadline for this thing."

He came to his feet. "All right, I'll leave. How about dinner tonight?"

She shook her head. "I can't. I'll be working late as it is. I'm behind schedule."

She had to give him credit for not insisting. He didn't even ask if he could take her out another night. He just left, saying he'd give her a call.

She felt oddly disappointed. She thought of the pink roses, feeling a twinge of guilt. It wouldn't have hurt to go out to dinner with him, would it?

Yes, it would.

She closed her eyes and groaned. On an instinctive level he made her uneasy, yet she was beginning to like him, too. It was hard to deny his primal male appeal. The expression in his dark eyes made her acutely aware of herself as a woman. Not that there was anything lecherous or licentious in the way he looked at her—it was simply the way a man looked at a woman he was attracted to.

He was getting to her. She could feel herself weakening and she didn't like it.

It wasn't part of the plan.

It wasn't going to be easy. Trevor drove his rental car back to the sailing school where his boat lay moored. Of course it hadn't been easy from the start. Who in his right mind would fall in love with a photograph? No sane man.

But then, perhaps he wasn't sane. Suzanna had had her doubts. Maybe that's why, wisely, she hadn't married him. His parents and brother had also indicated that they were not sure he was playing with a full deck. Why else would a native New Yorker hide on some obscure island?

Sane or not, he was here now. And he was staying until...until what?

She hadn't given away much personal information, which wasn't surprising, of course. *I grew up in Chicago. After college I went to work for my aunt.* There was a huge, painful gap between those two innocent statements.

He felt a pang of guilt at his secret knowledge and tried to force it down.

He would have to take it carefully. Try not to be too pushy. Go slow.

He went cruising the next day, exploring the lakes and mooring in a small-town harbor overnight, sailing back the following day. He made himself wait one more day before calling her.

"How about dinner tonight?" he asked when she answered the phone.

"I'm afraid not." Her voice was cool and businesslike.

"Playing hard to get?"

"I *am* hard to get."

He laughed, he couldn't help himself. "I appreciate your honesty. What would be an appropriate time for me to try again?"

"How about nineteen ninety-seven?"

For a moment he was lost for words. "That's five years from now."

"Very good," she said with exaggerated praise.

"Why is that?"

"Until that time I shall be too occupied to be able to accept your invitation."

"I see," he said. "Planning a trip around the world, by any chance? A mission into space?"

There was a moment of silence. "Something like that, yes. I'm afraid I can't fit you into the plans and I'm sorry to disappoint you. Goodbye, Mr. Lloyd."

The line went dead.

He stood with the receiver in his hand, staring at it like a fool. Damn that woman! Was he losing his touch or what?

He didn't have a lot of experience with this sort of rejection, low-level as it might be. Women in general usually accepted his invitations to dinner. Not that he'd given out many lately. In the year since his breakup with Suzanna, he'd not been interested in pursuing another relationship.

And here he was, finally interested again, if that was the word, and the woman was giving him the brush-off.

Well, he wasn't brushed off that easily.

Raine stared at the blank screen of her computer and let out a deep sigh.

"Dear Wanda," she typed. How many times had she typed that? She couldn't begin to count.

I want to write you, but whenever I try, I can't find the words. There's something I want to say, but I'm not altogether sure what it is, and in any case, I keep thinking you'll rip it up before you read it anyway.

No. No good. Wrong tone. Too defensive. She deleted it.

Dear Wanda,
There's a question I'd like you to answer: Is what you said to me final and irrevocable?

No. Don't put her on the spot.

Dear Wanda,
I know you feel I have been very ungrateful, as well as irresponsible, but having a disagreement does not necessarily mean...

A disagreement? Was that what it was? Raine sighed heavily, deleted the last attempt and closed out the computer. Fiction was a lot easier to write. You could make it up as you went along.

* * *

"I don't understand you," Kim was saying to Raine. "Why don't you want to go out with him? You need a social life. All you ever do anymore is write."

"That's what I came here to do." Raine sipped her iced tea. They were sitting on the farmhouse terrace, basking in the afternoon sunshine.

"And you put the rest of your life on hold?"

Raine shrugged. "Men take too much energy."

Kim grinned. "Trevor might take a lot."

"I rest my case."

Kim sighed. "Raine, he's gorgeous, and he's interested in you. He gave you those roses, for heaven's sake. Can't you spare him an evening?"

"No." Raine drained her glass and put it down. "There are fourteen of them. Roses, I mean. Is there something significant about the number fourteen in this country?"

Kim slowly shook her head. "No. Ten or twelve is usual, or fewer, if you want, but fourteen seems strange." She shrugged. "Maybe that's all the florist had and he tossed the extra two in for free."

"Maybe." Absently, Raine watched a white butterfly flutter around the scarlet geraniums. Why was she being so suspicious?

"Raine, why don't you just go out with him and have a good time?" Kim asked. "You don't have to stop writing just because you're seeing a man."

"You know my plan." Impatiently Raine swung her hair back over her shoulders. "Too many women get sidetracked when they fall in love, get married, have kids. I can't afford to."

"*Sidetracked?*" You call getting married and having children *sidetracked!* Isn't that what life is all about?"

"Oh, for heaven's sake, Kim, don't sound so clucky! You know what I mean. Women quit college, they stop their careers, they sacrifice themselves for hearth and home and then their husbands divorce them and they end up with two rotten kids and no money and no career."

Kim laughed. She just sat there and laughed. "I don't believe this! Raine, you sound like a cliché! Good Lord, not all men divorce their wives!"

"No, some wives find it necessary to divorce their husbands." Raine smiled, then laughed. "Okay, okay, so I am exaggerating."

"I should hope so."

"I've got plenty of time. I do want a man, and a family and all that, but not now. If I don't concentrate and discipline myself, I'm never going to be a writer. I've got to know if I can do it before I make any other major decisions in my life."

Kim grimaced in distaste. "Hence the infamous Five-Year Plan. You're lucky your parents left you with enough money to keep you alive for that time."

Raine shook her head. "Not luck, Kim. Fate, destiny." She gestured theatrically.

"Raine, you're nuts. You've got to be flexible. Life doesn't necessarily accommodate your fancy plan."

Kim's own life, of course, being a case in point, of which Raine was very well aware.

Once, Kim had had a life plan too, not one that included a Dutch husband and life among the Friesian cows, nor having a wonderful mother-in-law who was both a midwife and a justice of the peace, nor having a brother-in-law who owned a sailing school. Kim's plan had been to travel all over the world and write profound articles—and one day a book—about the social and economic conditions of humankind. Possibly she might hook up with a photographer, which would be an ideal union. Together they could do marvelous things. Children would be rather an inconvenience, and would have to wait until such a time that she was ready, which might never come.

And here she was, basking in domesticity and impending motherhood, writing fluffy little articles about the quirks of the Dutch people and life in the Netherlands, which she sold to American magazines and papers. Having studied years of Spanish and French in college, she was now spending endless hours mastering Dutch, a language completely useless on the international scene.

And she was Happy—Happy, indeed, with a capital H. Raine couldn't help feeling an odd mixture of emotions at times—annoyance that Kim had so easily abandoned her dreams and envy because it did seem quite a wonderful thing to be so in love. Of course she did want to be in love herself one day, but it simply wasn't the right time now and Trevor Lloyd simply wasn't the right man.

"I have to do what I have to do," she said stubbornly. "I'm not going to allow Trevor to screw up my plans." Her new life, her newfound independence were too precious to put at risk.

"And you're going to live like a nun for all that time?"

"I didn't say that."

"Then go out with Trevor Lloyd and have a little fun."

"I don't want to go out with him. Why ask for trouble?" Kim rolled her eyes. "What are you afraid of?"

"I don't want to get involved. He's here on business and vacation, and in a couple of weeks he's off to his little island again."

"So it's perfect."

"Flings are a waste of time." And a waste of emotions, she added silently. She doubted that a fling with Trevor Lloyd would be simple and innocent. No matter how short, a relationship with Trevor was going to have a price, and she wasn't willing to pay it. It wasn't worth it.

Kim threw up her hands in despair. "I give up."

The summer-like weather held for the next three days and it was difficult to stay indoors and work at the computer while the sun shone outside and the fragrant breezes stirred the trees. She worked till late at night, woke early, fed the animals and went back to work. The office was a small alcove off the sitting room, without a door, but with large windows offering a view of the green meadows. The windows were wide open most of the time and as she worked, she vaguely heard the background sounds of the outside world—the mooing of a cow, the twittering of the birds, the hum of bees.

She'd never felt more at peace. Gone was the busy office where she'd worked for Wanda, gone was the noisy, smelly traffic of Chicago in which she'd spent an hour every day coming and going from office to home. Gone was the swanky high-rise apartment where she'd lived with Wanda—sleek, sterile, expensive.

It had all come together so nicely. She wanted nothing to disturb her newfound equilibrium, especially not a man like Trevor. Dark-eyed pirates had a talent for rocking boats and causing great upheavals in people's universes.

She missed nothing. She regretted nothing. She wasn't even lonely. Apart from several phone calls from Kim and a quick trip on Femke Beintema's bike into the village for bread and milk, she saw no one for the next three days. Her writing was going well and she felt a growing excitement about her book. There just didn't seem much time for anything else just now.

Maybe one day she would be able to truly make peace with her past. Make peace with Wanda. Her heart cringed.

Several times over the past months she'd tried to write a letter, but the words had eluded her. Every time she sat down to try, Wanda's face appeared in front of her. She could see again the fury in her eyes, hear again her voice, the bitter, angry words.

And again she would feel the terror.

It was still difficult to think about that awful scene without emotion, difficult to try to see the reasons. She hoped, one day, it would be possible.

On the evening of the third day someone knocked on the back door, loud and insistent. She was so engrossed in her writing that it took her a moment to clear her head from her imaginary world to get up to open the door.

Eight-thirty, she noticed with amazement as she glanced at the clock in passing. Good Lord, where had the time gone? She hadn't even had dinner yet. Through the window she caught sight of a figure by the door, but didn't recognize the man until she'd opened the door.

Trevor. She gasped at the sight of him. "Good God, what happened to you?"

Chapter Three

He was soaked through and filthy, and he looked like he'd crawled out of a swamp. His shoes were clumped with mud, his face streaked with dirt. He raked a hand through his wet, disheveled hair and smiled.

"I hardly dare ask if I can come in."

"What happened to you?" She was staring, still standing in the doorway, not believing what she was seeing.

"I dragged a drowning kid out of the water." He shifted his feet and winced. "I wonder if I could clean up here."

"Yes, sure." How could she refuse aid to someone who'd just performed an heroic act? His cabin cruiser probably lay moored at Max's sailing school, more than half an hour away. She stepped aside to let him in. "Is the kid all right? Did you save him?"

"Her," he corrected. "Yes, she's okay, but only barely. Her parents got there after she came to, and an ambulance came and took her to the hospital in Sneek." He didn't make a move to come into the kitchen. "I'll take my stuff off here so I don't drag all the muck in." He began to untie his shoes, and she saw him wince again.

"Are you hurt?"

"Twisted my ankle. It's not bad. I can walk on it." He pulled his sweater off over his head.

"What happened?"

"She was out with her two cousins, two boys, in an old rowboat. They tipped it over and she didn't know how to swim. One of them stood by the road, screaming and waving and I stopped."

Raine shivered. "Lucky for her."

"Damned lucky."

"I'll get you a towel. You'd better have a shower."

He didn't look in the mood for further conversation, which under the circumstances was understandable.

She went upstairs and got a towel and a bathrobe that belonged to Kees Beintema. When she came back, Trevor was in the kitchen, stripped of shirt, socks and shoes, with only his muddy slacks clinging wetly to his hips and thighs. He was standing by the sink washing his face and hands. Her mouth went dry and her pulse leapt. She tried not to look at him, at his brown, muscled torso, his broad chest covered with a light mat of dark curly hair. It was not good for her peace of mind. She did not want to be disturbed by brown, muscled male torsos, but she couldn't help being a woman, could she?

She handed him the towel and the robe. "The bathroom is up the stairs, first door on the right."

"Thanks."

"Would you like some coffee when you get out?" He looked like he needed a bit of reviving.

He grimaced. "A shot of Scotch will do me more good, if you have one."

Of course Scotch would do a better job. "Anything you want. They've got a well-stocked bar here." The Beintemas had told her to use whatever she wanted, but except for the occasional glass of wine, she wasn't much of a drinker.

"Good," he said, and limped off.

She went outside and gathered up his muddy clothes and dumped them in the washing machine. Maybe she could find him something to wear in Kees's closet.

She'd met the Beintemas only once. She felt like an intruder going through the drawers and closets in the master bedroom, but under the circumstances she hoped she'd be forgiven. She also hoped she would not accidentally discover anything embarrassing or revealing, some indiscreet secret she would feel compelled to carry with her to her grave. Fortunately she found nothing but the expected. The Beintemas apparently were what they had seemed to be: solid Dutch citizens with no dirty little secrets.

She found Trevor some underwear still in its package from the store and a teal-and-white track suit and put the things on the bed in her own bedroom, which adjoined the bathroom. When she heard the shower stop she knocked on the door.

He opened the door, dressed in the robe, toweling his hair. Clouds of steam fragrant with soap and shampoo billowed forth. "Yes?" he asked.

"I found you something to wear. It's on the bed in the room next door. And if you give me the rest of your clothes, I'll run them through the washer and dryer."

"Thank you. You're being very nice."

She made a face. "A good samaritan I am." She went back down the stairs with his wet things, started the washer and stood in the kitchen, unsure about what to do next. She was hungry, she realized suddenly. Engrossed in her writing she'd clear forgotten to eat. Damn, it had been going so well. An interruption wasn't what she needed right now. Well, maybe later she'd get a chance to finish the chapter she was working on.

The sun was low, bathing the landscape in a golden glow. Two teenagers on bikes pedaled by on the road, side by side, holding hands. Raine watched them, smiling. The girl had brown hair flowing loose over her shoulders and the long strands moved in the wind.

She heard a sound and turned away from the window. Trevor limped into the kitchen.

"I'll get you some ice for that ankle," she said.

"I don't need ice." His mouth curled. "Stop fussing."

"Oh, you're one of the tough ones, are you?" she said with mild mockery. "Suffering through it all the way, teeth grinding. How brave."

"I'm not suffering."

"Is that why you're limping?"

He lowered himself onto a chair, giving an exasperated sigh. "Are you a frustrated mother?"

She stared at him, for a moment at a loss for words. "Oh, go jump in the lake," she said finally.

He laughed. "I just did. I'd rather sit here and bicker with you."

"Funny, funny."

They looked at each other, challenge between them. And something else—a faint but undeniable tension of another sort. Then he sighed and leaned back in his chair. "I was coming over to ask you out for dinner."

"I have no time, Trevor. I've told you that."

"You didn't give me a good reason."

"I have a lot of work to do." Which was true, as far as it went.

"At night?"

"Anytime."

"You don't want to go out with me?"

"Right now it's out of the question. You can barely walk. I'll fix us something to eat, if you're hungry."

"I'm hungry." His eyes taunted her. She ignored it. He got up from the chair. "I'll get myself a drink if you don't mind."

She watched as he hobbled into the living room, favoring his right leg. If he weren't so pigheaded, she'd have offered to get the drink for him, but apparently he did not expect any help.

They had soup and thick crusty bread and aged Gouda cheese and some white wine. She'd bought the bread in a bakery in Sneek, where a variety of fragrant dark loaves filled the shelves and delicious pastries tempted the weak. Being weak, she never passed up the opportunity to be tempted when she was in town.

He said little as they ate and seemed occupied with his own thoughts. He looked tired and troubled, and deep lines ran beside his mouth. Raine wondered what he was brooding over. After all, the girl was safe. She hadn't seen him in this solemn a frame of mind, but then he probably didn't save little girls from a certain death on a daily basis.

"What's wrong?" she asked.

He looked up from his plate, frowning. He waved his fork. "Nothing." He stood up, restless, wincing at the pain in his ankle as he moved over to the kitchen window. For a moment there was silence as he stared out the window.

"This incident brought back some memories," he said slowly. "Not very happy ones. I'm having a hard time shaking them."

"I'm sorry," she said. She had some troublesome memories of her own.

He said nothing further and she got up and cleared the table.

"Would you like some coffee?" she asked.

He shook his head. "No, thanks. I'll have another whiskey, if you don't mind."

"No, go ahead."

She poured herself some more wine and took the glass and the bottle into the living room. He followed her, helped himself to another drink and sat down beside her on the couch.

"She was unconscious when I dragged her out," he said tonelessly. "I had to resuscitate her. She was a scrap of a little thing, skinny." He closed her eyes. "She could have been dead."

"But she isn't," Raine said quietly. The incident had shaken him badly, that was clear.

"I had a little sister about the age of that little girl." The words came slowly, as if he had to drag them out. "She drowned when she was five."

"Oh, how horrible," she said softly, feeling compassion stir.

"I was eight. I was there when they got her out of the water. It was . . . awful." He closed his eyes. "I keep seeing that image. I was seeing it as I fished that little girl out a couple of hours ago."

She cradled the wineglass between her hands. There was nothing to say but platitudes, so she said nothing.

"Damn those kids!" he muttered. "I can just see what happened. Taking out that old rowboat, goofing off, seeing if they could make it tip over. Scaring her to death, thinking it was funny. Probably never even thought about whether she could swim or not. They can probably swim like rats themselves."

"They're just kids," she said gently.

He stared at her for a moment, not really seeing her. "I gave them quite a lecture. They couldn't understand a word

I was saying of course, but it made me feel better. They looked at me as if I were a raving madman. Of course I *was* a raving madman." He picked up his glass. "Sorry," he muttered, and tossed back the last of his drink. "Well, I'd better go." He came to his feet, grimaced, gave a smothered curse and sagged back onto the couch.

"You don't have to go," she heard herself say. "You've had two drinks within an hour and you're tired." She sensed the sadness inside him and she didn't want to think of him going back to his small cabin cruiser alone. Besides, with that ankle he probably wouldn't be able to drive.

He lifted his head and looked at her, searching her face. "You're sure?"

She gave a half smile. "No."

His mouth curved. "You're very brave."

"Stupid, you mean."

"You're not stupid."

She smiled. "Thank you. There's an extra bedroom upstairs."

There was a glint of humor now in his eyes, which made her flush a little. It annoyed her.

"Just making sure you don't misunderstand the nature of my invitation," she said, trying to keep her voice level.

He touched his fingers to his temple as if in a salute. "Understood."

She sipped her wine, aware of the quiet man next to her, wishing she could erase the brooding sadness from his face. "I know how you feel," she said quietly. "At least I think I do." Her heart began to beat rapidly and she bit her lip.

He met her eyes. "You do?"

She looked down into the golden liquid swirling in her glass. "I had a baby brother who died when he was a year and a half. I was fourteen."

Again it was silent in the room. His body had gone very still. She felt his gaze on her face.

"Tell me about it," he said.

She kept her eyes down, seeing not the wine, but the small, sweet face of her baby brother. "There isn't much to tell. It was a car accident, very bad. My parents, my sister, who was twelve, and my little brother, they all died." Her voice was soft and toneless.

"My God, what a tragedy," he said softly. "You weren't in the car?"

"No. I was at a friend's house." For years she'd had nightmares about the accident, about her family being trapped in the car. About blood everywhere.

She focused her eyes on the pink roses on the table and forced the image out of her mind. Pink. Pink was soft, sweet, gentle.

She glanced over at Trevor and met his eyes. "I can still see him, you know, my little brother. He was such a sweet thing, so full of life." She put the wineglass on the coffee table. "I can see what must have been going through your mind when you saw that little girl drowning."

His big hand enveloped hers and it felt warm and dry. She was aware of the vibrations between them, some connection, as if he was a stranger no longer. She had seen a part of him, a tender, vulnerable part.

When she stole a look at him, he was smiling. "We're a funny pair, aren't we?" he said.

"If you say so."

He tugged at her hand. "Come here." He took her in his arms and kissed her, gently at first, as if he was afraid he'd hurt her. She did not resist, didn't even want to, feeling herself respond to him, answering his kiss. Reaching up, she put her arms around him, flattening her hands against the strong muscled surface of his back. He lifted her closer against him, his mouth hungry now and no longer gentle.

It felt good, so good. A warm tide of longing swept through her, an urgent, clamoring need. Her body trembled and she felt him move away from her, releasing her mouth, yet not letting go of her completely. She leaned against him, eyes closed, not wanting to leave his embrace.

"We did that very well," he said on a low note.

She felt dizzy, breathless, her heart pounding restlessly against her ribs. "Yes," she said lightly, hoping her voice sounded as casual as she intended. She straightened slowly, not looking at him, running a hand through her hair.

"Look at me, Raine."

She didn't dare, afraid of what he might read in her eyes. She got up and went into the kitchen. She had to get away from him and the emotions he stirred in her. It was frightening, the intensity, the depth. In the kitchen she began to put the dishes in the dishwasher, but there wasn't much to do. She cleaned the counter and the table, rinsed the cloth, draped it carefully over the edge of the sink. She was falling for him like a brick. She liked him, liked him way too much for having known him such a short time.

Chemistry. Chemistry knew no time, no place. There was no way to fight that, was there? He kissed her and her blood went wild. He touched her and every nerve tingled.

Was there any reason she should fight it? She straightened the toaster and absently wiped some crumbs off the counter. Maybe he was married. He was only here on a vacation. Soon he'd be gone again, back to his little island in the Caribbean, broad chest and all. She had to be nuts to let this go any further. She was asking for trouble.

She heard him come in. "What's the matter?" he asked.

"I forgot to clear things away," she said casually. "And I still have to check on the animals and feed them. I forgot." She smiled at him. "Make yourself comfortable, watch some TV. I'll be right back."

It was a relief to be out in the dark, away from him.

She'd fallen in love before, but never quite with such instant fire. She felt out of control and the feeling terrified her. *Control,* she thought, *I've got to stay in control.*

Michael, too, had swept her off her feet, but she had been younger then and eager, so eager for what love could offer her: escape, freedom, security, a life of her own.

Love, a husband, children, a family of her own, a home. A home with color, lots of color. And a wood stove for warmth. Color and warmth. Images whirled like a kaleidoscope in her mind.

"Oh, damn," she muttered fiercely, slamming the gate shut. She put the feed back in the storage shed and went inside. Trevor was watching an English sitcom on TV.

"Come sit," he said, and patted the seat next to him. His voice was level, as if nothing had happened. He picked up the wine bottle and filled her glass before she could refuse. She shouldn't have more wine; two glasses was enough. Well, she could manage three.

"Thanks." She took the glass from him and took a sip. "Tell me, what terrible deeds did you do when you were a boy? I'm sure you were no angel."

His mouth twitched at the corners. "No." There were memories in his eyes, cheerful ones now, the devil dancing among them.

"So tell me."

His smile widened. "I used to climb on top of the roof and sit there, king of the hill, so to speak. Our house was three stories high and the roof was plenty steep. And I used to hang on to the back of delivery vans and hitch a ride down the street."

Raine made a face. "You could have killed yourself."

"Of course not, I was immortal," he said dryly and she laughed.

"Well, you were right, here you are, alive and well, apart from your ankle."

"So, what about you? What did you do when you were a little kid?"

"Nothing life threatening. I read a lot." She'd also been a daydreamer, making up fantastic tales and wonderful stories in her head, then writing them down in notebooks. "My friends and I would make up sketches and plays and make our own sets in the basement of our house, or in the yard. Very elaborate ones sometimes. Then we'd invite the whole neighborhood to come and watch." The memories made her smile. "We felt quite the *artistes.*"

He smiled back at her, his eyes holding hers. "Very creative. It must have been a lot of fun."

"Yes." She was beginning to feel warm. She was beginning to feel annoyed. *Get a grip on yourself.*

"I think," he said, as if reading her mood, "I'd better hobble on upstairs."

His choice of words made her think. "On second thought, I think you'd better stay down here. You won't be able to make it up the stairs with that foot." She jumped up, glad to have something to do. "I'll get you some bedding." She skipped up the stairs, found a pillow, sheets and a blanket and carried them down to the living room.

"If you move to the chair, I'll make up the couch for you," she said.

He did as she requested and she quickly made up the sofa.

"Looks very cozy," he said, dark eyes amused.

She gave him a blank look in return. "I'm going back to work now, but feel free to watch TV as long as you like."

"You put in long hours."

"When I need to."

He nodded, the humor still in his eyes.

He thinks I'm just doing it to escape him, she thought. *Well, let him think what he wants.* She gave him a level look. "I won't ask if you want ice for your ankle."

"Good."

"I'll see you in the morning, then."

"All right. And thanks."

"No problem." She swung around the corner into the small office, relieved to be alone, although there was no door to close. She was conscious of his presence around the corner in the living room, but she couldn't see him. She switched on the desk lamp. The computer was still on, the text on the screen right where she'd left off. She sat down and reread the last few pages. After that she was not aware of anything. She was back with Elizabeth and her Gypsy pursuers. The next time she looked up it was well past midnight. The chapter was finished and she switched off the computer with a sense of satisfaction and grinned at herself. No mere man was going to keep her from what she wanted to do.

The house was silent. She did not hear the TV; Trevor must have gone to sleep.

She tiptoed around the corner into the living room. Only a small reading lamp was left on, perhaps so she wouldn't have to stumble through the room in the darkness. Trevor lay on the couch, asleep on his back, his face turned slightly to the right. The sheet and blanket were pulled up to the middle of his bare chest.

She stood by the couch and looked at him, her heart in her throat. He looked very relaxed, his hair rumpled, the rough, hard lines of his face softened in sleep. His chest was sinfully tanned, a deep, sexy bronze. She felt the sudden urge to touch the springy hair on his chest, to feel the warmth of his skin under her hand. She took in a slow, deep breath. She watched the easy rhythm of his breathing, the rising and falling of his chest. His bare arm lay on the blanket, the fingers of his hand gently curled in relaxation, the nails short and square.

It was quite an intimate thing to do, to stand there and watch him, and she felt vaguely indiscreet, but not enough to move.

She wondered what kind of lover he was, the thought alone bringing heat to her skin all over. This was crazy. What was she thinking of? Even silent and asleep, he was affecting her. It was absurd; she didn't even know him.

Except that it disturbed him to drag little girls out of the water. And that he'd had a little sister who had drowned. And that he'd climbed on steep roofs when he was a little boy and hung on to the back of delivery vans. She smiled. She could see him in her mind as an eight-year-old, eyes full of adventure and mischief, thinking he was immortal.

Taking a deep breath, Raine moved away from him, out of the room and into the kitchen. She looked around aimlessly, not knowing what to do next. She didn't feel tired. She brewed a cup of tea and poured some rum into it. *Dutch recipe from my mother-in-law,* Kim had told her. Kim's mother-in-law was a justice of the peace as well as a midwife. She married people she'd helped bring into the world twenty-some years ago. Kim adored her mother-in-law, which was very convenient, if not plain lucky, considering Kim was separated from her own mother by an entire ocean and half a continent. Mrs. Boersma had helped her set up house, helped her sew curtains and draperies, told her where to shop and in general helped Kim get adjusted without ever being overbearing or intrusive. The woman was a marvel, said Kim. Raine, having been invited over for coffee or tea at Mrs. Boersma's many times, could only agree. She possessed a genuine *joie de vivre,* possibly punctuated by the fact that she'd recently found a new man in her life after being widowed for seven years. Love, Kim had said, does wonders for a person.

Despite the tea and rum, sleep did not come easily, and Raine lay awake for a long time. When she finally slept, restless dreams full of disturbing images haunted her. Trevor kissing her. Trevor asleep on the couch downstairs. Trevor helping her hang curtains in a house she didn't recognize. Trevor saying, "Love does wonders for a person."

At four in the morning she was awake again, so awake she knew she would not go back to sleep. She forced images of Trevor out of her mind and thought about her book, writing scenes in her head. It came with surprising ease. When light began to creep through the curtains, she got up, put on a warm terry robe and slipped quietly down the stairs.

Opening the kitchen door, she inhaled the clean morning air. It was cool and clear like champagne, and the world lay bathed in the new light like a promise. Birds chirped in the trees and the chickens cackled. The meadows looked impossibly green. Dewdrops sparkled like jewels in the yellow climbing roses by the door. She felt suddenly, wonderfully, gloriously alive. *I'll never want to live in a city again,* she vowed.

She made a small pot of coffee, and while it was dripping she took Trevor's clothes out of the washer and put them in the dryer. With a hot cup of coffee in her hand she carefully made her way through the living room. He was sound asleep, on his side, this time, his brown back turned toward her. There was a small birthmark under his left shoulder blade. She swallowed and moved quickly past him into the office.

She sat down at the computer, closing her eyes in concentration, trying to recapture the inspiration she'd felt earlier. She thought of the story in her head, taking a deep breath, and suddenly it was all clear again. She knew how to write the next chapter and she saw in her mind the Gypsy camp, the blond English girl, the dark, dangerous hero holding her captive in one of the wagons at the edge of the camp near the woods.

She typed, absently taking sips of coffee, her mind a thousand miles away, until suddenly a sound made her look away from the screen. She gave a start, seeing the dark man, the black eyes, the unshaven chin—seeing the Gypsy rather than Trevor.

"Good Lord," she said, letting out a sigh. "You scared me half to death."

Trevor was leaning against the wall, wearing only the bottoms of the track suit. He rubbed his chin. "I seem to be making a habit of that, sorry." He glanced at the screen.

She felt an irrational annoyance at him for having startled her, for standing there, bare chested, reading her writing on the screen. She stabbed a few keys and the screen went blank.

"Don't stop on my account," he said.

"I'm not. I've been slaving away here for hours and I need some nourishment. I'm starving."

He grinned at her. "It was interesting to see you so engrossed and so oblivious to the world. You didn't work all night, did you?"

"No. Just until twelve-thirty, and then I was up again at five."

"A true, unadulterated workaholic."

She got up from her chair and tied the robe closer around her. She should have put on some clothes. She should have at least combed her hair. Not that he had. He looked rather a sight with the dark shadow of beard on his chin and the rumpled, dark hair falling over his forehead and that damnable bare chest.

"How's your foot?"

"Still a little sore, but I'm managing."

"I'll make breakfast," she said, stepping past him out of the office, her robe flapping around her ankles.

"I'll help," he offered, limping after her into the kitchen. "Just tell me what to do."

"Put on a shirt," she said, sorry the moment the words were out. She didn't want him to know he was disturbing her peace of mind.

He gave a hearty laugh. "Bothers you, does it?"

She gathered her composure and gave him a level look. "I prefer not to have the view of a hairy chest while I eat in the morning."

He frowned. "Mmm, never had that complaint before."

"Are you in the habit of eating your meals half-naked?"

He gave a lazy grin. "You know how it is, life's easy in the islands."

He was laughing at her and she had asked for it. She should have just shut up and endured his naked chest. Turning her back on him, she poured herself another cup of coffee. She heard him yawn elaborately.

"Well, I'll go up and make myself presentable. I wouldn't for the world want to offend the tender sensibilities of my hostess."

She would have liked to have thrown the coffee at him, but she managed to control herself. Instead, she walked out of the kitchen and sat down on the old wooden school bench and took deep breaths of the crisp morning air.

He was getting to her and it was unnerving. In his presence she felt completely off balance and acted like a fool. God, it was embarrassing. He was a smart man and there was no doubt in her mind that he knew exactly what was going on.

What *was* going on? She watched one of the chickens pecking in the dirt. *Nothing* was going on.

Twisting an ankle wasn't what one did for fun, but it had come in handy. Trevor grinned at his image in the bathroom mirror as he scraped the razor across his cheek. More and more he was beginning to have confidence in Fate. Certainly something outside himself, some mysterious cosmic force, was at work here. There was a reason why he had ended up here in the Dutch countryside. He grimaced at himself. Next thing he knew, he was going to hang a crystal around his neck to bring him further good fortune.

Chapter Four

"Nice morning." He stood next to her on the terrace, hands in the pockets of the teal sweat pants, looking spic-and-span and smelling of soap. He's shaved and brushed his hair and put on the T-shirt she'd given him last night.

"Yes. And then to think I could have woken up in Chicago and have had to battle the traffic to get to work." She shuddered. "Well, let's have some breakfast."

He asked her what he could do to help and she said he should just sit down and keep his weight off his foot.

"Yes, Ma," he said, and sat down. She glowered at him and he laughed. "What is it about you women, wanting to take care of perfectly mature, grown males?"

She looked at him haughtily. "Nature knows you must need it. Your average life span is years shorter than ours."

He grinned. "Touché. But rest assured, I won't die from a twisted ankle. It's not even swollen."

"Good. Then you won't have trouble driving the car?"

There was the most infuriating glint in his eyes. "Don't worry, I'll leave right after breakfast. I don't want to get in the way of your lofty pursuits."

She ignored the taunt and broke four eggs into a frying pan. "Do you have help in your house on the island?" she asked for something to say.

"Only for cleaning and washing laundry. I do my own cooking. My life is so irregular, it's easier that way."

"Are you married?" It didn't sound like it, but she wanted to pose the question, if only for the record. Not that she actually cared about his marital status, of course. As a matter of fact, if he were married it would make things a lot easier. She didn't get entangled with married men.

His eyes gleamed. "No."

"You could be lying."

"Yes, I could," he agreed.

She sighed and he grinned.

"I will admit to a long-term relationship however, which was terminated a year ago—painfully, but peacefully."

She would have liked to know why and how, but wasn't about to ask. "How do you like your eggs?"

"Anyway but cooked to death."

At least he wasn't picky. She liked that in a man.

"And you?" he asked.

"How do I like my eggs? Anyway but cooked to death."

"How about that. But actually I was referring to your earlier question. Are you married?"

She widened her eyes. "Me? Of course not."

He shrugged. "Why of course? Maybe you ran away from him."

"I ran away from Chicago, the business world, and my dear aunt Wanda. Wicked Wanda, Kim calls her."

"Sounds like a lovely person, Wicked Wanda."

Raine picked up a spatula. "She's beautiful, elegant and very smart." None of which had anything to do with being lovely. She slipped the fried eggs onto the plates and took the toast out of the toaster.

He looked at her closely, eyes narrowed slightly.

"Don't look at me like that!"

"Like what?"

"Like you're trying to read my mind." Like he *was* reading her mind. It was unnerving to see.

He sighed elaborately. "I wish I *could* read your mind."

"Don't even try." She began to eat.

He grinned. "Touchy, touchy."

She ignored him and went on eating.

"You do have quite an appetite," he commented. "I like to see a woman eat."

"Using your imagination burns up lots of calories. I'm starving." She pushed her chair back. "You want more coffee?"

"Please."

The cat slipped in through the door and curled himself around her legs, miaowing, while she refilled Trevor's coffee cup. She thought of Wanda's cat who'd wanted nothing to do with her. Her loyalties had been strictly for Wanda, who adored the little thing. Attila was less discriminating. He'd curl himself around anyone's legs if he thought it might get him what he wanted.

"Attila is hungry. I'd better feed him." Raine went outside and fed the animals. When she came back in, Trevor had cleared the table and put the dishes away. He was making himself useful, which was good. He was not giving his foot a rest, which was bad. Oh, well, he wasn't her responsibility.

"How about going out to dinner Saturday night so I can repay you for your hospitality?" he suggested. "My ankle should be all right by then."

"There's no need to repay me." She washed her hands and took out a clean towel and dried her hands.

"I'm not asking because it's *necessary,*" he said patiently. "I'm asking because I'd like to. I was on my way here to invite you last night, but I had to play the rescuer instead. Let's go for a nice leisurely meal somewhere and talk."

She hung the towel on its hook with careful precision. It was a perfectly reasonable invitation. There was also a perfectly good reason why she shouldn't accept.

"Is there a problem?" he asked.

"I told you. I'm not in the market for cozy dinners until nineteen ninety-seven."

"You can't be serious."

"I'm very serious. I haven't got time."

He moved a little closer, trapping her against the counter and putting his hands on her shoulders. "Then make time," he said softly.

She said nothing, aware of the warm weight of his hands on her shoulders, his closeness, the smell of soap.

"I like being with you," he went on, quiet and insistent. "I enjoy talking to you, and I think you feel the same way."

He was much too close for comfort, his eyes hypnotizing her. Her pulse was leaping madly. Her tongue wouldn't move.

"What are you afraid of?" he asked.

"I'm not afraid." That was a lie; she was petrified.

"Then let's have dinner."

She closed her eyes for a moment. "All right then," she heard herself say. "One dinner and then we're even."

He stepped back, letting her go, the gleam of triumph in his eyes unmistakable.

Later, after he'd put on his own clothes again and left, she was sorry she'd let him pressure her into it. It was a bad idea, she could feel it in her bones, but it was difficult now to back out.

Surely she could manage one more evening?

And why not? What was she afraid of? She didn't know. She felt an instinctive, growing uneasiness she could not explain.

Oh, don't be a sap! she told herself. What's there to worry about? Trevor is an interesting, intriguing man, but that doesn't mean you have to fall in love with him, for heaven's sake.

You are *not* going to fall in love with him.

You haven't the time. He's no good anyway; he's out for a good time, you can see it in his eyes. In a couple of weeks he'll be gone and that'll be the end of that. All he wants is a vacation fling. He'll be a waste of good time. Time is precious. All you have is five years. Well, at least that's what she had given herself.

She had it all planned, her Five-Year Master Plan to Fame and Fortune, or at least to bread and butter on the table. It had been a high to put it all on paper, realizing that for the first time she was taking complete charge of herself, that no one was pushing or pulling her or making demands. This was hers, this plan. Hers alone. And she was in control.

Control. What she wanted was control, and now, ever since Trevor had come on the scene, she had the terrifying feeling that she was losing it. She wasn't sure how and when it had happened, but it had.

He phoned on Saturday morning. "Don't dress up too much," he said, "and bring something warm to wear—a sweater, or a jacket."

"Why?"

"It's a surprise. Oh, and don't wear heels."

Here you go, she said to herself. *You accept one miserable dinner and he's dictating to you what to wear, or not to wear. There goes your independence. Before you know it he'll have you barefoot and pregnant in the kitchen and from there on it's all downhill.*

"Why is that?" she asked, annoyance in her voice. "We're going out to dinner, so why can't I dress up and wear heels?"

"Trust me," he said.

"Yeah, that's what all you guys say. So what's the big deal here?"

He laughed. "Do you want me to give the surprise away?"

"Yes!"

He gave a dry chuckle. "Well, I'm not going to."

"You're infuriating. I should never have agreed to come."

"Sure you should," he said calmly. "You'll enjoy it."

"Don't be so certain." How did he know what she liked or didn't like?

He laughed again, not at all put out. "See you later."

Trevor went back to his cruiser and sat down in front of his computer and frowned. It was time to send word to Wanda, but he felt reluctant to do so, and he was not sure why. Yes, he did know why.

There was something not quite right about talking about Raine behind her back. He had initially assumed he would give Wanda a call, but later had decided against it. He did not want to deal with her questions and end up in a discussion he was not prepared to have. A fax would do. He began to type.

> To: Wanda Strickland
> From: Trevor Lloyd
> Re: Raine

No. He deleted the "Re: Raine." It made her sound like a case, a subject of discussion, which of course she was, but he didn't like it. He typed in the date and sat back, taking a swallow of coffee, contemplating what to write.

> Dear Wanda,
> The Antilles project is interesting and the work is going well. I have recently found some time to go in search of your elusive niece. She was not at the friend's house and it took me some time to figure out where she was and . . .

He groaned in disgust. He didn't like the sound of it. It made him seem some sort of a conspirator, which, in actual fact, he was. He deleted the letter and started over.

> Dear Wanda,
> My work is going well and I have recently found some time to look up Raine. She is well and happy and there is no reason for you to worry about her. Regards, Trevor

He sat back and reread the short note. Well, that would have to do. It was what she had asked for, but nothing more. He printed it out and took it to Max's office and sent it off.

Wanda's voice echoed in his head. *I know she's never coming back.* He wondered for the umpteenth time what had transpired between them.

Raine's mood during the rest of the day did not improve. Her writing was not going well. Every sentence seemed a struggle. She couldn't keep her mind on the story. The Gypsy hero looked too much like Trevor with his wild black hair and dark eyes. Her thoughts kept driving off to Trevor, seeing his mouth, his hands, remembering again his kiss. This was crazy. She felt like pulling her hair in frustration. Outside, the sun mocked her.

Later, as she was trying to find something to wear, she was really losing her temper. Casual, he'd said. But how casual? Jeans? No high heels. Then what? Sneakers? Where was he taking her, for Pete's sake?

She settled for a jean skirt, a fashionable flowered silk blouse and flat shoes. Long dangling earrings, hair swept to one side completed the picture. An oversized black sweater-jacket should keep her warm.

She was ready when he called. It struck her again as she opened the door how tall he was, and how irresistibly intriguing with his rugged features and black eyes. She felt a shiver of apprehension, then squared her shoulders and looked at him.

"I'm ready."

"Good." His gaze swept over her appreciatively. "Very nice," he said.

"Thank you. I was hoping this would meet your specifications."

His mouth quirked. "It does. Well, let's go." He made a sweeping gesture, motioning her to precede him to his car. He opened the door for her and Raine sat down in the passenger seat, feeling for all the world like a convict being carried off to some unsavory prison.

It was a wonderful summer evening. The sun was still shining and the balmy air was fragrant with summer scents—fresh-cut hay, clover, flowers.

He turned onto the road and Raine looked out the window at the green expanse of meadows, the peaceful cows, the rustic buildings of the villages on the horizon.

"So you're not going to tell me where we're going," she stated.

He gave her an innocent look. "Why wouldn't I? It's a restaurant on the water in a small village. We can eat outside, if it's not too cool."

It sounded nice, she had to admit. She looked at him surreptitiously, wondering what it was about this man that intrigued her, what it was that made her apprehensive.

"What do you do all day?" she asked. "Just cruise around the lakes on your boat?"

He nodded. "I do a lot of that, yes, and I read and I even put in a few hours of work now and then."

"Work?"

"I have a laptop computer and Max lets me use his fax machine. Right now I'm finishing up a report for the World Bank, and I have meetings in Rome and Geneva coming up. And I'm still working on the preliminaries for the Antilles project. There seem to be a few problems."

"How long will you be here?" It would be useful to know.

He shrugged. "I'm not sure. Maybe another month, maybe longer. I'm in no particular hurry."

Oh, great, she thought. A whole month or more. I hope I'll live through it. Yet at the same time, she felt a thrill of anticipation. Oh, damn, she thought, don't get any crazy ideas.

Trevor turned off the highway onto a narrow country road winding through the fields in the direction of the lake.

"We're going to the sailing school," she said, recognizing the road, feeling suspicion rear up again. "There's nothing around there in terms of restaurants, is there?"

"We'll take the cruiser and go across the lake."

She stared at him.

He laughed. "I'm not going to kidnap you," he said, as if he read her thoughts.

"Well, that's a relief."

"I thought a little trip on the water would be nice on a night like this," he said smoothly.

That all depended on what he had in mind, alone with her on his boat in the middle of the lake. Don't be paranoid, she told herself.

He gave her a quick sideways glance. "Is there a problem?"

"No. How long will it take?"

"Why? Are you in a hurry to get back? More work?"

"I'm just asking."

"Only about twenty minutes. It's not far. It's a place that caters to boating people. It's quite upscale and the food is definitely gourmet."

At the sailing school students were mingling around, outside. They were a cheerful bunch of German kids, laughing and singing, their hair windblown, their cheeks red, looking wholesome and healthy.

Trevor leapt easily on deck of the cruiser and reached out to help her in. His big hand, strong and warm, closed over hers. She avoided his eyes as she jumped on board. He let go of her as soon as she had regained her balance and gestured at the chairs and table on the deck.

"Have a seat," he said. "I'll get us a drink before we get started. Or, if you'd like, you can come in and have a look around."

"All right." She followed him inside the cabin, which seemed roomier than she had expected. There was a tiny galley with a small refrigerator, a sink and a stove that ran on gas. There was a table with comfortable benches all around, which somehow could be folded and made into a big bed. Everything looked neat and clean. There were little curtains, a tablecloth, stoneware dishes. A laptop computer was perched on the table.

"Very cozy," she said, feeling uncomfortable being so close to him in the small space.

"Yes it is," he said, "if you don't suffer from claustrophobia."

"Do you?" she asked.

"Only sometimes. It was nice spending the night at the farmhouse, having space around me." His eyes met hers and his mouth curved in a smile. "It was nice being with you."

She tried to move away a little, but it was hopeless and he noticed her futile effort, his smile deepening. She felt like hitting him. He knew what she was feeling and thinking, and he thought it was funny.

To his credit, he did not touch her, or say anything. Instead, he opened the little fridge and extracted a bottle of white wine. "Bulgarian," he said, "quite good. Would you like a glass or would you prefer something else?"

"Wine would be nice."

They took their glasses back on deck and he started the engine and moved slowly away from the dock into the open water of the lake.

She had to admit it was glorious. The low sun on the water gave everything a deep golden glow. The clean, fresh breeze cooled her cheeks and lifted her hair playfully away from her face and neck. She was glad she hadn't put it up in some more elaborate fashion. It would be easy now to fix it when she got to the restaurant.

She thoroughly enjoyed the little trip across the lake and was almost disappointed it was over when they arrived at the dock by the restaurant. It was a rustic building with an old-fashioned thatched roof and a large outdoor terrace with small tables covered with white-and-green cloths. They were offered a table near the water's edge, which gave them an unobstructed view of the shimmering lake.

"This is wonderful," she said, surveying the terrace with its profusion of blooming plants in wooden barrels and hanging baskets. The table, too, was graced with a small bouquet of flowers and the waiter was lighting a candle, protecting it with a glass globe to keep the breeze from blowing it out again.

Trevor leaned comfortably back in his chair, stretching out his long legs. "I thought you might like this."

Over a glass of French wine and a light appetizer, he amused her with some island stories, telling her of the people and the culture and the easy pace of life. He enjoyed sailing among the islands, fishing and snorkeling on the coral reefs.

"Your life sounds just about perfect," she said. "A challenging job and all the freedom you want."

"Not perfect," he said, giving a half smile.

"No? What's not perfect?"

"No life is perfect," he said noncommittally.

The waiter appeared with their main course. He placed the food in front of them, poured wine into their glasses, then left them with a smiling *eet smakelijk*.

Raine wondered what was not perfect about Trevor's life. Maybe it had something to do with the broken relationship he had mentioned. Had the woman lived with him on the island? There was no discreet way to ask about it and besides, she didn't want to appear too interested in the intimate details of his love life. Of course, she wasn't actually interested. She was merely searching for appropriate topics of conversation, and other people's love life did not fit that category.

She looked down at her plate. Grilled salmon with a generous pat of melting herb butter. It looked delicious. She took a bite of it. It was.

"Why did you leave New York to live on that island of yours?" she asked.

He shrugged. "The rat race in New York drove me crazy. I don't like the frenzied life-style of the big cities. I work damned hard, but when I'm not working I like to relax in more peaceful surroundings." He wiped his mouth with his napkin and took a sip from his wine. "So, about three years ago, I made my escape. Living on St. Barlow, I'm closer to where I need to be and it cuts down on the travel and the stress."

"What about your job? Did you just pick up and... what?"

"I'd built up a reputation. People had no trouble finding me. Most of my assignments originate in Washington or New York, but the actual work is in the islands and with fax machines, computers and telephones there's no need for me to live in the States and travel back and forth to the islands all the time. Now when I come home, I go to my own little beach and a clear sky."

She sighed, thinking of the pace she'd worked at herself in Chicago slaving for Wanda. She could well understand him. Since coming here she'd felt so much more relaxed. She was her own boss now. That, and peaceful country living had soothed her frayed nerves.

"You don't get bored?" she asked.

He shook his head. "No. If I want more exciting entertainment I hop on a plane and visit friends. Usually I make the rounds between the States and Europe a couple of times a year, to keep the network oiled, or to pick up new contacts. I'm not a recluse."

She smiled. "So here we are, two rat race escapees."

"What did Wicked Wanda think of your taking off?"

Raine bit her lip, remembering Wanda's face when she'd told her she was leaving, remembering the bitter, painful words. "She was furious," she said.

"Why?"

"She likes to control everything, including me. She had my whole life planned out for me. When I quit working for her and left, she lost that control. It made her . . . I don't know. Maybe it made her feel like she'd lost, or like a failure." She put her knife and fork down. "She doesn't know where I am." She wondered, as she heard her own words, why she had said that.

He met her eyes. "Maybe she's worried about you?"

Her heart contracted. She looked down at her plate. "No."

"What makes you so sure?"

She felt her body tense, but the pain was still there. "I know." She picked up her glass of wine and took a long swallow, avoiding his eyes.

"How long are you going to be here?" he asked.

She was relieved he did not pursue the subject of Wanda. "For another three months at least, maybe longer. It will depend on when the Beintemas come back. They're not sure."

"What will you do then?"

She hadn't given it a lot of thought yet. Staying here wouldn't be a problem; there were winterized summer cottages for rent everywhere. It didn't matter much where she lived as long as it was in the country somewhere and she could write. Writing was the only thing that mattered.

"I may stay here, I don't know. I'm a Gypsy now." She smiled. "I can stay, or move on, it doesn't matter." It didn't sound as light as she intended, because of course it did matter. It did matter not to have a place to call your own, a place to belong, a place to come home to. "I do know I'm not going back to Chicago."

He took a sip of his wine. "You know," he said evenly, "I think you'd like living on St. Barlow."

Chapter Five

"You think so?" she said lightly, determined to be perfectly casual about it. Did he think she was interested in a summer fling on his beautiful island? Or was there more to it than that? Her heart beat crazily in her chest. Don't be an idiot, she told herself. It was just a casual statement and it means nothing. Yet there were so many undercurrents between them. Maybe...

"I'm sure of it." He smiled confidently. "The weather is almost always nice and—"

"Apart from your occasional hurricane that flattens the place and wipes out the crops," she added helpfully.

"The chances of that happening are actually very small. The last one that hit St. Barlow was over fifty years ago."

"Then you must be due for another one soon," she said, feeling a little devil stir inside her.

He gave her a narrow-eyed look and she bit her lip trying not to laugh.

He held her gaze. "Do you want to hear about my island or what?"

"Please tell me about your island," she said demurely. "The countryside must be gorgeous."

"Yes. Massive volcanic hills covered with rain forest and beautiful coral beaches. There are exotic flowers and coconut palms and cinnamon trees and wonderful fruit and all kinds of birds and butterflies. If you get high on nature, St. Barlow is the place for you."

"Are you a consultant for the local board of tourism, by any chance?"

He laughed. "We don't have a board of tourism. Amos Kadell handles anything that might pop up. He's the minister of finance. Also the minister of commerce and industry."

"He sounds like a busy man," she said.

He grinned. "Not too much. He plays a lot of tennis with Darnell Robertson, who is the minister of education and child welfare, as well as the minister of cultural affairs and sports."

Raine laughed. "An interesting political scene, I can tell," she said.

The waiter brought their dessert, a luscious strawberry mousse with thick cream and fresh berries.

"We can go hiking in the rain forest," Trevor went on, "and we can go sailing and fishing and swimming."

She met his eyes. "Is this an invitation?" She might as well get it out into the open.

His mouth tilted at the corners and his dark eyes gleamed devilishly. "My house is big enough for two. Have you ever been to the Caribbean?"

She shook her head. "No." She dug her spoon into the mousse.

"Maybe you should try it," he said evenly. "It's the perfect place to write."

It was a real invitation all right—an opportunity many women would seize with both hands.

"I'll have to think about it." Good Lord, what was she saying? She was nuts, getting swept up in a crazy idea like this. Well, why was it crazy? She was free to go where she pleased. She could write wherever she wanted. No more Wanda to guide her career and determine her schedule. No more business meetings, no more financial reports and advertising campaigns. Ah, freedom!

Her new life still seemed a miracle at times.

She could go and stay at a tropical island if she wanted. She could do her writing in a white room cooled by the tradewind breezes. She could go sailing and fishing. She could go hiking in the rain forests.

Rain forests. Trevor. Visions of the two of them wandering among the massive, ancient trees filled her mind. Adam and Eve in Paradise—a world alive with magical species of birds and insects and animals; exotic flowers and mysterious plants with wondrous medicinal powers growing in lush profusion everywhere.

"I never think of Caribbean islands as having rain forests," she said.

"Not all do. Some are purely coral islands, flat and fairly unexciting apart from the beaches." He took a bite from his strawberry mousse. "The rain forest is fascinating. No, that's not really the word. It's...overwhelming, awe-inspiring. It makes you think about how magnificent creation is, how little we understand, and how stupid and shortsighted we humans are not to respect our environment more."

She nodded. "I've been thinking about it more since I've been here. I never lived in the country, but now all I have to do is look out the window, and there is all that glorious green and gorgeous blue. Sometimes I sit by the pond and watch what goes on there. It's amazing to see all that tiny busy life." She smiled. "I like it here. I've felt much more in tune with myself, much calmer."

"That's what nature will do for you. It's too easy to lose touch with nature when you live in a big city." For a while they talked about the need for global measures to protect the environment, the destruction of rain forests and the loss of fauna and flora through extinction.

"Enough," he said after a while, leaning back in his chair. "No more gloom and doom. Look at the sunset. All is not lost."

The sun was slowly drifting down, washing the placid lake in glimmering gold. "Magic," she said, smiling. *He's special,* she thought. *I like him. He cares about things that matter.*

Like him? Oh, come on, she told herself, you know it's more than that. Liking doesn't make you feel as if you had champagne flowing in your veins. Liking doesn't make you feel like touching him. Liking doesn't make you wish he'd kiss you—now, right here.

Oh, God, I can't let this happen. I don't have time for this. It's not in the plan. I've had enough of men for a while.

Well, maybe soon fate would come to the rescue and she would discover Trevor had some odd fetish, or some disgusting habit that would turn her off. Kaboom—done, over, *finis.*

There were no such signs. He did not eat with his mouth open, or slurp his wine. His conversation was intelligent and amusing. He gave no indication of dangerous political leanings. Apparently he did not belong to any type of radical religious cult. But then you would never tell, could you? Some of these guys were real con artists and you didn't find out their dirty little secrets until you were celebrating your fifth wedding anniversary.

She'd better just watch out.

He liked watching her, seeing the rich copper of her hair gleaming in the candlelight, seeing the various emotions cross her features. He liked listening to her voice, which had a light melodious sound to it that sometimes wavered a little. She appeared so tough and determined, but it didn't cover up the fact that underneath it all she was vulnerable and uncertain. Her green eyes were like windows. She was struggling with something, trying to hold on to something. He wasn't sure what.

It was interesting getting to know her, like exploring an exotic new country, a faraway place with intriguing customs and fascinating landscapes. Ah, the mysteries of her thoughts and feelings! He smiled at the image.

He liked the way she dressed, colorful, casual, but with a sophisticated touch for color and design—an artist at work. There was none of the elegant but calculated austerity that marked Wanda's clothes. Raine's appearance showed a kind of unselfconsciousness, cheerful stylishness and he liked it.

He could not help noticing her hands while she ate, beautiful hands, the nails not too long and polished a soft shade of burnished coral. She handled her fork and knife with confidence and elegance. No insecurities here. She was no stranger to expensive restaurants and sophisticated surroundings—Wanda had taught her well. The sad little sparrow had changed into a beautiful bird of paradise. The thought made him smile.

"Tell me what it is that you like about writing," he asked, wondering what made her sit for hours at the computer, completely absorbed.

She tilted her head a little, her green eyes fixed on her plate. "Because I can make it all up." She looked up, her smile widening, humor shining in her eyes. "I can create my own little universe and play God with it."

He laughed. "Power hungry, are you?"

She frowned. "I hadn't thought of it that way. I think of it as...I don't know, having freedom, being in charge, something like that."

He studied her serious face. *Being in charge.* The words lingered in his mind. "I see what you mean," he said.

She pushed her dessert plate aside and rested her arms on the table. "That's why you are an independent consultant. Because you like your freedom, because you want to be in charge of your own life. You don't want the restrictions of working for a large company and following their policies and rules. You like to pick your own projects. Save little islands and rain forests and do good works."

"I'm a prince," he said lightly. She gave him an odd look and he wondered what she was thinking.

"Don't let it go to your head," she said.

Dessert finished, they ordered coffee, small cups of strong fragrant brew. Raine laced hers liberally with cream and sugar. She had to admit to herself that she was enjoying this meal a whole lot more than she really wanted to. It was dangerous.

I'm a prince, he'd said, be it with a note of self-derision. He did look more like a prince than a toad, but you could never tell.

As they drank their coffee, they talked, and the words and thoughts came easily. His eyes would meet hers, dark and full of mystery.

Mystery. What made her think there was mystery in his eyes? Something he knew, or could see, something he wasn't revealing. He took her hand across the table and all her nerves began to jump and spark.

"We'd better go," he said. "It's getting late."

Darkness had fallen, a darkness vibrating with the sounds of insects and the gentle lapping of the water. They strolled up the winding path to the dock where the cruiser lay tied up.

She stood next to him at the wheel as they boated back to the sailing school. The lake surrounded them, quiet and peaceful, and the expanse of sky was alive with the gold-and-silver light of stars and moon. It was an oddly exciting feeling to realize how very much alone they were in the darkness. She felt a glow inside her, a lightness in her head. Her body tingled with the awareness of his presence. She caught herself smiling at the water.

The trip back was too short. He tied up the boat and took her hand as they walked past the sailing boats with their colorful sails tied down, around the building to where the car was parked. But instead of opening the door for her, he leaned her up against the car and kissed her. His mouth was warm and sensuous and her heart began to race.

She knew it had been inevitable. The tension had been there all evening, only barely hidden beneath the civilized conversation.

She felt his body tremble, or was it her own? She felt powerless against the urgency of his kiss, helpless against her own clamoring emotions. Her body responded as if she'd been waiting for this to happen for a long time.

Which was ridiculous. She hadn't been waiting at all. She didn't want this. She'd been stupid, stupid...

She tried to speak, but the words would not come. His hands cupped her head and his mouth took hers again, warm and insistent. She kissed him back, fire rushing through her. Her arms curved around his back, her hands feeling the muscled strength beneath his sweater.

They drew back at the same time, gazing at each other in silence.

"Stay with me on the boat," he said, his voice low.

She swallowed, leaning weakly against the car door. She wanted to, but the strength of her emotions terrified her. How was it possible to feel this way about him so soon? How could his touch be so shattering? Was it just the pure physical appeal of him? She wanted to think, she wanted to have time. It was madness to sleep with a man she'd known for only a short time. It was irresponsible.

Yet the thought was wildly exciting and all her primitive instincts clamored for his touch. She wanted his arms around her in the dark, his strong, male body close against her own.

No! her inner self said.

She forced herself to look at him, then shook her head slowly. "No," she said, her voice husky, alien to her own ears. She bit her lower lip, feeling miserable, feeling like a tease. She wanted to explain, but the words would come out wrong and make everything even worse.

He moved to open the door. "I'll take you home, then." His voice was even.

They drove without speaking and the silence was nerve-racking. The evening was ruined, the magic lost.

She didn't want magic. Magic was dangerous and mysterious and sapped all your strength and control. It trapped you in a beautiful cage and then you were lost, no longer yourself, no longer in charge.

She glanced at him, but in the dark she could only see the angular outline of his face—a strong profile made up of hard, rugged lines. There was nothing wishy-washy about it. There'd been nothing wishy-washy about his kiss, nor his invitation. He was looking straight ahead. Why didn't he say something? Anything. Was he angry? He probably wasn't used to women rejecting him. Must be quite a shock to his ego. Well, to hell with him and his tender male ego. If he wanted to be offended, he could go right ahead.

The tension in the car was unbearable. Her every muscle felt strung tight and it was hard to breathe.

"I didn't mean to make you angry," she said at last. It was the truth, and it wouldn't hurt to say it.

"I'm not angry." His voice was calm. "But I know I didn't read you wrong."

Her hands tightened in her lap. She was a grown woman. She was not going to play pretend games. The electricity between them had been obvious all evening. He had held her in his arms. He had read her reaction to him perfectly well. "No, you didn't," she said.

"Then why?"

"I don't want a summer fling. I don't want to get pregnant."

"Do you think I would have taken the risk of your getting pregnant? I'm not eighteen, Raine."

"Not all men are as enlightened as you and a woman should never take anything for granted."

"True."

"Even so, I hardly know you." Which was not exactly the truth. She knew quite a bit about him and his convictions, the things that mattered to him. She had certainly caught some intimate glimpses into his soul. "I wanted to make love, of course I did. I'm not going to deny it, but fortunately for me my brain took over. I didn't mean for this to happen. I don't want to get involved at the moment. And I don't want a meaningless fling just to pass the time."

"Ah, yes, I remember now. I can try again in five years."

"You've got it."

He laughed, a truly unrestrained, amused sound holding no rancor. "You've got to be kidding."

"There are other things in life besides sex." *Oh, God,* she thought, *I sound like a repressed maiden aunt.*

"I couldn't agree more," he said smoothly. "However, making love is a nice, pleasant diversion from cerebral pursuits, and a natural enough activity for normal healthy people."

"So is swimming."

He gave a hearty laugh. "But not nearly so satisfying."

"I'm sorry I can't be your partner in your quest for satisfying exercise." She smiled sweetly. "You'll just have to make do with swimming."

"What do you intend to do about your natural, physical urges in the next five years?"

"The greatest power is of the mind, not the body," she said loftily. "I read that somewhere."

He laughed again. "It's going to take quite some power to restrain all that lovely passion of yours. A great pity."

"Oh, shut up." She glanced away, hearing his dry chuckle. He certainly was amused, and she couldn't even blame him. Had she not been so aggravated by his arrogant male attitude, she might have found it funny herself.

So what was she going to do in the next five years? Certainly she didn't intend to ban all male contacts, was she? Writing her book and planning her work had taken so much energy, she really hadn't thought through all the ramifications. All she knew was that getting involved with this big, dark pirate with the devil in his eyes would be disastrous. All her instincts told her so. He was too pushy, too overbearing. Something just wasn't quite right. Something bothered her, made her feel uneasy, but the reason eluded her.

They drove on in silence until they reached the house. It lay like a dark shape amid the meadows; she'd forgotten to switch on a light for her return.

She hoped he wouldn't get out of the car, but he did, walking her to the back door and taking the keys from her to unlock it. He strode in right after her, closing the door firmly behind him.

She turned to face him, apprehension dawning. The closed door was not reassuring. He leaned against it, feet planted slightly apart, thumbs tucked into his waistband. Six foot plus of primitive male aggression.

He did not look like a male ready to leave.

"Thank you for the nice dinner," she said politely. "I liked the cruise on the water. I think we're even now." Even a fool would get her message, but Trevor seemed unimpressed.

His eyes gleamed darkly. "We're not finished, you know," he said in his low, gravelly voice.

His arrogant pose irritated her. It also made her distinctly uncomfortable, but she was determined not to show him. "I have no idea what you mean," she said coolly.

One black eyebrow rose in mock surprise. "Do you think you can just push me out of the way with some silly story?" A smile tugged at the corners of his mouth. "You're not getting rid of me that easily, you know."

Chapter Six

The words dropped like icicles into her consciousness. Her body froze. Her mouth went dry. She could not believe what she was hearing. *You bastard!* she thought wildly. Unsavory visions blossomed in her mind. Fear ran rampant for a moment, then she struggled to contain it, hoping he wouldn't notice.

He noticed. The smile vanished from his face. He muttered a curse, closing his eyes briefly. "I'm not going to hurt you, for God's sake! Don't look at me like that!"

Her muscles turned limp at the sound of the shock in his voice. She sagged into a chair, seeing the astonishment on his face. He raked a hand through the unruly mop of his dark hair, a gesture that seemed oddly unsure and confused.

He stared at her. "What the hell did you think I had in mind?"

She drew in a ragged breath. "Use your imagination," she said dully. "What am I supposed to think when you march in uninvited, stand there as if you own the place and give me a line like that?" He was big and intimidating—it didn't take much for him to look damned threatening.

"I wasn't contemplating rape and pillage."

"*Thank* you," she said acidly.

He searched her face. "You didn't actually think—"

"I didn't *think,*" she snapped. "It was a gut reaction at seeing you stand there like that." Well, perhaps she had overreacted, but he had that effect on her. It seemed impossible to feel neutral about him. Her feelings were like a yoyo going up and down from one extreme to the other. Weariness overtook her. She closed her eyes and wished he would just go away and leave her alone.

When she opened her eyes a moment later she caught him watching her, his dark gaze intent on her face.

"I'm sorry I upset you," he said.

She shrugged. "I'll live." She met his eyes. "So what did you have in mind?"

He moved over to the table, took a chair and straddled it. "I would like an explanation."

"For what?"

"What is all this nonsense about waiting for five years? What is wrong with me being interested in you now?"

"I can't imagine why you're interested." She couldn't. She'd hardly been encouraging. What could he possibly see in her? She had red hair. She was slim and attractive. She was no nitwit. All right, fine, but that was hardly enough to keep him coming after her without any incentives from her. Yet there was an unmistakable magnetism between them—something indefinable drawing them together, tugging at their senses.

"I don't know," he said. "Fate, kismet, but you're changing the subject. Why can't you be available until five years from now?"

It did sound rather crazy, she had to admit. He must think her a nut case.

"Actually, it's four and a half." She didn't know what made her feel like taunting him. *And,* she added in silence, *in four-and-a-half years I'm going to have a book on the New York Times bestseller list. I'll be famous. I'll be interviewed on TV and appear on "The Tonight Show." But if I hang around with you I'll never make it. You disturb my peace of mind and ruin my concentration. I wouldn't want you to have that on your conscience.* She smiled at him sunnily.

He closed his eyes and groaned.

"I've told you, I'll be too busy," she said when he looked at her again.

"Writing books?"

Inspiration hit and her spirits began to rise. "Actually," she said, lowering her voice, "it's a cover." Imagination began to flow freely.

He lifted one mocking eyebrow. "You're working undercover? Spy stuff? National security?"

She nodded solemnly, feeling humor take over, a magical relief after the craziness of a few minutes ago. It was hard not to laugh. "Yes. It's very secret, and I really shouldn't even be telling you this at all, but I just don't know how else I can convince you to leave me alone." She gave him a wide-eyed, innocent look. "It's for the best, honest. You don't want to ruin the project. It's going so well right now. Just leave and forget you ever knew me."

He came slowly to his feet. "Not a chance." He moved around the table, pulled her out of her chair and held her against him in an iron grip, all in a flash of a moment.

She could barely breathe.

"You've got a great imagination," he said close to her ear.

She bit her lip. "Sometimes it comes in handy," she murmured. "I'm a writer, you see. I'm a very creative person." Her face was crushed against his shoulder and the warm, male scent of his body was intoxicating.

"But you're a lousy liar."

With determined precision he planted his mouth on hers. Don't give me any more nonsense, his mouth said. Just you stand there until I kiss you senseless and we'll talk some more about that five-year plan of yours. Oh, she heard the words all right, even though he didn't speak them out loud. And then she heard nothing, because his mouth was doing magic. It was a shattering kiss, as it was intended to be. Heat rushed through her as his mouth explored hers in fierce demand. His hands pulled her blouse loose from her skirt and slipped across the bare skin of her back, warm, possessive hands making her senses reel.

Her blood pumped wildly through her body and with the last shred of willpower, she tore away from him. She couldn't let it happen. She could not make him think that all he had to do was touch her and she was putty in his hands.

Well, she was, almost.

"Stop it," she said huskily. "Just because—"

He laughed, stopping her in mid sentence, infuriating her.

"You think this is funny?" she asked with cool disdain. He thought she was amusing. He thought he could do whatever he wanted with her no matter what she said.

He lifted one quizzical brow. "Where's your sense of humor now?" he mocked.

She lifted her chin and produced a drop-dead look. "I don't like to be mauled and pawed by some Neanderthal male who thinks he's—"

"Quit the melodrama, Raine. You can do better than that."

She crossed her arms in front of her chest. "What do you think you're proving? That you're irresistible? That you know all the tricks? Well, you don't impress me. I told you, I don't like pushy men."

He put his hands in his pockets and surveyed her calmly. "I'm merely trying to show you that you are not indifferent and not uninterested. No matter what you try to make yourself believe."

"So you kiss well. Big deal."

There was a pregnant pause. His mouth quirked as if it took an effort to contain his mirth. "I kiss well," he repeated. "Is that all it is?"

She shrugged. "I certainly have no idea what else it could be."

A brooding darkness suddenly lurked in the depths of his eyes. "Use your imagination," he said. He turned on his heel, opened the door and was gone. Outside his car engine leapt into life. The car rumbled down the drive, the sound fading into the night. Then there was silence. She sank down on the chair, leaned her arms on the table and lowered her head.

Good God, what was she going to do?

She dreamed that night of walking with Trevor in a magical forest. Giant butterflies fluttered around them and fruits she had never seen grew on the trees, sweet and succulent.

This is Paradise, she said. *Look at the birds, the flowers.* She picked an orchid and smelled it. *What color is this?* she asked, and he said there was no name for that color because the world had never seen it before.

We should not wear clothes in Paradise, she said, and he smiled at her and began to take off her clothes very slowly, his eyes full of dark, smoldering passion.

They lay down on a thick carpet of soft moss and held each other close. *I want to make love,* she said. *Please, please, I want...* His fingers played her body like a delicate instrument. Her blood sang and all around was beautiful, sensuous music, music that had color and taste—music of the soul.

Horrible, raucous, screeching sounds awoke her with a start. She sat up in bed, her heart pounding.

Cats. Cats fighting outside her window.

"Damn," she muttered, dropping back onto the pillow. "Damned cats."

The next several days went by peacefully. Her writing was progressing nicely, apparently not affected by her stormy evening with Trevor. She forced herself not to think of him and concentrate only on the imaginary story in her head. Enough storm and disaster there to keep her mind occupied. Poor Elizabeth had been captured by the Gypsy men.

There was no way to escape. The wagon they'd put her in wasn't much more than a tent on top of some sort of farm cart, but there was no way to escape. Outside one or two of the men were guarding the wagon. They changed every few hours. The man bringing her food was the same one every time, the one she wanted to see the least, the one with the flaming eyes and the wolfish grin.

Elizabeth peered through the opening by the front flap that served as a door. It was almost dark. There were other tents and carts gathered around in a circle, and a fire burned in the middle, a pot suspended over it. People mingled around, the women wearing colorful clothes and head scarves. She wondered what was in the pot. She shivered.

She was cold and hungry, but she feared the sight of the big dark man. What if the man came into her wagon at night and demanded her body? The thought made her tremble with fear.

Raine's fingers flew over the keyboard, her mind engrossed in her own fantasy, the Gypsy camp surrounded by dark forest, the Gypsy man with his burning eyes who had captured Elizabeth. It was just after six on Tuesday when she finished another chapter. Getting up from her chair, she stretched, feeling a great satisfaction and a pain in her back. And she was hungry. She thought of the Gypsy cooking pot. Wild rabbit stew. Sounded great. Maybe she ought to find a recipe and try it out one day.

She was in the kitchen looking for something to eat when Trevor's rental Peugeot came up the drive. Her body tensed all over in instinctive defense. The man was not good for her health.

It wasn't possible. What could he conceivably still want with her? Was he deaf, dumb and blind? He stood in the open door, a cardboard box in his hand.

"How about some steak, wine, strawberries and cream?"

"I don't understand you," she said slowly. "Is it the hunter in you?"

He laughed. "The game is fascinating, elusive, beautiful." The look in his eyes taunted her.

She rolled her eyes heavenward, saying nothing. Beautiful, he said. She wished she'd paid more attention to her appearance, but she hadn't expected anyone today. Faded denim shorts and a turquoise T-shirt, comfortable though they were, were not the height of style. She'd piled her hair loosely on top of her head and strands of it were coming down. And no makeup. She groaned inwardly. She looked like a slob, but when she was writing she didn't feel like spending precious time to primp just for a meeting with a computer. Well, she didn't care what Trevor thought. Maybe he'd change his mind about her seeing her in this state, flee in horror and never come back.

As it turned out, her appearance did not send him screaming out the door. Instead, he came into the kitchen and deposited the box on the table. "Actually, this is a peace offering," he said. "I admit to being too pushy and too demanding and I'm sorry. The only excuse I have to offer is that all my primitive male instincts start galloping out of control when I'm near you. It brings out the caveman in me and I apologize."

She raised her brows in mock surprise. "Wow. That must be painful for you to admit."

"Excruciating," he said, deadpan. "Now, I would like to make amends."

"How would you like to do that?"

"First this meal. I will prepare it while you can go on doing whatever secret spy stuff you're doing in that little office of yours. Then, while we eat, I have a proposal I'd like you to consider."

She became suddenly aware of a sweet, flowery perfume wafting in the air, an intimately familiar scent carrying with it memories from long ago—her mother, the luxuriant flower garden of her childhood.

"Is that freesias I smell?" she asked.

He reached into the box and carefully lifted out a bouquet wrapped in florist paper. "For you," he said, handing it to her with an exaggerated, sweeping gesture.

She took it from him, inhaling the lovely scent of the flowers. She smiled at him. "Freesias. I love freesias."

He was watching her with a strangely intent look in his eyes. She felt a flutter of apprehension.

"Why are you looking at me like that?"

He shook his head, as if to shake a thought. "It's nothing," he said, reaching into the box again and taking out the makings of dinner.

She stood very still. There was something strange going on, something she couldn't put her finger on. She stared at the flowers in her hand. Why freesias? Why not roses or carnations? The florist shops and market stalls overflowed with an endless variety of fresh flowers, many of them larger and more dramatic than freesias. Fresh flowers were a fixture in Dutch living rooms, like the cozy lamps and bookcases full of books. Flowers were bought like bread, because you need them.

She inhaled the scent, remembering the freesias on the coffee table in her childhood home, remembering the entire house pervaded with the lovely scent.

Trevor was at the counter unwrapping the steak. She stared at his back. "Why freesias?" she asked.

He didn't turn around. "Why not? They smell nice." His voice was light. Too light.

"Yes, they do," she said slowly, still staring at his back. She felt an odd premonition, a fleeting feeling she could not grasp or identify. It flitted away in her mind, leaving a vague unrest.

Bringing her freesias had been a mistake. God, he felt terrible—dirty, dishonest. He crumpled the butcher paper and tossed it into the garbage can with vicious force. It bounced right back out and dropped onto the floor. He wished he could come clean with her, tell her the truth. But he could not. There was no way in the world he could do that now, not if he wanted any chance at all to make it into her good graces.

He rested his hands on the counter and closed his eyes. If only he didn't feel about her the way he did. If only he didn't know deep in his gut that she was the woman he could be happy with.

If only, if only... If only he could just walk out of here and forget the whole bizarre business. If only he had met her some other way, some other place.

Taking a deep breath, he pushed himself away from the counter. If he wanted her, he'd have to stick it out, keep his mouth shut and hope it would all work out in the end— somehow. Yet the whole affair left him with a bad taste in his mouth. He was a despicable rat.

But what choice did he have? What choice had there ever been?

None.

Raine was working on her notes for the next chapter when Trevor called her forty-five minutes later. He'd set the table outside, with the freesias in the middle. The wine had been poured and the smell of steaks on the grill filled the balmy evening air. A basket of French bread was on the table, as was a wooden bowl of mixed salad.

She'd considered changing her clothes, but had decided against it. It might give Trevor ideas. So she'd simply washed up and brushed out her hair before putting it back up. She'd even resisted putting on makeup, which was rather heroic. Facing the world without it was not one of her habits; it made her feel not quite dressed.

"Sit down," he said, "the meat is just about ready." He lifted his glass. "How about a toast?" He clinked her glass. "To a stimulating friendship," he said.

"A stimulating friendship?" she repeated. "I thought you were more in the market for a torrid love affair."

He put his glass down and laughed. "Torrid? Do I look—"

"Yes," she said, cutting him off.

He sighed. "Well, since I'm not going to get a torrid love affair out of you, I was hoping you'd settle for a stimulating friendship."

"You could try and peddle your passion somewhere else with more luck." She made a sweeping gesture. "Loads of nubile Dutch women out there, redheads included."

He narrowed his eyes. "I want you."

It thrilled her to hear the words; she couldn't help it. The sound of his voice and the way he looked at her made lovely music in her soul. Why was she resisting him? What woman in her right mind would refuse a man like him? What was she afraid of?

A good question. A thousand fears flitted in and out of her consciousness. There was something secretive and elusive in those dark eyes. He would look at her sometimes as if he could see right inside her head. It was disturbing, to say the least. It made her feel like drawing away, hiding in the darkness so he couldn't see anymore whatever it was he was seeing.

She took a drink from her wine, saying nothing.

"So," he went on, "I would like us to get to know each other better. I will make every effort to keep my hands to myself, if you'll agree to see me now and then, when you have time, of course."

She stared at him. "Why?"

"Why what?"

"Why do you care? In another month or so you'll be gone."

"Not to another planet." He inspected the two steaks, then placed one on each plate and sat down in his chair opposite her. "Besides," he went on, "I might persuade you to come dally in Paradise with me."

"Paradise?"

He grinned. "St. Barlow."

It was the second time he had mentioned her coming to the island. "Do you invite all women who cross your path to your island?"

"Only redheads who think I kiss well."

"You hardly know me."

His eyes held hers. "Let's work on it then, shall we?"

She didn't know what to say.

"I'll stay out of your way when you have to work," he promised. "But I'd like to take you out on a real sailing boat one of these days, and share dinner now and then. Perfectly innocent entertainment."

Innocent. Trevor Lloyd and innocent were not two compatible concepts. She couldn't help but laugh.

He smiled crookedly. "You don't trust me, do you?"

"I'm not some naive schoolgirl, Trevor."

"I know. You're an experienced, world-wise, undercover agent."

She groaned. "Oh, be quiet and let me eat my food."

"Is it a deal?"

She sighed. "Is what a deal?"

"We'll get to know each other and I'll keep my hands to myself. Give me a chance to prove it to you."

He had to be kidding. A man like him with all his vibrant sexuality would not be able to keep that up for long. And what about herself? How easy was it going to be to spend time with him without getting disturbed by all the dangerous stirrings he caused in her? She gave him a skeptical look. "That could be very interesting."

A devilish glint shone in his eyes. "Yes it could."

She closed her eyes, sighed and capitulated. "Okay, okay. It's a deal."

It wouldn't work. Never.

It *had* to work. Trevor was determined. He sat on the empty sailing school terrace, laptop computer in front of him, his hands idle. The sun was warm and mild. Flowers bloomed in tubs and baskets and a breeze blew off the lake. It was quiet at this time of the morning with everyone out on the lake sailing.

It had to work, because he wouldn't allow it not to.

Raine was scared of something, but he couldn't figure out what or why. If he genuinely thought she didn't want him, he would have been long gone. Back to St. Barlow, back to his work in the islands. Not that he was wasting his time here—networking and making contacts was an essential part of his work and his writing could be done here as well as anywhere else. Besides, he owed himself a month of vacation, at least. Being an independent agent, vacations sometimes went by the board and he hadn't had any real time off for a while.

His parents and brothers said that his whole life was a vacation, but that was to be expected. They were architects and had plush offices in a prestigious New York building. His office was a room in his private villa on a tiny tropical island. Everybody knew you couldn't do a stroke of honest work in such idyllic surroundings. You could not blame them for their ignorance. He grinned to himself and typed a few more sentences, all about creative financial planning and capital equipment. If only they could read this paper he was presently creating while sitting in the spring sun in Holland—no, Friesland. That would show them. Then again, it might not, but it didn't matter. They liked him anyway.

His thoughts returned to Raine, as they invariably did.

She was afraid. Of what? Of him? Of a relationship?

I don't want a summer fling. He couldn't blame her. He himself had no taste for summer flings. She, however, had no reason to take his word for it. Even if he were seriously interested, she had let it be known she had no time for men in the next five years. No, four and a half. So she said. Not exactly a believable story, but she seemed to believe it herself. Of course the human mind was a magic machine. A person could make himself believe any crazy or impossible thing as long as he was determined enough to believe it. Or she, as the case may be. Society was full of people deceiving themselves to make life more bearable or just more interesting. The world was full of Picassos and Napoleons and people who believed they had no problems while gambling away the house.

Raine had convinced herself she didn't want a man in her life. He didn't believe it for a minute. The question was, why did she think this?

The logical train of thought would lead to the assumption she'd had a traumatic experience with a man and she didn't want a repeat. Fear of intimacy, fear of being hurt again, fear of commitment. A common enough story. So common, in fact, that he hoped it was something a little more interesting.

Maybe it was part of the problem, but not the whole problem. His gut told him something else was going on.

Having freedom, being in charge. Her words came back to him, wafting in on a breeze of memory. She liked being in charge.

He saw Jannie, Max's wife, walk across the lawn toward him, the baby on her hip. She had very short, very blond hair cut in a sportish style and she had an open, smiling face. She was the bright, sparkly type, and he liked her. Her blue skirt flapped around her legs in the breeze. It was a good day for sailing and windsurfing, and bright sails dotted the water.

"I have the coffee ready," she said. "Would you like a cup?"

He looked at his watch. It was just after ten. Time for mid-morning coffee. The Dutch had tea for breakfast, coffee in the middle of the morning, coffee after lunch, tea at about four in the afternoon and coffee again after dinner. Very organized people, the Dutch.

Trevor looked down at his computer. He had not done a staggering amount of work. As a matter of fact it was stunningly little, so he definitely needed a break. He smiled at Jannie.

"I'd love a cup of coffee." He ducked to escape the baby's hand, which was reaching for his hair. The kid had strength, he had discovered, and could give you a real yank. Jannie laughed and grabbed the little hand in mid-air.

With a couple of strokes he closed out his computer. "I'll be right over," he said.

Jannie made for the school. "I have to steal some sugar. Don't tell anybody."

He laughed and began to gather the loose papers on the table held down by a monstrosity of a stone ashtray somebody had brought back as a souvenir from some mountainous region across the border.

He could smell the coffee as he entered the house a little later, hear voices and laughter coming from the living room. He caught a fragment of conversation, Kim saying something about Raine being determined to finish her book.

"That child looks as if she needs some good old-fashioned loving," Mrs. Boersma was saying, speaking with the authority gained from many years of mothering. Trevor sat down and Mrs. Boersma poured him a cup of coffee, giving him a warning look.

He raised his brows at her in question. "What did I do?" he asked, and Kim chuckled.

Mrs. Boersma offered him a slice of ginger cake. "Raine's not my daughter," she said, "but I'm very fond of her, so I warn you, don't play games with her."

He suppressed a smile and nodded solemnly. "I keep asking her to play, but she refuses, so I'm out of luck. Like Kim said, she wants to write her book."

Jannie gave her mother-in-law a reproving look. "Raine can take care of herself."

"I'm not so sure," said Mrs. Boersma.

After which the discussion changed to the weather, which was amazingly beautiful this spring. Back at the computer forty-five minutes later, fueled by strong coffee and conversations, Trevor's thoughts turned back to Raine.

Was he crazy to pursue a woman whose entire attention was focused on the writing of a book? Was he nursing an obsession of his own? This was not a pleasant thought, but not the first time it had occurred to him. He was not normally an obsessive man. He understood the meaning of the words yes and no. What he was getting from Raine was yes and no at the same time, which was rather confusing. He should just go back to doing what he was good at—rescuing islands and rain forests and goat farmers instead of chasing after a red-haired woman who didn't want to be caught.

So he typed another brilliant paragraph about tropical fruits and vegetables and hoped perhaps later he would come to his senses.

But of course he did not. He had offered Raine a stimulating friendship, a scheme he couldn't believe he had actually dreamed up, but the only thing he had been able to come up with that would possibly convince her to keep him around without constant conflict.

A stimulating friendship. Friendship in a love relationship was of course extremely important, and he doubted that any true love relationship could exist without the core of friendship. However, friendship alone was not what he wanted—he had friends aplenty already—but for now it would have to do. Hands off.

She didn't believe he could do it, not in a thousand years. The expression on her face had been very clear. Well, he would just have to prove it to her. It might well be the most difficult assignment of his life.

In the next couple of weeks, Trevor took her sailing on the weekends or they took long drives through the countryside visiting small village markets and eating leisurely meals in cozy restaurants. Sometimes during the week he would arrive in the early evening with the makings for dinner. He was absolutely the perfect man to have around when you were creating the novel of the year. He never came during the day, leaving her to do her work.

He kept his word: He didn't touch her. He did not kiss her, but he might as well have. His eyes, his voice, the very way he treated her were saturated in romance and seduction. She'd never thought it possible that a man could thrill her so deeply without even touching her. *The forbidden fruit.* Was that it? How did he do it? It was driving her crazy. *He* was driving her crazy.

A memory floated into her consciousness. A memory of his eyes and face the first time she had seen him—across the crowded room at the party. *I knew from the start*, she thought. *I knew from the start he was trouble.*

Yet she could not complain—after all, he was keeping his promise. Still, she was falling deeper and deeper in love with him. She felt devastated; she hadn't planned it. It was happening whether she liked it or not and she *didn't* like it. It made her feel vulnerable and off balance. But there it was.

Trevor was the most interesting man she had ever met, a fascinating combination of laid-back calmness and energetic ambition. He was deeply committed to his work in the islands. She liked listening to his stories, his views and opinions, feeling a growing respect.

They'd often eat dinner at her house, dinner he would fix, then watch the BBC news on television and discuss the state of affairs in the world, which usually was not good. War, poverty and ignorance were on the menu daily or so it seemed.

"I think we ought to figure out a better way of dealing with each other," said Raine one evening, disgusted by more bloodshed and intolerance. "All this fighting is so *primitive.*" She'd had two glasses of expensive French wine with dinner and she felt very clearheaded.

"You have any ideas?" asked Trevor, filling up her glass.

"Yes. I've thought about it a lot. It's called the Raine Plan for Eternal Peace." She gave him a solemn look.

"Fascinating. Tell me about it."

"Ignorance is the root cause of hate and strife," she said, sounding rather like a preacher giving a sermon. "We are afraid of what we don't know or understand. We don't like what we fear, which creates hate, which triggers the fighting instincts, which are evolutionary leftovers from our caveman days when we had very small brains and no intellectual capacity. With all those fighting instincts revved up in the body, adrenaline flowing, chemicals gushing, we are merely prey to our bodies and in order to get this boiling chemical soup to cool off we've got to fight and cause mayhem, so we start wars or inflict injuries on others." She took a swallow of her wine. "If we could just get rid of ignorance, we'd have the problem solved."

"And how are you going to do that?"

"It's very simple," she said, taking another swig of wine. "Every teenager at the age of eighteen should do a year of mandatory traveling around the world, carrying very little money and a lot of Pepto-Bismol," she improvised. "He would have to rely on the kindness of strangers. We hope of course that the strangers will be kind, but by and large people are. In that year he will learn about the goodness of people, even people wearing funny clothes and eating disgusting food. He will come home with a profound love for his fellow man. In twenty years or so we'll have peace, prosperity and brotherhood all over the world."

"Brilliant," he said. "Have another glass of wine, sweetheart."

She produced a look of great disdain. "I'm not your sweetheart and it's a sound plan."

"But totally impractical."

"It's not impractical. It is simple. Politicians and economists and educators get confused when they see things that are simple. They don't know what to do with them because they are all used to problems and solutions described in highfalutin language that they don't understand and therefore consider important. If it is simple, they don't value it, because it makes them feel stupid."

"The ones doing the traveling will be the rich kids. The poor kids can't even figure our where their next meal is coming from. So you'll have all the rich kids traveling around the world sponging off the poor people."

She glowered at him. "You're trying to confuse me."

"I'm just trying to keep it simple. No highfalutin language or nothing." He poured her another glass of wine.

"I don't want any more," she said. "I already had two."

"Three. And I'd like to hear the riveting stuff you come up with after you have four."

"You're a terrible person, leading me astray."

"Is that what I'm doing?" His eyes were laughing.

"Yes. You know you are. One more glass of wine and you'll try and seduce me."

"Will I succeed?"

"No, because I'm not having a fourth glass of wine." She came to her feet and straightened her spine. "I'm going to feed the animals and then I'm going to bed with a cup of tea and a good book." She sounded like a little old lady. She smiled sweetly.

He sighed. "In other words, get lost, buster."

"You've got it."

Not having a passionate love affair, they did a lot of talking. She asked him questions. He asked her questions. They were trying to draw each other out, which was, of course, quite acceptable since they were seriously working on a stimulating friendship.

"Have you ever had a grand passion?" he asked one day after they'd seen a torrid movie about a grand passion in the Amicitia theater in Sneek.

"I'm not sure," she said.

"How can you not be sure? A grand passion doesn't pass you by while you are asleep."

"Well, I was deliriously in love when I was twenty, but I don't know if it qualifies as a grand passion. It was the first time. I never had a boyfriend in high school. I was sort of a nerd, I guess. Straight A's. I was shy and scared to death of boys." She spooned whipped cream into her mouth. A mound of it covered the *appeltaart* she was having with the coffee they'd ordered in the cozy little restaurant not far from the theater. It was a place as ancient as the town. The tables were covered with thick imitation-persian rugs, a strange thing to have on a table, but there they were. There was dark paneling, old paintings and antique brass lamps.

It looked like something out of a movie set in the last century. It was interesting to visualize that a hundred years ago, maybe two hundred years ago, people had entered this place, sat down at a table and had a meal or some refreshments.

"What happened?" he asked.

"He dumped me and moved out of town. I cried for two months solid, lost ten pounds and then a much-drooled-over football player asked me out and I was too overwhelmed by the honor to go on crying."

"And you fell in love with the football player," he concluded.

"No way. I had learned my lesson. Besides, he was too much in love with himself already. All I did was bask in the glory of his fame for a while, until I got tired of him. He was a conceited jerk."

He laughed. "And after that?"

"Oh, let's see." She forked up another bite of the apple cake and contemplated the various men who had passed through her life, leaving few, if any, tracks. "There was Donald. He was rich and he traveled a lot. He had a collection of obscene oriental carvings—jade and rosewood and extremely expensive. He was very proud of them. And then there was Jerry. He was a vegetarian veterinarian." She grinned. "A lethal combination. I applaud the love of animals and I applaud vegetarianism, but I like a piece of red meat on occasion and he set out to convert me and I didn't want to be converted. He said I was a sadist, so that was that." She paused. "Oh, yes, Chuck. He had a really disgusting-looking teddy bear left over from his childhood. He still slept with it and he carried it around in his car in the daytime. Then one day he said Teddy was lonely and jealous and he wanted me to bring a girl bear to keep it company. I decided it was time to find greener pastures."

He put down his coffee cup and laughed.

She leaned back in her chair and sighed. "That was it. The grand total of my love life. A very sad story, I know."

"Why did you pick those losers?"

"I didn't pick them. They picked me."

"Hah. You allowed them to pick you."

"Don't you play Freud with me."

"It's true. Why didn't you find yourself a decent, normal guy?"

"There weren't any around, obviously, or I would have had one by now. I would have been married with a baby and a house in the suburbs."

"Is that what you want?"

She sensed a trap. "Eventually. Some variation of that at any rate."

"Not until five years from now."

"Right. I want to be in charge of my own life for a while and not have to worry about other people's needs and wishes."

"Are you afraid," he asked then, his voice quiet, "that if you have a relationship with a man you won't be in charge of your own life anymore?"

She shrugged. "Something like that, I suppose."

There was a silence. So she'd told him. It didn't matter; it didn't change anything. She didn't want any pirates rocking her boat.

Only, her boat was rocking already.

Chapter Seven

Kim could not understand what was going on. Then again, maybe she did. "It's all Michael's fault," she said late one afternoon when Raine had dropped by. "He ruined everything for you."

"Michael?" Raine could not have been more surprised. "What has Michael got to do with this?" Michael had been her first love, when she was twenty, and Kim had suffered with Raine through the eventual misery of its collapse. "I fail to see what Michael has to do with anything," said Raine.

"He was a toad. He treated you miserably."

This was true. Michael had not deserved her love and devotion. She had been so eager, so willing and hopeful and romantic. She'd dreamed of her own house, a house with color. In her head she'd already picked out the furniture, the color of the draperies, the sheets and towels. She would prepare lovely, home-cooked meals, nourishing and delicious. She could picture the two of them at the table, set with flowers and candles every night, discussing the day's events. Michael would amuse her with the stories of the guests of the hotel where he was an assistant manager. She would tell him about her writing, the people that she made up in her head.

Then one evening, over chicken cordon bleu, he'd calmly told her he needed his freedom back and was leaving Chicago and he hoped she would understand.

She did not.

Something alien had taken possession of his senses, a demon, an exotic virus. Why was he leaving Chicago? Why was he leaving her behind? What about the love they shared?

He was going back to California, he said. He had found a new job in a luxury resort hotel and it was a great opportunity. He belonged in California, in the land of eternal sunshine. *I can come with you,* she'd said, desperate, devastated. *I'd follow you to the moon!* she'd added.

It was not possible, he'd said, sounding like a patient father speaking to a dimwitted child.

But I love you, she'd whispered, feeling as if the ground had been ripped away from under her feet. He'd said she'd get over it.

In a trance she had finished her meal, while he went on making casual conversation as if for all the world they had merely dealt with a business matter and it had been concluded. It had not occurred to her to get up from the table and walk out. Wanda's training had worked well. Good manners and iron control till the bitter end.

At home she had cried. And cried and cried. Her sweet dreams and happy imaginings lay like wilted flower petals at her feet.

"I told you so," Wanda said, which indeed she had, many times. "He wasn't to be trusted. You're well rid of him."

This was true, of course, but it was not a truth that Raine had been ready to accept just then. She had been able to accept Michael's unworthiness a lot better after she did the desperate thing of getting on a plane and seeing him in California, hoping against hope that he might change his mind about her joining him there once he saw her again. He would realize how much he had missed her, how pretty she was with the sun shining on her copper hair, how much he loved her.

She'd made the journey half in a trance, a sort of daze of hope and euphoria: All would be well. She was already feeling his love surround her again. It had all been an ugly dream and soon it would be over.

A taxi dropped her off at the hotel. He had certainly done well for himself. The luxury resort hotel was opulent, the lobby awash with tropical trees. Having come so close, the daze cleared somewhat and her courage almost failed her. What would he say when he saw her? He might, after all, not be pleased. She sat down on one of the rattan chairs to collect herself.

She couldn't go through with it. Yes, she could. She hadn't come all the way to California and spent all that money just to flee like a scared rabbit. Love demanded courage.

What was the worst that could happen?

It happened right then, a nightmare in slow motion. The elevator door opened and Michael walked out. Tall, handsome, sophisticated in his expensive suit and tie. She wanted to jump to her feet and rush into his arms. Instead, she sat frozen in her chair, aching, wanting to cry out, but not a sound would come from her mouth.

He glanced around the lobby, looking right past her, not even noticing her. A woman walked in through the large main doors, carrying a small child. Michael's face brightened and he smiled. The woman put the little boy down and he toddled over to Michael.

"Daddy!" he called, his small face happy and smiling. Michael bent down and held out his arms and the boy almost fell into the embrace. Michael lifted the boy up and the small arms wound around his neck. The woman walked over and Michael kissed her. The three of them disappeared out of the main doors, into the bright California sunshine.

And that was that. The end of an illusion, the end of hope. Michael was, had been, a married man all along, and the father of a small child.

He's not to be trusted, Wanda had said. *I told you so. You're well rid of him.* Wanda was right. Wanda was smart. Raine had no trouble admitting it.

It had not been one of the better times in her life, but it had been years ago and she could look at it with the wisdom of increased age and without going to pieces over it. She should count her lucky stars the man wasn't *her* husband.

Raine looked at Kim and sighed. "You're right, he was a toad." Toad, of course, was an understatement, but she had no energy to spend on calling Michael names. Michael was history.

"And you know what happened afterward," Kim went on. "All those losers you had."

"Obviously, I am not lucky in love."

"Obviously you don't want to take any risks. None of those guys were serious and you knew it from the beginning. Maybe not consciously, but certainly subconsciously. You didn't want to take the risk of going through another Michael fiasco again."

"You've been reading pop psychology. Come on, Kim."

"And Trevor threatens your peace of mind," Kim went on doggedly. "He doesn't sleep with a teddy bear or have any crazy quirks that turn you off. It scares you to death, doesn't it?"

"Yes," said Raine, "but I'm not sure it has anything to do with teddy bears."

"Then what is it?"

"I want to be free."

"Free for what? To grow old alone? You need somebody to love, somebody to love you. I know that's what you want. That's all you ever seemed to want. And telling me that you can't have a man and write, too, is baloney. It's just an excuse."

Raine said nothing. It's just an excuse for what? she asked herself.

"Loving takes risks," said Kim, warming up to the subject, "and a lot of faith. And I know all about it. Look at me, I married a foreigner and moved to this country where they talk funny and put cornflakes on their yogurt and eat it for dessert."

"*You* put cornflakes on your yogurt and eat it for dessert."

"Well, yes, I happen to like it. And of course I picked the right foreigner and I quite like this country and I love my in-laws. So, all in all, I made out like a bandit. But it was a *risk.*"

"I know," said Raine. "And now you're determined to see me happy with a man and you like Trevor." She was well aware that Trevor spent considerable time with Kim and Menno and with Max and his wife, Jannie, and that they all got along like a house on fire.

"Yes. If I didn't have Menno, I'd go for him like a shot. And now I'm going to make us some coffee and shut up."

* * *

"You said your life wasn't perfect," Raine said to Trevor one day. It was Sunday and they were out on the lake in a small sailing boat. "What is it that you're looking for? What's lacking?"

"I don't enjoy being alone, living alone," he said.

His words surprised her. She'd thought of him as the independent type. The kind of man who liked to travel and not have too many strings to hold him back.

"Why not? You have your freedom. You can go where you want, leave when you want."

He shrugged, tipping back his can of beer and taking a drink. "I enjoy having somebody in my life. Somebody to talk to, to wake up with."

"I see." She glanced at the water glittering in the sun. There was a nice breeze, perfect weather for sailing. "So," she said slowly, "why didn't you marry the woman you were with for a long time?" If he wanted a wife, or a live-in partner, surely a man like him had plenty of choices and opportunities. "Not that I mean to pry, but since I told you about my torrid love life, you owe me."

He laughed. "Suzanna was very involved in her career. She lived in Miami and we had some sort of commuter relationship. Not ideal, but it was the best we could do. Then she was promoted and moved to New York, a year after I'd left there and moved to St. Barlow. It complicated matters a great deal. No way did she want to live on the island for any length of time. She was not enamored with the place— she's very much a big city person. She called it my 'Rotten Rock.'"

"I see. Basic incompatibility." The wind felt good on her face. She tucked an errant strand of hair behind her ear and studied his face.

He nodded. "On more than one front. Also, she didn't want children."

"And you do?"

"Ten or twelve."

Raine groaned. "No wonder no woman wants you."

He smiled. "I was only kidding."

"I sure hope so." She wondered what kind of father he would be. A good one, no doubt. He'd take them fishing and sailing, teaching them what he knew. She visualized him sitting in the boat with a couple of boys and a girl. It wasn't difficult.

"What about you?" he asked. "You want kids?"

"Not until I'm thirty and then only if they'll come with a written guarantee that they'll turn out right."

He threw back his head and laughed. "Have another beer," he said, lifting his own can.

He looked hopelessly sexy in his white shorts and shirt, which set off his tan to perfection. She enjoyed watching his strong arms and legs at work when he handled the sails, the muscles flexing and relaxing. His hair was windblown and his whole body looked at ease; he was in his element here on the water in this boat. She felt like touching him, feel the sun-warmed brown skin under her hands.

"So it didn't work between you and Suzanna," she asked, not wanting to continue her train of thought.

He shrugged. "The relationship sort of died a natural death. We saw each other less and less. It was a mutual decision to call it quits. I think the expression is we were not made for each other."

"Fate. Do you believe in fate?"

He met her eyes. "I didn't used to."

"But you do now?"

His eyes were suddenly hard to read and for a moment he was silent. "Yes, I do," he said then.

She felt a strange lightness as his gaze held hers. "Why?" she asked, her voice soft and husky.

"I think it's fate that we should be together."

Again the fleeting feeling of apprehension, the feeling that she couldn't tell what was in his mind—some secret knowledge he was keeping from her.

"Why do you think that?"

He shrugged lightly. "I just do. There's no way to explain it. I knew it the first time I saw you."

Romantic nonsense, she thought, yet the idea was exciting. *Love at first sight,* Kim had said. Could there really be some truth to it? Chemistry, some might call it. Or a sense of connection people were aware of on some deeper, spiritual level.

"Maybe," he said, a glint of humor in his eyes, "we knew each other in another life. Maybe we were lovers."

"Who knows," she said. "Maybe we were slaves in ancient Greece, or maybe you were a rich Chinese merchant and I was your concubine. Or, let's see. Maybe *you* were a lowly Aztec laborer and *I* was a princess." She grinned. "The possibilities are endless."

"So is your imagination."

"You started it. I can't help it. It just sort of comes rushing out." She swept a strand of hair out of her face. "Anyway, why does it matter now what we were in another life?"

He looked at her solemnly. "There's a belief that if you had a tragic love affair in a previous life, or a love affair that did not have a chance to bloom properly, you get another chance to make it right."

"How nice. So that's what we're doing? Or let's say that's what *you* would like us to be doing? Making right what we didn't get to do in a former life?"

"Don't you think it would be a very nice thing to be doing?" He was smiling at her, an intimate smile that made her grow warm all over. Her pulse raced. It wasn't hard to tell now what he was thinking. It wasn't hard to know what she wanted herself.

She averted her eyes, focusing on the orange-and-white sails of a boat not far from theirs. She willed her heart to calm down. Her skin burned despite the cool wind.

I wish he would touch me, she thought. I wish he would kiss me.

But he did neither. Instead, he adjusted the sails, slightly changing course. For a moment the sails flapped joyfully in the wind, then tightened and billowed again.

Amazingly, her writing went well. She'd thought her turbulent emotional life would sap her of inspiration and concentration. The opposite was true; it seemed to fuel her imagination. Writing passionate love scenes wasn't nearly as difficult as she had anticipated. The Gypsy hero was a wonderful lover, and although Elizabeth had fought him tooth and nail she'd had to succumb to him eventually. Also, totally against her will, Elizabeth was getting enchanted by the wandering life, the spirited women, the dancing and the singing. She was beginning to understand why the Gypsies lived the way they did, felt the way they did about *gorgios*.

Sometimes Raine would look up, surprised she'd toiled for hours on end without even knowing it, wondering if her work was any good. Fear would clutch at her. What if she was no good? What if all this was only an unrealistic dream? But her fears never lasted long. She could not afford to give into fear—she just had to keep going. Ever since she was a little girl she'd wanted to write books. Now she was going to do it. Whether she'd ever be able to make a career of it was still uncertain, but she'd never find out if she didn't try.

One Saturday morning they visited the Jopie Huisman museum in Workum at Raine's request. Jopie Huisman was the artist who'd done the painting of the dolls hanging in the living room at the farmhouse. "He used to be a junk collector," Raine told Trevor. "Kim says he does lots of paintings of old junk and they're wonderful. I'd love to see them. He doesn't sell the originals, they're all in the museum."

Workum was a lovely picturesque town, centuries old, with narrow streets and interesting houses and flowers in tubs and planters everywhere. The museum building was an historical house with narrow passages and staircases and small rooms. They moved from room to room, looking at all the marvelous paintings of old and forgotten things the painter had picked up in his cart, the stuff people threw out and didn't want anymore—worn-out work shoes and rusted farm tools and broken toys and ancient knit wool underwear, darned and faded.

In one of the rooms, they found the original painting of the dolls, and Raine stood in front of it, smiling.

"I really like this one," she said. "You can see the love in it, and the sadness. It's almost as if these dolls were human, with real feelings. As if they're really hurting because somebody threw them away."

"If only they could talk," he said evenly. "They could tell you their sad story. I'm sure it would be riveting."

She glowered at him and he laughed. "You're such a sentimental romantic," he said.

"Don't you see it?"

He was standing very close to her, his eyes smiling into hers. "Yes, I see it."

"I had an old doll once, not one like these, but I'd had it for ages and my mother had given it to me. Wanda threw it away when I moved in with her."

"Not nice. Why did she do that?"

"She said there was no need for me to keep all that junk. Her apartment wasn't very big and we had to get rid of as much of my stuff as possible. She threw it out and I didn't know it was gone until it was too late.'' She paused for a moment, not seeing the painting, but her own treasured doll. ''I didn't play with dolls anymore, of course,'' she went on, ''and it was pretty ratty looking, but this one had been my favorite and I'd wanted to keep it.'' The hurt over her loss was still there, silly perhaps after so many years, but she could feel the sadness of it still in some deep, hidden part of her heart.

She remembered vividly the moment she had discovered the doll was gone, remembered the horrible mixture of anguish and fury. It had seemed to her at that moment that Wanda had purposely wanted to rob her of her past, of all that represented her life with her parents, her sister, her little brother. She had taken over, buying her new clothes, getting her a new hairstyle, telling her how to act and what to say. Trying to mold her into something new, a person Wanda could approve of.

He was silent for a moment. ''Maybe she didn't understand what it meant to you.''

''No.'' She glanced at him. ''She isn't the sentimental type.''

''Like you,'' he said, his hand squeezing hers for just a fleeting instant. Her heart did a crazy somersault. It was the first time he had touched her in weeks and every nerve in her body jumped to attention at the touch. *Good Lord, control yourself,* she admonished herself.

''The day after Wanda threw the doll out, she gave me a pair of real gold earrings. Very beautiful. I think it was to make up for throwing out the doll, but she never said it, never apologized.''

''What did she say?''

''Just that she had a present for me, and that it was important for a girl to have good jewelry.''

"But the earrings didn't make up for the doll."

"No." She sighed. "It was her way of saying sorry, I think. She gave me a lot of things, a lot of presents, but I never wanted them."

"Some people aren't good with words, or showing emotion."

"I know. She never hugged me or kissed me. I came from a very affectionate family, and I think I had trouble with that. I've tried—I *am* trying—to accept Wanda for what she is, but it was very difficult when I was younger."

Now that she lived here, with the help of time and distance, she was trying to see Wanda more objectively, but it still was not easy. She wanted to understand Wanda, wanted to understand the dynamics of their relationship. *It's too late,* came the unbidden thought.

"Sometimes accepting is all we can do," he said.

They moved on to the next small room. The paintings were full of emotion—sadness and nostalgia and lost love and forgotten joy and memories that made people smile. The old darned wool underwear on a washing line made people smile.

Junk, Raine thought, all that junk and the artist had seen something in it—the history, the stories, the love, and he had made something beautiful out of it, images and pictures that touched people's hearts.

She wished she could take all that was old and broken in her life and make something new and beautiful out of it.

Wanda is not the sentimental type. The words echoed in his mind. Good God, what an understatement. He remembered the cool gray eyes, the calm controlled voice.

I wanted what was best for her, Trevor. When she came to live with me she was a mouse, silent, skinny. I had to do something. A woman has to be able to take care of herself in this world, be assertive, speak up. She never spoke up. She didn't know what she wanted. It seemed to me that she just tried to fade into the wallpaper.

What Raine had tried to do, no doubt, was to get away from her overbearing aunt, those cool eyes, that calm voice. Fourteen years old she'd been, suddenly robbed of family and home, full of despair and pain. She'd been in need of love and compassion and what she'd received was instructions and advice on her wardrobe, her school curriculum, her behavior.

He saw again the spacious office with its Italian designer furniture, the beautiful woman behind the desk in her haute couture clothes, the immaculate makeup. And there had been that cat in her office, that small, nondescript gray cat. It had jumped onto her lap, and she had pushed the chair away from the desk and leaned back, stroking it slowly, sensuously. Something about the image struck him as slightly off-key, but he could not put his finger on it. He had watched her, wondering what had gone on in her head, what her motives had been.

There were other images, pictures of Wanda sitting in the middle of the room with Raine's papers strewn around her, a wild look in her eyes. *I have to find her, Trevor. I've got to find her.* And the memory of his own feeling of pity for her. Pity he couldn't quite understand. Somewhere under all the hard gloss of her life, there had to be a soft spot, some feeling.

I think of her as my daughter, she'd said.

You couldn't look into the souls of other people.

He glanced over at Raine studying another painting. She no longer faded into the wallpaper. She was striking with her flaming hair and green eyes. She was plenty assertive and she seemed quite sure of what she wanted. But a few moments ago he'd glimpsed another part of her, a part she was very good at hiding. For a fleeting moment there had been pain in her eyes, the pain of memories from long ago. He had taken her hand, but what he'd wanted to do was hold her tight against him, feel her heartbeat against his own. It had been a long, long time since she had been loved by anyone. If only she would let him near.

Chapter Eight

May, sunny and bright, danced into an equally cheerful June. Flowers bloomed everywhere. Kim bloomed. Her pregnancy made her glow and shine and she looked wonderfully well. Raine felt quite aglow herself; she was in love with Trevor and there was no way to deny it. She felt exhilarated just being with him. Yet the fear remained, and sometimes she would lie awake wondering where the fear came from, why she was afraid.

"Tell me," she said one day, "don't you have anything better to do than to pursue a neurotic, obsessive writer who doesn't want to sleep with you?"

"No," he said, "this is an opportunity of a lifetime."

"How's that?"

"I get to observe you, talk to you, get to know you as a person without all those distracting sexual games that cloud a man's mind and sanity and interfere with his reasoning. It's very refreshing."

Sure it was. Nothing sexual going on between them, not a bit. They were like brother and sister, like innocent lambs frolicking in the clover.

"Very refreshing indeed," she agreed.

"And so mature and adult. Think of how much pain and anguish could be avoided if more people would take this sensible course of action instead of going off the deep end and getting swallowed up by the frivolous rapture of sexual pleasure and shallow passion. Sleeping together in the same bed, sharing sublime physical intimacies." He smiled. "True friendship and an intellectual and spiritual bond are so much more satisfying."

"Quite," she said.

"Of course," he went on, "any time you feel you'd like to explore the more intimate side of this relationship a bit further, don't hesitate to let me know. I might be persuaded to accommodate you."

"I wouldn't want to cloud your brain." She smiled benevolently. "I wouldn't dream of being so selfish."

He adopted a pensive look. "Then again, it is quite possible that after I've studied you sufficiently I will agree with you that right now is not the time for a passionate relationship and bid you a fond farewell."

"I will miss our intellectual conversations, but think of all the time I'll have to write. Would you like another beer?"

And so it went.

Sitting on the terrace one early evening, fish on the grill, a glass of wine in her hand, she found herself telling him about Wanda.

"I had to leave," she said. "I was beginning to feel like a doormat. I couldn't stand myself anymore."

He gave her an amused look. "You, a doormat? It's hard to imagine."

"Oh, there's a doormat in all of us," she said lightly. "All it takes is the right person to bring it out."

"And there was Wanda."

"The perfect bringer-out-of-doormats. She's very intimidating. She's a master of manipulation, knows exactly how to make people do what she wants them to do."

"You don't seem like someone who lets herself be manipulated easily."

"I am a recovering doormat, so to speak. I had to learn that it wasn't all Wanda's fault. I *allowed* her to manipulate me. I should have stood up to her much sooner. But I was only fourteen when I came to live with her, you know. I'd just lost my whole family and I was terribly vulnerable then. I was numb and I just let her make decisions for me. I didn't have the strength then and nothing much seemed to matter anyway. I didn't care about anything for a long time." She shrugged. "And then we were in a pattern and I didn't know how to get out of it. Of course, while I was away at college, I began to see things a little differently, although I still felt I owed her."

"Why did you feel you owed her?"

She sat back and took in a deep breath. "Well, think about it," she said lightly, determined not to get maudlin. "She'd taken me in. I mean, it must have been very hard for her. She never had any children of her own. She was a businesswoman running her own company." She grimaced. "Having a teenage girl around must have been the *last* thing she wanted. I cramped her style, no doubt."

"You were her *niece*."

Raine nodded. "Right. So she did what she had to do. She took in the poor waif and did the best she could."

"Did she ever say how she felt about your living with her?"

"No, but it was obvious. She's not the maternal type."
She made herself grin. "She's very...eh, sophisticated, very
glamorous in an offbeat sort of way. Very much her own
person. There are always men around. She's been divorced
for years, but she's never remarried. I don't think she ever
will. What I mean to say is that she's totally independent
and she expects people to perform, no excuses."

"So why did you go to work for her? Why didn't you get
away and do your own thing?"

She extended her hands, palms up. "Because that had
been the plan for years. Because she expected it. Because it
was a great opportunity." She made a face. "And because
I felt I owed her." She dropped her hands. "So I decided to
at least give it a chance. And I tried, I really did, but... It
just didn't work out."

He'd been listening intently, his dark eyes never leaving
her face. "So here you are," he said, "playing spy, just what
you always wanted to do."

She gave him a taunting look. "Right," she said, not rising to the bait.

"Has it occurred to you," he said slowly, "that your reluctance to let me close has something to do with all that?"

"Like how?"

"You are afraid, if we get too close, that I'll manipulate
you. That you'll lose control." He glanced around the
room. "You've left everything behind and started over, and
you've built yourself your own little universe and you're
worried it might collapse."

She felt her heart beat against her ribs.

"There's nothing wrong with being in charge of your own
life."

"No, there isn't. What makes you think, Raine, that if
you let me into your life you'll lose control?"

She remained silent.

"I like you for what you are, Raine. I wouldn't ask you to be different, to change in any way. I have no desire to take over your life, or anyone else's, for that matter."

The phone rang, startling her. She scrambled to her feet to answer it. It was Menno, and as soon as she heard his voice, she knew something was wrong.

"Kim's in the hospital in Sneek," he said, his voice toneless.

Raine felt her heart turn over in her chest. "What's wrong, Menno? What's wrong with her?"

"She had a . . . uh . . . mis . . . mis-something. *Miskraam.* Damn, I can't think of the word in English. The baby, it's—" His voice broke and he was silent.

Raine grew icy cold. "Oh, Menno," she whispered. "You mean she lost the baby?"

"Yes," he said, and his voice sounded unsteady. He cleared his throat. "What do you call it?" he asked in an obvious effort to regain control over his emotions with a cold, academic question.

"A miscarriage. Oh, Menno, I'm so sorry. How is she?"

"Physically she's fine, but emotionally she's taking it very hard."

Raine felt a wave of grief for Kim. "Can I go see her?"

"Yes, of course. Please do."

"I'll come right over."

She replaced the receiver and looked at Trevor. "I've got to go to the hospital." She swallowed hard. "Kim lost the baby."

"Oh, no," he said, his voice low. "Poor Kim. Would you like me to come with you?"

"No, no. It's all right." She turned and ran up the stairs, changed her clothes and came back down. "I don't know when I'll be back."

"It doesn't matter."

Kim's mother-in-law was in the room with her when Raine arrived at the hospital. "I was just leaving," she said and smiled at Raine. Then she kissed Kim and squeezed her hand. "See you later."

Raine went up to the bed and hugged Kim and promptly broke into tears. "Oh, Kim," she whispered. "I don't know what to say."

"There's . . . nothing *to* say." Kim was crying, too. Raine straightened and wiped her eyes. "I made you cry, I'm sorry."

"Crying is all I've done. I'm such a mess. Oh, I'm so glad you're here." She took a tissue and blew her nose. Raine did the same. They gave each other a watery smile.

"Well, there goes my eighteen-year plan," said Kim in a voice thick with tears.

"Eighteen-year plan? What are you talking about?"

"I had this baby going to Harvard on a full scholarship." She gave Raine a tearful smile. "As you see, life does not accommodate our plans always. You may think you're in charge, but you're not, Raine."

Raine's heart contracted. She felt a mixture of emotions—pity for Kim, fear for herself. She didn't want to feel helpless. The idea was terrifying. She clenched her hands as if grasping something, holding on to something for dear life.

She sat down on a chair and forced herself to relax. She glanced around. It was your average generic modern hospital room. There was a picture on the wall with large sunflowers on it, a Van Gogh reproduction. Fresh flowers were sitting on the window sill.

"So how are they treating you here?" she asked lightly.

Kim made an effort to smile. "Everybody is really nice, I can't complain. Menno is a rock, but he's upset too, and my mother-in-law is wonderful." Her eyes filled with tears again. "Oh God, I wanted this baby. It was real to me,

Raine. I know that's hard to believe, but it existed and it was mine and it was real." Tears ran down her cheeks. "I talked to it, can you believe that? I talked to it all the time."

Raine felt her heart contract. "It was real, Kim. Of course it was real."

"And now it's gone. And I'll never hold it. I wanted so much to hold it, Raine."

When Raine left, after Menno had arrived, she felt worn out with emotion. She crossed the front lobby in a daze, surprised to hear her name called. She stopped and saw Trevor getting up from a chair. He scrutinized her face.

"Are you all right?" he asked.

"I'm fine. What are you doing here?"

"I thought you might want a drink." He draped his arm around her shoulders and steered her out the door.

They had drinks and a late dinner. The food, which was delicious, was wasted on her, as was the ambience of the restaurant. All she could think of was Kim's anguished face. She felt an aching sadness and she didn't feel like talking. Trevor seemed to understand it and spoke little himself. Yet she was grateful he had come to the hospital to wait for her.

He wanted to drive her home in his car and take her to pick up her car at the hospital the next morning, but she refused the offer. He took her back to the hospital parking lot. It was a little windy and chilly and she shivered in her dress as she searched for her keys in her bag.

He took them from her and wrapped his arms around her and held her tight, saying not a word. There was comfort in his embrace and she felt the urge to hold on to him and not to let go. Then he released her, opened the door for her and handed her back the keys.

"I'll see you tomorrow," he said.

Kim was tough, at least she seemed so on the outside once she was back home and life resumed its normal routine.

She'd stopped crying, but there was a sadness in her eyes and Raine knew that for a while Kim wouldn't be her usual bouncy self.

You may think you're in charge, but you're not, you know. The words kept echoing in her head. And there were other things Kim had said about plans. About making adjustments, about accommodating fate, making the best of things. *Don't let something good pass you by because it isn't part of your plan. Make room for it.*

Prioritize. In five years' time Trevor would not be around. Trevor was here now. She watched him as he played the piano, listening to the music, feeling her soul fill with some new emotion.

Was she letting something wonderful pass her by?

She was feeling at peace sitting here listening to him playing music, watching his hands move over the keys with grace.

What makes you think, Raine, that if you let me into your life you'll lose control?

Why was she afraid? She was a doormat no longer. She'd stood up to Wanda. She was a strong person. There was no reason to be afraid. If she didn't lie down, no one could step on her. It was as easy as that.

The last notes floated away in the air. Trevor got up from the piano bench and sat down next to her.

She sighed. "I could listen to you play all night," she said. On impulse she took his hand, turned it palm down and smoothed the fingers straight with her own. It was a big, masculine hand, a good, strong hand not afraid of work, not a delicate pianist hand you'd associate with exquisite music, tender melodies. Still, that's what this hand had created on the piano. "Magic fingers," she said, smiling at him.

He smiled back, his hand turning slowly, fingers curling around hers. The mood changed subtly and the silence quivered with tension.

The ringing of the phone made her jump, and he laughed softly, releasing her hand. Reluctantly, she uncurled herself from her comfortable corner on the sofa and went to answer it. It was Max.

"Is Trevor there?" he asked. "I had an agitated Spaniard on the phone looking for him. Wants him to telephone him right away."

Raine handed the phone over to Trevor who jotted down a number.

"Do you mind if I use your phone?" he asked after he hung up. "I'll pay for the call."

She gestured in approval. "Go ahead. Is it personal? You want me to leave?"

His brows shot up in surprise. "No, no. Business." He began to dial.

"I didn't know you had business in Spain."

"Spain? I'm calling the DR—the Dominican Republic."

Raine watched him as he talked, seeing his relaxed pose disappear, his face harden. His whole body stood at attention, tall and in control. He spoke in fluent, rapid Spanish—much too fast for her to follow. She sipped her wine absently. He began to scribble numbers and words on a pad. A series of emotions crossed his features—surprise, anger, frustration. Watching him, she was glad she was not on the other end of the line. It was fascinating to see this other part of his personality, the man at work, strong, in command.

She felt a tightening of her stomach muscles as she watched the dark, flashing eyes and the hard, determined line of his chin. She closed her eyes for a moment. Sometimes she wished he wouldn't keep his promise. The growing tension was getting on her nerves. Maybe that's what he had intended.

She took another slow sip of wine. The Dominican Republic: a Caribbean country sharing the island of Hispaniola with Haiti. She knew that much, but she hadn't realized people spoke Spanish in the DR. It was appalling how little she knew. She got up and found an atlas on the bookshelves that ran the length of an entire wall. It was large and heavy and she put it on the thick Berber carpeting on the floor.

Sitting on her knees in front of it, she found the Caribbean. The island chains stretched across two pages. The DR was easily found, but she couldn't locate St. Barlow.

As she was studying the maps, she heard Trevor replace the receiver.

"Is there a problem?" she asked, looking up at him. He towered over her, gazing down at her. The frown was gone and his face was magically relaxed again.

"No," he said, "it's straightened out." His mouth curved in a half smile. "I just had to remind somebody who was boss."

"You were very impressive on the phone."

"That was the whole idea." He glanced down at the map on the floor. "What are you looking for?"

"Your precious island. I don't see it anywhere."

"It's probably not there. There are hundreds of tiny islands that aren't on a map like that."

"I didn't know there were so many."

"You can even buy your own island, if you want to. There are real estate agents specializing in the sale and resale of islands." He sat down next to her on the rug. He was very close. So close she could feel the warmth of his body radiating onto her bare arm.

Don't let something good pass you by because it isn't part of your plan. Make room for it.

Was she too inflexible? Was that the problem? Certainly it had been proven that Trevor was no threat to her creativity. In fact, his presence in her life and thoughts had acted as a stimulus—she couldn't deny it. He was not going to keep her from reaching her goal; he might very well help her reach it sooner.

It all seemed so simple. What wasn't simple was the fact that she still felt scared in the depths of her being, a dark spot of uncertainty and fear. Why was she afraid? Where was the threat?

He reached out and pointed at the map. She stared at his big brown hand, feeling her pulse quicken. All she had to do was reach out. She wanted to touch him, run her hand over his muscled arm to his neck, let her fingers creep into his thick hair. There was nothing wrong in loving a man like Trevor. Nothing wrong at all. It should, in fact, be supremely right. She swallowed and focused on the place where he was pointing.

"It's about here," he said. "Lots of little islands all over the place here."

He turned his face to look at her, his dark eyes holding hers. Warmth suffused her. One part of her wanted to move away, just so they wouldn't accidentally touch. His eyes smiled into hers and her breathing stuck in her throat.

She dropped her gaze and glanced back at the map.

"If I wanted to go there," she heard herself say, "how would I get there?" She glanced back at him.

His eyes met hers, the smile deepening. "You'd fly from Miami to St. Thomas and from there you'd take a puddle jumper, a twin engine with just a few seats, like a small bus."

"I see," she said, feeling strangely breathless. She reached out, her finger searching the map for St. Thomas.

"Here," he said, pointing.

There hands touched. She did not withdraw. Her blood roared in her ears. His hand slipped over hers, covering it lightly. Still she did not withdraw. The warmth of his hand sent sparks of fire shooting through her.

"Have you decided?" he asked, his voice deep and low. His fingers curved around her hand, holding it. The air between them pulsed with sudden tension.

"Decided what?" It took an effort to talk. There seemed to be no air to breathe.

His mouth was close to her ear. "If you'd like to come to St. Barlow," he said softly.

"It seems like such a beautiful place from what you've told me." It was a struggle to utter the words.

"Yes, it is." His mouth touched her cheek, a feathering of wine-cooled lips, teasing, tantalizing. "You haven't answered my question."

Silken threads of tension drew them closer, closer. It was hard to breathe. "What was the question?"

"Would you like to come to Paradise?" His mouth was near hers, touching the corner. Her skin tingled with his touch.

She closed her eyes, afraid to move, afraid to breathe. Her heart was racing, all her senses acutely aware of his strong male nearness—the clean, warm scent of his body, the sound of his voice, the touch of his mouth. Shivering sensations captured her body. She longed for him to hold her, to feel loved and desired.

She wanted so much to be loved.

She longed to touch him, feel his strong, hard body against her.

Paradise. Did she want to come to Paradise?

"Yes," she whispered, "yes, I'd like that."

Chapter Nine

His mouth moved over hers and his kiss, deep and urgent, shook her. There was passion, yet no forcefulness—a wild need, somehow still controlled. He nudged her back until she lay on the rug. He went on kissing her, his hands sliding under her shirt to stroke her bare skin, eager, gentle hands. Releasing her mouth, he lowered his face against her breasts, expelling a soft groan. His body stilled. "I want you so much," he whispered huskily. "I've wanted you for so long, so long."

"You . . . how—"

He silenced her with a gentle finger. "Shh." He took her hand and held it to his chest. "In here," he said. "In here, I've known you for a long time."

She smiled and closed her eyes. "Very mysterious, very romantic."

His fingers curled into her hair. "I knew you in my dreams. I saw your face, your eyes."

"Maybe you knew me in another life, like you said," she whispered, relishing in the feel of him against her, her body stirring restlessly, a frantic need surging through her. "Do you believe in that? Do you think it's possible?"

"I don't *not* believe it. I don't know anything about it. All I know is the present and it's all I care about now." His tongue traced the contours of her mouth. She let out a soft sigh, relaxing back against the rug.

"Let's go upstairs," he said into her ear. "I don't want to fight with the legs of the coffee table."

And of course they could not allow themselves to be swept away by passion as if they were nothing but fluff caught by surprise in a tropical storm. They were not, of course, caught by surprise. They'd known the storm was brewing for a long time and that the crucial matter of precautions needed to be dealt with. So they dealt with it, like two mature adults, and it was done very sweetly and responsibly.

Her room under the eaves was no longer the same with Trevor in it. It seemed transformed into another, secret world, away from everything that was normal and routine. The moon spilled its silver light over the bed and the air was filled with the flowery perfume of roses growing below the open window. They stood by the bed, arms around each other.

"I dreamed of you, too," she whispered, her face against his shoulder. "Of you here with me, in this room." The words came with surprising ease, spinning a delicate web of intimacy. It was true, of course. She'd dreamed many dreams, and edited versions of some of them had even ended up in her book, which had made her feel a little funny, but that's the way it went with a creative mind.

"I'm glad," he said on a low note, his mouth against her temple. "I'm glad you're telling me that."

Over his shoulder she could see the moon and the swaying of the branches of the old apple tree. She could hear the rustling of the leaves and the eerie call of some nocturnal creature. All her senses seemed sharpened as if her awareness of him made everything else come alive around her.

"Let me take off your clothes," he murmured, reaching for the buttons on her blouse. "I want to see you, all of you." His fingers worked with slow deliberation, and the soft movements of his hand against her breast set small flames of fire licking at her senses. His eyes smiled into hers, dark and full of tender promise, as little by little he slipped off her clothes. It was difficult to stand still, difficult to breathe. Every nerve tingled with the touch of his hands.

She helped him with his clothes and an endless, tantalizing eternity later they were both naked, looking at each other. Her heart was in her throat, her eyes drinking in the sight of his strong, aroused body washed in moonlight. Adam in Paradise, she thought, feeling a smile tugging at her mouth, feeling love and wonderment suffuse her. Surely there was nothing more beautiful than a man and a woman and the magic of love.

Love. And trust. It was time to trust again, to let go of old suspicions and fears. And as she looked into his eyes, she felt no barriers, no apprehensions, knowing in the depths of her soul that this was right, that what was between them was real and true. Underneath his lighthearted teasing and seduction of the past weeks, she'd sensed a deeper emotion, something more substantial than simple physical desire. It was obvious in the way he listened to her when she spoke, his interest in what she told him of herself.

She reached out and put her hand flat on his chest, feeling the rapid beating of his heart under her palm.

"I want to make love," she whispered, feeling a need to say the words, wanting to see his expression when he heard them.

His eyes darkened, and the strong lines of his face twisted, softened, as if her words had struck a nerve and for a moment his control was gone. He drew her to him with a groan, pressing her against him until every inch of her touched him. His body was hot, the rough hair of his chest tickled her breasts, and a flash flood of heat rushed through her. A moment later he lifted her effortlessly onto the bed and lay down with her. He leaned over her, his eyes holding hers, dark and intent.

"This is not a summer fling," he said, his voice rough. "I want you to understand that."

She smiled. "It would be an awful expensive one considering the investment of your time and patience."

"And I know all about investments and I only invest in worthwhile, long-term ventures."

"Like small islands and rain forests."

"And you, for the long haul." His mouth claimed hers, then slowly moved down, dropping kisses on her chin, her throat. His hands and mouth began a sensuous exploration, caressing her breasts, her stomach, his tongue leaving damp trail across her skin. He wasn't rushing, his slow, movements gentle and caring. It amazed her to feel the tenderness of those big hands.

"How's that?" he whispered. "Do you like this?"

"Yes, yes." How could she not? She had never been touched like this before. Time was standing still and all was sweet, delirious sensation. She felt as if she'd found water after a long drought, as if suddenly she was coming alive, feeling exquisite sensations, her body full and warm and lush with loving, blooming under his hands.

She swallowed. "I didn't know..."

"Know what?" he said softly.

"I didn't know . . . it could feel like this."

He laughed softly. "Magic."

"Yes." She turned slightly so she could reach him better, wanting to feel him under her hands, touch him as he was touching her, making him feel what she was feeling.

They pleasured each other for a long time, as if performing a mysterious ritual, ancient and intimately familiar, as if they'd been together for a thousand years.

Her body turned into fluid motion, aching, wanting, searching. Pressure built in the vibrant, liquid core of her and her body trembled with a dizzying hunger.

"Trevor," she whispered, "Trevor . . ."

They clung together, melting into each other, and all dissolved in fire and passion.

The early light and bird song awoke her. The window was open and the fresh morning air filled the room. Trevor was next to her and she lay still, eyes closed, knowing that if she opened them he would be there. She reached out her hand across the bed, finding the solid warmth of him and she smiled, eyes still closed. This was the way it was supposed to be, this feeling of love and warmth, this sense of connection with another human being.

He shifted closer to her, drawing her to him, his legs tangling with hers. She opened her eyes and looked into his face. Dark eyes studied her, eyes full of love and amusement.

"Did you think I'd be gone?"

"No. I could feel you were there, even before I touched you."

"And you had no objection?"

"Objection?"

"To finding me still in your bed."

"Where else would you be?"

"I could have gone back to the boat."

"Did you want to?"

"No, I did not want to." He kissed her. "But I don't want you to worry that I am going to interfere with your independence. I am a very liberated man."

"How liberated?" she murmured.

"I wash my own socks."

She laughed. His mouth was warm against her throat and new desire swept through her. Wrapping her arms around his back, she pressed him closer to her. "Trevor?"

"What?"

"Make love to me, please."

He gave a low grumble. "Do I have to?"

For a fraction of a second she was speechless, then she heard him chuckle. She tried to push herself away from him, but he held her easily, refusing to let go. "You . . . !" He silenced her protests with his mouth, kissing her, covering her body with his, pinning her against the mattress. She struggled against him, laughing now, knowing it was hopeless, doing it anyway. Her squirming body did nothing to calm desire.

In the new light of day, they made love again, playfully, joyfully, until, their passion spent, they lay quiet and exhausted in each other's arms.

"Will that do?" he asked, pseudo-polite.

"Oh, go away," she said, pushing at his chest. "I want to sleep. You've worn me out. Keep this up, and I'll be spent and wasted before I'm thirty."

He laughed as he leapt out of bed. She threw a pillow at him, which he caught neatly and threw right back at her. He left the room and Raine curled up under the covers, too drowsy and languorous to get up.

She hadn't really meant to fall asleep again, but when she looked at the bedside clock the next time she opened her eyes, she knew she must have. Quickly she jumped out of bed. She glanced out the window. His car was still there. She showered, pulled on a pair of shorts and a T-shirt and raced down the stairs. The smell of coffee greeted her. It sure was nice to have a man around who wasn't helpless when it came to domestic chores. He seemed to do them completely naturally, thinking nothing of it.

He wasn't in the kitchen or on the terrace, but she found him standing in her office with a sheaf of white papers in his hands.

Her manuscript.

She froze and for a moment she couldn't breathe. He'd gone into her office and he was reading her manuscript. The heat of anger rushed to her face, made her heart race.

He glanced up. "Hello again," he said softly.

She moved toward him, her body rigid. "What do you think you're doing?" Her voice shook. She snatched the papers out of his hand, but her grip was awkward and the stack of loose pages slipped out of her hand and dropped in disarray on the floor. "Oh, damn!" she cried. She went down on her knees to gather the papers. "This is my office! This is my work! You have no right to go snooping around in here!" Her sense of joy and elation had evaporated. Outrage replaced all the other feelings. Furiously she snatched up the papers.

"Raine, please," he said. "I wasn't—"

"This is invasion of privacy!" she said fiercely. "You have no business coming in her and reading my stuff!"

"I wasn't reading it," he said, an odd tone to his voice.

Still on her knees, she stared up at him. He was standing perfectly still, his face tense.

She came to her feet, the manuscript clutched against her chest. "You sure could have fooled me!" She dropped the untidy, crumpled papers next to the computer on the desk.

"I came in here looking for a pencil to do the crossword puzzle," he said quietly. "There was one right on top of those papers on the table here. I wasn't anywhere near your desk. I picked up the pencil and the top part of the pile slipped off and all I did was pick up the pages and put them back. I wasn't aware I was committing any sin."

"It's private!" She turned and stormed out of the house, taking in the cool air in big gulps. *Calm down!* she admonished herself. She was an idiot to blow up over this, she knew, but she couldn't help it. The office was hers; it was the place where she spun her dreams, the place that was all hers, where she worked by herself with no one telling her what to do and how to do it. The place where she was in charge.

She took a deep breath and went back inside. He was in the kitchen pouring coffee. He handed her a cup and she sat down at the table.

He searched her face. "Raine, I didn't read your manuscript, but I'd like to understand why it upsets you so much to think that I had."

"I didn't ask you to read my writing. My office is private, my work is private. I am not ready for anybody to read it until it's finished."

"Does it embarrass you?"

She shrugged. "You may not understand this, but it's like going out in public without your makeup on. No, more like you're standing naked in the street in broad daylight for everybody to see you in all your imperfections."

He smiled at that. "I don't think anybody would do much criticizing seeing you naked."

She scraped her chair back and walked off. "Leave me alone!"

Fortunately he didn't follow her. She went to the barn and got out the feed. So he thought it was funny. He seemed to take life the light way, didn't get all worked up about things, liked to see the humor in a situation. Well, it was an admirable quality and one that made life in general a whole lot easier for himself as well as those around him. But a few minutes ago she simply hadn't had any humor in her. She sighed heavily. She had to admit she sometimes envied Trevor his easygoing ways, although, come to think of it, last night on the phone to the DR he had not seemed all that laid back. There were of course matters that needed to be taken seriously. And certainly it was an art, a talent, to know which matters needed the serious treatment and which did not.

Was she too touchy?

She took her time feeding the animals and filling their water troughs. One of the goats nuzzled her hand. She patted her head; the hair was coarse but smooth under her fingers. "So, what do you think, Sheba?" she asked. "Did I overdo it? Am I too sensitive?"

The goat gave her a blank stare.

Raine let out a sigh of defeat. "You're a big help." On her way back to the kitchen, she heard a car engine start up and moments later the blue Peugeot came into view going down the path to the road.

He was leaving. She didn't know if she was relieved or upset. Last night had been the most beautiful night of her life, yet now she just wanted to be alone and think.

There was a note on the kitchen table. *I think you're perfect naked. When will you let me read your book? I'm intrigued. See you later. T.*

She crumpled the paper and tossed it into the garbage can.

"When hell freezes over," she said out loud, and then, in spite of everything, she smiled.

Trevor drove through the peaceful countryside, regretting his lighthearted note. Maybe that's not what she had needed. What he was sure she needed was to be left alone for a while. She needed a chance to calm down. He hoped she believed him when he'd said that he hadn't read her manuscript.

Not that he hadn't been tempted, of course. He'd stood there with the stack of loose pages in his hand, staring at the title page, wanting more than anything to read her work, yet knowing also that he would not.

The look of anger and mortification on her face when she'd discovered him in her office had not been a pretty sight. He could only imagine how she would look if she knew the truth about him. His chest tightened. Damn, damn.

Unbidden, unaccountably, the image of Wanda floated into his consciousness. Wanda. Wanda taking charge of Raine's life. Wanda manipulating her. Raine, feeling obliged, giving in.

I want to be in charge of my own life.

Well, she was, and she was scared to death to lose her independence. Scared to death someone else would take over and manipulate her. Wanda had done a great job on her.

He was sick and tired of the whole affair and his role in it. What he wanted was to have everything out in the open. He kept thinking of Raine in his house on St. Barlow. It was an image that wouldn't leave him alone. He wanted her with him.

But first he would have to tell her the truth. And he'd have to tell her soon. He had to find the right moment and make sure she would understand. If she didn't, all might be lost.

Tentacles of fear gripped him. His hands clenched on the steering wheel.

Well, this is what happens when you have less than honorable little secrets, he told himself. They come to haunt you. However, even now he didn't see that he'd ever had an alternative. Telling the truth might not always be the best policy. But owning up to the truth now was rapidly becoming a serious necessity.

And he wasn't looking forward to it.

Chapter Ten

Raine was too distracted to write. In the quiet house her thoughts kept going back to Trevor and the love they'd made the night before. Such utter joy and delight. And then this morning—everything smashed to pieces. How could it all change so quickly? Why were love and happiness so fragile?

What is the matter with me? she asked herself. *Am I looking for things to go wrong?* She felt as if she had a lump of cement lodged in her chest.

Outside, the jubilant chatter of the birds mocked her. It made no sense struggling with the words; she wouldn't get anywhere. The Gypsy hero was resisting her—he had a mind of his own and the words that came out of his mouth onto the monitor screen weren't the ones she wanted to be there.

It was Tuesday, market day in Sneek. She called Kim and they decided to meet for coffee, then go shopping in the market. Raine closed out the computer and drove into

Sneek. The narrow streets were busy with morning traffic. Eight-hundred-year-old towns had obviously not been built with the movement of modern transportation in mind. Along with all the cars and delivery vans there were the bikes. At this hour the women were out shopping, babies and children strapped in seats on the back or front of the bikes, sometimes on both, shopping bags dangling from the handlebars. It seemed rather a contortionist exercise maneuvering around in the traffic without losing balance, but with ease born from long experience, they handled it effortlessly. Raine found it quite a sight.

She met Kim at the coffee shop cum bakery near the already crowded market. All along the edge of the canal, covered stalls had been set up, some complete with electrically refrigerated display cases. Flowers, cheese, fresh fish and meats, vegetables and fruit, clothes, knickknacks, bread, cakes and pastries, leather bags, music cassettes, towels, and a hundred other things were displayed for sale, all of them loudly praised by their owners, who joked and laughed with their customers.

The coffee shop was small and cozy, the tables covered with tablecloths and decorated with small bunches of fresh flowers. They ordered coffee. Of course it was impossible to just have a cup of coffee; it simply wasn't done. You needed something to go with it. "In this country, that's the law," Kim had explained the first time she'd taken Raine out to experience the delight of *koffie met gebak*.

They scanned the trays of artfully decorated confections—apple cake, strawberry cream cake, mocha hazelnut torte, fruit flan, chocolate mousse cake. The variety was astounding.

"It's enough to make you drool," Raine said. "They don't believe in just ordinary donuts, do they?"

"Who wants donuts when you can have true, unadulter-ated decadence?"

They made their choice and sat down at a table to await their order. Small cups of strong coffee were placed in front of them a few minutes later along with the plates with their pastries.

"So what's the matter that you couldn't write this morn-ing?" Kim asked. "Writer's block?"

Raine shook her head. "No. I was mad. I found Trevor in my office reading my manuscript, or at least that's what I thought he was doing."

"This morning?" Kim's face broke into a wide grin. "I see. Hallelujah. I'm glad you weren't immune to him. I was beginning to be seriously concerned about you."

"Oh, be quiet, Kim." Raine stabbed the little pastry fork into her mocha hazelnut torte. Kim watched her, humor in her brown eyes.

"It's not funny!" Raine forked a bite into her mouth.

Kim laughed. "I know, I know. It's very serious, very profound. I was laughing because I liked the way you at-tacked your cake. What did you do when you saw him?"

"I yelled at him. I said he'd invaded my privacy, words of that nature." Raine sighed heavily. "He said he hadn't read it. I suppose I overreacted. It just...I got so mad when I saw him standing there in my office with my work in his hands."

"Well, if he wasn't reading it, why did he have it in his hands? What was he doing in your office?"

"He was looking for a pencil to do *The New York Times* crossword puzzle and there was one on top of the manu-script and the stack fell and he gathered it up and then, of course, right on cue, I marched in and caught him red-handed with it in his hands."

"And all that misery because he wanted to do *The New York Times* crossword puzzle," said Kim. "Tragedies born from tiny, insignificant incidents. There's an article in there somewhere, maybe a book.''

Raine grimaced and drained her cup. "I need another cup of coffee. These cups are too damned small.''

"More cake?"

"Don't tempt me. You'd have to roll me out of here.''

More coffee was brought to their table. They laced it liberally with cream and sugar.

"I wonder if you'd read my manuscript for me," Raine said. "I think it's time for me to get another opinion.''

"I thought you'd never ask," Kim said evenly. "I offered, remember?"

"I know. I just wasn't ready.''

"Did you finish it?" Kim took a bite of her strawberry cream cake. Raine's cake was long finished, gobbled up with relish. Kim took her time, savoring every bite, driving Raine crazy.

"No, I'm about three-quarters done. It's pretty rough, still, but I want you to tell me what you think about my writing and the story line itself.''

"Your writing was always good," Kim said bluntly. "In college you won every short story contest in sight. Why would your writing be bad?"

Raine shrugged. "So I suffer from galloping insecurities. Maybe my writing is good but the story is lousy.''

"Well, I don't know anything about history or about Gypsies, but I'll bet the story is interesting.''

"If it isn't, I want you to tell me. I want you to take a red pen and mark every single place where you fall asleep or where you get bored. I need you to be brutally honest.''

"You know me," Kim said. "Brutal is my middle name.''

"I mean it. If you tell me it's wonderful just to be nice, it won't help me.''

Kim gave her a pitying look. "What's the matter with you? Am I dumb or something? Am I not a writer myself writing magnificent pieces of literature? Do I not know the value of true constructive criticism? The pitfalls of empty flattery? I'll be brutally honest, don't despair. If it's a lost cause, I will tell you and spare you years of anguished struggling trying to make it in the jungle of the publishing world."

Raine made a face and groaned. "Then I'll have to find another job."

"Or you could marry Trevor and have babies and I'll come visit you in your tropical paradise and we'll compare notes while we laze on the beach in the shade of coconut palms drinking rum punches and watching our beautiful children play in the turquoise waters—"

"Oh, shut up, Kim," Raine said. But she couldn't help laughing.

Then she swallowed her laughter and looked at Kim. They stared at each other for a few silent moments.

"Well," said Kim, and her voice sounded a little too bright, "I'm going to go on talking about babies and children. It's not taboo."

"It's not a subject easily avoided, I'm sure," said Raine carefully.

"I'm not going to try. I'll just have to adjust my life to the reality of events and keep on going. I won't have this baby, but . . ." Kim's voice broke and her eyes flooded with tears. She swallowed and fought back the tears. "I have a husband and a future and I have to go on living, don't I? Oh, damn, I'm sorry. I didn't mean to get all weepy." She found a tissue in her bag and blew her nose.

"Don't apologize, for heaven's sake."

"It's probably just my hormones. I suppose they're still all screwed up." She took a drink of her coffee. "Do you know that sweet little old lady across the street from me? The one that still grows all her own vegetables?"

"Yeah, the one with rhubarb up to the roof."

"She came up to me yesterday, and said she was sorry to hear about the baby, and then she said not to worry, I'd have another baby soon probably, and I know she meant well, but I wanted to sock her one. Think of me, abuser of old ladies." Kim grimaced and tried to smile. "It's one of those things people say and I knew somebody was going to say it sooner or later and still it made me see red. We're planning on having other children, but I still never will have this baby and it hurts. Does that sound crazy?"

"No, it doesn't."

Kim sighed again. "Anyway, where were we? Oh, yes, you and Trevor. I still think it's a good idea, and of course I'm not at all selfish about this. You marry Trevor and live on the island and I'll promise to come visit you at least once a year for an extended period, bringing along my brood."

"Oh, stop it, you're raving," said Raine.

But the image was, somehow, very tempting.

Trevor came by late that afternoon, carrying a huge box of chocolates with an enormous red bow on top. It was so ridiculously extravagant, it was hard not to smile.

"I'm sorry I upset you," he said.

"You think you can sweeten me up with chocolates?" she asked lightly, giving him a faintly mocking look.

He sighed. "Obviously it didn't work." And then, before she realized it was coming, he took her in his arms and kissed her, a deep, lingering kiss that devastated her completely.

He released her mouth and smiled into her eyes. "Am I forgiven for trespassing into your holiest of holiest?"

She took in a shaky breath. "You made sure you kissed me before asking that, didn't you?"

He grinned. "Of course. Am I forgiven?"

"No." She broke free and walked out the kitchen door, into the late-afternoon sunshine. He followed her out and she began to run, around the pond to the back of the barn. He caught up with her easily, pushing her down into the long grass, holding her hands down.

He was leaning over her, looking down into her eyes and it was hard to keep her face straight. She was out of breath from running.

"What do I have to do," he asked, "for you to accept my apology?"

"Let go of me!" She struggled, but he lowered his body on top of hers and there was no way to move.

"Answer me!"

She pressed her lips shut.

"I'm sorry you don't trust me." His eyes locked with her and she saw a flash of pain cross his face.

Her heart contracted. "It has nothing to do with trust." But if it wasn't that, then what was it? What was it that made her angry when he got into her personal space?

"Then what is it?" he asked.

"I don't know," she said on a low note. "I don't know, Trevor." There was a mysterious core of fear lodged deep inside her and she couldn't get rid of it. She could ignore it sometimes, but it never really went away.

He looked at her for a long moment. "Well," he said at last, "let me know when you find out."

"All right." She closed her eyes. "I will."

His mouth came down on hers, softly, tenderly. She felt her muscles relax, felt herself melting into the soft grass. There was the scent of clover in the air, and the warmth of the sun stroking her skin. A bee buzzed lazily nearby.

"I want to make love to you," he whispered. "Right here." He began to take off her clothes, then stood up and quickly took off his own. His naked body was beautiful in the golden sunlight and her hands traced the contours of him, the flat, hard planes of his muscled chest and stomach. She stroked his arms, feeling the soft, springy hair under her hands. His body tensed with urgency and his breathing grew shallow. Aching to feel him closer, she put her hands behind his head and drew it against her breast. His mouth captured a nipple, sending a tingling sensation all through her. Her blood sang and she closed her eyes with a sigh, giving herself up to the rapture of loving.

Raine and Trevor were invited to Mrs. Boersma's house for Sunday morning coffee. Raine, as Kim's friend, had been made part of the family circle as soon as she'd arrived in the country, and she liked their casual get-togethers, enjoying the love and warmth of family life. Trevor too had been easily accommodated. There was always another chair and another plate and the snug little house seemed to expand as need demanded.

Raine watched as Trevor played with Max and Jannie's baby boy, holding him on his lap and tickling him. The baby was handed around all morning since everyone wanted a chance at holding him, and he loved all the attention. She watched Trevor. It was a touching sight to see such a big, tough-looking man being so gentle with a small baby. She caught Kim's eyes, and Kim smiled at her meaningfully. *See*, her smile said, *he's a prince, too*.

They drank pots of coffee and ate plates full of cake and cookies. There was a lot of talking, a lot of joking, in a crazy mixture of Dutch and English that seemed to come easily and unselfconsciously and was cause for some hilarity when meaning and interpretations got lost or corrupted along the way.

The closeness of the family was good to see. *I made out like a bandit,* Kim had said, and so she had. Raine felt a twinge of envy, and an emptiness she didn't want to feel. She came to her feet and gathered up the cups and saucers and followed Mrs. Boersma into the kitchen to help her wash up.

"You have a wonderful family, you know that?" she said, taking a dish towel from its hook.

"Oh, yes, I know that," she said calmly. "I am very lucky. These two sons of mine, well, I despaired at times, like I'm sure every mother in the world does, but they did all right for themselves. They certainly found themselves the right girls to marry."

Raine carefully dried a delicate china cup and put it on the tray. "You didn't mind Menno marrying a foreign girl?"

Mrs. Boersma put more cups into the sudsy water. "I never looked at it like that. He married Kim, and Kim is Kim first, and she just happens to have been born in another country. I think it's an adventure, actually. I might never have learned how to make American apple pie."

Raine laughed. "A great loss it would have been. A life without apple pie is not a life."

Later, Trevor drove her back to the farm. "You're quiet," he said. "Something wrong?"

She shook her head. "No. I was just thinking how lucky Kim is to have such a nice family here." She tried not to think how it would have been if her own family had lived, but sometimes she had trouble suppressing the longing and the regret. Her family would never know whom she married. They would never know her children. Her children would never know their grandparents. She had no family to offer them, to enrich their lives. Not even Wanda.

He took her hand. "I have a very nice family, too," he said, "even if they are all architects with illusions of grandeur."

She gave him a look of surprise. "You knew what I was thinking," she stated.

He smiled crookedly. "I know you better than you think."

"Your family may not like me, you know."

"Well, yes, there's that," he acknowledged. "You are, after all, a redhead, and gorgeous and smart and independent and you're crazy about me. They might find it difficult."

She laughed, leaning her head against his shoulder. He did know how to cheer her up.

They found Attila on the doorstep with an offering of a dead baby mole. It was not a pretty sight. Raine made a face. Attila looked at her with arrogance and pride.

"You're an ugly monster," she said and Trevor laughed.

"Nature is not all just sweet flowers and cute calves and pretty sunsets," he said. "Cats may be domesticated animals, but they still have their primitive instincts. You can't blame him. He's programmed to go after baby moles."

"I should lock him up in the house."

"That's not natural."

"Wanda has a cat and it's never outside. There are lots of cats that are never outside. She even takes it to the office with her."

He made a sweeping gesture, indicating the great outdoors and all its summery beauty. "What a shame. Think of what it misses."

She gave a half smile. "I don't think Bijou suffers much. She's a very indulged creature. Wanda found her by the road and rescued her." She laughed at the memory. She went inside the kitchen, took a tablecloth off a shelf and draped it over the terrace table. She sat down. It was too nice to be inside.

"Your aunt Wanda rescued a cat?" he asked. "Tell me about it."

"She'd spent the weekend with friends at their summer house and she was driving back on Sunday night after dark in the rain no less and got a flat tire. She was in the middle of nowhere. So she changed the tire. She's very competent, you know. She doesn't believe in depending on men for that sort of thing. Anyway, suddenly there was that little cat miaowing at her, all skinny and wet and bedraggled and not a house in sight for miles. So she wrapped it up in her designer sweatshirt, put it on her lap and drove home." Raine laughed again. "When she came home, Wanda looked as bedraggled as the cat. I'd never seen her look like that. It was quite a sight."

Seeing the scrawny little alley cat had been quite a surprise. They'd fed it tuna fish and warm milk and cleaned it up and Wanda and the cat had been inseparable ever since. Raine had thought Wanda would take the cat to the pound the next day, but instead she'd taken it to her office and the subject of the pound had never come up.

"And what does she call it?" Trevor asked when Raine finished the story.

Raine chuckled. "Bijou. Means jewel in French, and also cute little thing, something like that. Just the sort of thing she would call a cat, only not that kind of cat. You'd see her more with, say, a Siamese cat, all sleek black fur and blue eyes."

Trevor spent the day with her and they made love that night, and afterward she watched him sleep, wide awake herself. *I have a nice family, too,* he had said, as if he had offered them to her for her own because he knew how much she longed for what she no longer had herself.

She had no family, not even Wanda, because Wanda no longer wanted her.

It had taken her a week to gather up enough courage to tell Wanda the truth. She had told herself she was merely looking for an opportunity to talk—the right time, the right circumstances. After a week or so, she'd come to the realization that there was no such thing as the right time and the right circumstances for what she had to say to Wanda. What she needed was courage and the conviction that she was a mature adult who had made a mature, adult decision on which she needed to act. However, the mere thought of facing Wanda made her shrivel into a trembling fourteen-year-old.

It was pathetic. She could not stand herself, could not stand the idea that Wanda could send her into a tailspin of panic and cold sweat. She was twenty-four years old and it was time to take charge of her own life.

It had been a cold November day, full of hard winter light, and all day, like the days before, she had felt slightly sick with nerves and stress. She'd waited until they were home in the apartment that night, feeling she needed a more personal atmosphere—after all, it was a personal matter as much as it was a business one.

She'd practiced in her head the words she would say, the sentences, the paragraphs—all carefully constructed so they would convey her message clearly while causing the least possible damage. Damage there would be, she'd known that. What she hadn't predicted was the full extent.

Wanda had listened, her face revealing no emotion. "You mean to say that you want no part of the business?" she'd asked coolly.

Raine felt herself shrink under Wanda's cold regard. "I'm not meant to have a career in business. I don't feel like I belong in the business world."

"Nonsense. You need to give yourself more time."

"I'm not going to give myself more time." Her heart pounded. "I'm sorry this ruins your plans. I'm sorry I can't be what you want me to be. I—"

"For years we planned for you to come into the business," Wanda said, cutting her off. "For years you studied business. For years I've counted on you and now, after working for me for barely six months, you tell me you don't want to go through with it."

Wanda was calm. Too calm. Raine sensed the cold fury beneath the carefully controlled demeanor. Her hands trembled in her lap.

"I'm sorry, Wanda. I need to live my own life."

"Then go live your own life." The quiet words were terrifying. "Go live your own life, by all means, but once you walk out of this door, don't expect to come back."

Raine stared up at the slanted ceiling, remembering the awful scene, her stomach still clenching at the memory of Wanda's words.

If only she could fix things up between Wanda and her.

A sleepless hour later, she slipped out of bed, careful not to wake Trevor, and went into her office and turned on the light and the computer. She put her fingers on the keyboard.

Dear Wanda,
Fearing that you will rip this letter up before reading it, I still feel the need to write and... No, too defensive. She deleted it.

Dear Wanda,
I don't know what to write or how to write it, but it seems that after all this time I ought to write something and . . .

No, too . . . what? Belligerent?

Dear Wanda,
In the months since I left Chicago, I have done a lot of thinking about what happened the day I told you I was leaving. You were very angry, which I can understand to some point.

No. Too accusatory. Oh, God, well let's just go on. Maybe I can fix it later.

I never meant to hurt you.

No. Who said Wanda was hurt? Wanda was mad. Being hurt was for weak people, like Raine. She'd gotten mad a lot, but had learned to hide it. One of Wanda's many lessons had been in self-control. It was very important for the outside world not to be able to read your feelings. Especially, of course, in business. It made you look weak and then the other guys would jump on you and throw you to the wolves.

She deleted the third attempt and stared disconsolately at the blank screen. *I don't know how to write her,* she thought. *I just don't know how to do this.*

Maybe you're not the one to write. Maybe it's up to her to write you.

Well, nice thought, but she doesn't know where I am, and what would it hurt for me to try and take the first step?

You are a noble person. Humility is a virtue.

Oh, shut up.

Dear Wanda,
You gave me a home when I needed one.

Oh, God, no. Not the poor waif stuff. She zapped it and once more stared at the blank screen. It wasn't going to work.

She heard a sound and turned her head. Trevor stood at the entrance to her office, looking sleepy, his hair rumpled, a towel wrapped casually around his hips.

"I woke up and you weren't there," he said, sounding vaguely accusatory.

"I couldn't sleep."

"Feeling creative?"

"Actually, no." She gestured at the blank screen. "I . . . I was trying to write a letter to Wanda, but I just don't know how." She closed out the computer. She'd have to try again another time. She got up and he opened his arms and hugged her.

"You were looking rather sad and forlorn sitting there at your desk. Come on back to bed and I'll make you feel good."

She smiled against the warmth of his neck. "Magic words."

Kim tossed the manuscript on Raine's kitchen table and hugged her. "It's wonderful! It really is!" Her brown eyes sparked with golden glints of humor. "That Gypsy hero, he's absolutely devastating. Where did you get your inspiration? Did you make him up?"

"Yes," said Raine.

Kim sat down and nodded solemnly. "I thought so. Imagination, a miracle of the mind."

Raine smiled breezily. "Isn't it though."

Kim smiled back. "Trevor must be quite a man."

"Yes, he is." Raine poured them each a glass of apple juice. "So, what did you think of the story? Apart from the hero."

Kim leaned her arms on the table. "It's a wonderful story, it really is. I can't wait to read the rest."

Raine studied her face. "Is that all?"

"What more do you want?"

"Kim! I told you! Please don't just try to be nice!"

Kim grinned. "Okay, okay. Nice is over. Now for the brutal part."

Involuntarily, Raine tensed. She would have to be able to take criticism if she wanted to learn anything. "All right, shoot."

"But not to kill." Kim tapped the manuscript. "It's very solid, most of it, and that Gypsy stuff is really intriguing." She frowned. "I didn't realize they'd been so horribly persecuted everywhere."

"Oh, yes, humanity at its best when it comes to hitting on the Gypsies," Raine said dryly.

"The other thing I found intriguing is how they treat each other, their code of honor. I mean, all we think of is how they're thieves, liars and swindlers and take you for a ride whenever they can."

"Well, they're good at that, too. Fooling *gorgios* is like a sport to them. Honor and fairness are strictly for other Gypsies and they'd better behave or they're in trouble." Raine looked down at the neatly stacked pages. "You haven't told me what's wrong with the story."

"Well, there are a couple of small rotten spots that you'll need to work on."

Raine frowned. "How rotten?"

"Not irredeemable, in my considered opinion. Here, let's go over this. Just remember, it's only my opinion you're asking for. I'm not an editor. Okay, let's see, Part One, the section when the heroine escapes from the palace and roams through the countryside and gets captured by a band of Gypsies. . . ."

Trevor managed to convince Raine that a week away from her work would do wonders for her creativity. He managed to convince Kim that driving to the farm twice a day to feed the animals would be an act of great friendship. All that accomplished, Trevor and Raine spent an idyllic week on the water in his cabin cruiser, going down rivers and across lakes, seeing the lovely countryside and picturesque towns and villages in a leisurely, relaxed fashion. Raine had never been so happy before; she marveled at the joy she found in being with him, making love with him, talking to him.

On impulse she'd taken the unfinished manuscript with her, tucked away at the bottom of her duffel bag. On their fourth day on the water they moored in a small town, earlier than they'd done the other days for they needed to do some food shopping before the stores closed at six. With her heart pounding, Raine dug the book out of the bag and took it on deck where Trevor was sitting finishing a beer.

Her hands shook as she handed him the open box containing the loose pages. "I'd like you to read this," she said, her voice husky and unsteady. She swallowed hard. Why did she have to have a case of the jitters doing this? Why couldn't she just be businesslike about it?

He put the beer can down and took the box from her. For a moment, he studied her face silently. "If it makes you uncomfortable, Raine, I don't want to read it. You don't have to feel . . ."

She moistened her lips. "I want you to read it."

His eyes held hers. "Are you sure?"

She nodded. "Yes."

He put the box down and pushed himself to his feet. He wrapped his arms around her, pulling her face against his shoulder. "Thank you," he said quietly. He held her tight, just a little too tight for an ordinary embrace, and he just stood there, not moving, holding her as if his life depended on it.

She closed her eyes, feeling the warmth of his body through her thin clothes, feeling emotion in him she wasn't sure how to interpret. Was it the fact that she had offered up her trust that moved him so? She felt her heart flood with love, and an odd sense of humility. Did her trust mean that much to him?

A moment later they drew apart. She lifted her hair back over her shoulder, feeling awkward. "I'll go into town and do the shopping, and I'll cook dinner when I get back. That will give you some time to get started, if you want to."

"I want to." He smiled, his eyes warm and full of loving. He touched her cheek. "Don't get lost."

She laughed. "Not on your life."

It was just past four. She walked into the small town, which had only one main street, lined with small shops and businesses. The buildings were centuries old with interesting gables and storefronts, many of them with window boxes full of scarlet geraniums and cobalt-blue lobelia trailing down over the edges. There was a small supermarket on the first corner, but she passed it by. There was no hurry to get back. It would be uncomfortable watching Trevor read her book, wondering what he was thinking. Not that she wasn't wondering now. She grimaced at herself.

The streets were full of people, many of them boaters and sailing enthusiasts. The ambience in the town was festive and relaxed, the restaurant terraces filled with people drinking tea or beer, chatting cheerfully, lounging in their chairs as if they'd parked themselves for life.

She found a bakery and bought a loaf of crusty brown bread and some large currant buns. At the butchery farther down the street she bought two pork chops and a piece of French country pâté to spread on crackers. The vegetable shop was next. Bins of fruits and vegetables were displayed on the sidewalk in front of the store. All of it looked fresh and luscious and beautiful, and it was an effort to keep her purchases down to broccoli and strawberries; there was a limit to what she could carry in her bag. It was nice to do the shopping the old-fashioned way though, going from store to store simply to get the ingredients for one single meal. She wondered how long the small shops would survive in Holland. Modern-style supermarkets carrying a large assortment of products from around the world flourished in all the larger towns and competition must be difficult for the smaller stores.

Slowly she made her way back to the harbor. A teenage couple sat on a wooden bench feeding each other thick brown french fries from a cone-shaped paper bag. They were oblivious to the world, seeing only each other.

Trevor was reading when she approached the cruiser. He didn't notice her and she stood still for a moment, watching him. He seemed relaxed, but certainly his eyes were intent on what he was reading. Well, she said to herself, he hasn't fallen asleep. At least that's one good sign.

"Hi there, sailor," she said. "You need a date?"

His head snapped up, his face blank for a moment. Then he grinned and jumped to his feet. "Best offer I've had all day." He took the bag of groceries from her, reaching out his other hand to help her jump on deck.

She cast a quick glance at the manuscript. There was a stack of turned-down pages next to his chair, obviously the ones he'd already read.

"You've read all that?" she asked, surprised.

He nodded. "I think—"

She held up her hand to stop him. "Don't say anything until you've finished it."

He raised his eyebrows, giving her a puzzled look. "All right, if you like." He sat back down and resumed his reading. Raine went into the small galley and started dinner, trying not to think of him sitting there reading her words. Close to two hundred seventy pages. How long would it take him?

He read all evening while Raine tried to concentrate on a murder mystery, sitting up in bed, sipping a glass of wine. She fell asleep while he was still reading.

She awoke to his touch, his hand caressing her body in slow, sensuous movements. Not opening her eyes, she lay still, relishing the feel of his hands as they roamed over her body. Then, giving a soft moan, she turned into his arms.

"You're wonderful," he whispered.

"Mmm."

"And you're a marvelous writer."

The words took a moment to sink into her sleepy brain. She drew away a little so she could see his face, but it was too dark to make out anything. "Did you finish it? That's impossible!"

He laughed. "I'm a fast reader."

"What time is it?"

"Almost three."

She groaned. "You didn't have to do that! I didn't mean for you to—"

"I wanted to do it. And it wasn't any hardship, Raine. I can't imagine what you were afraid of, why you are so insecure about your work."

"I just am." It was almost three. He'd read for hours on end and he hadn't fallen asleep. "I can't believe you read it at all," she murmured.

"It's a fascinating story—you did your research, I can tell. And your imagery is wonderful. It was all totally real to me." He trailed his mouth across her cheek. "No wonder you didn't stick it out in the business world. You have no business doing anything but writing."

Relief flooded her, making her giddy with joy. She laughed. "Not even making love?"

"Mmm, all right. Writing and making love, but that's all." He teased her breast with his thumb. "I'm interested to see what will happen. Your Elizabeth is on a path to self-destruction, you realize that?"

She laughed, pushing his hand away. "Why do you think that?"

"She's altogether too pigheaded when it comes to her relationship with the hero. Her pride is going to do her in. She's going to have to give up her pride or lose her man."

"Hah! Her pride is what kept her going all this time. Pride is what made it possible for her to live through the whole ordeal."

He nibbled her ear. "Pride, my love, can be a good thing up to a point, but it needs to be managed or controlled or it's bad news." His hands began to move over her body.

"Your wisdom leaves me breathless," she said, squirming beneath his hands.

"My wisdom? I thought it was my macho male sexuality."

"You're insufferably conceited," she said, trying to push him away. She was not successful.

"I'll let that pass," he said generously. "I think what we ought to do is turn back in the morning so you can go home and finish your opus."

"What?"

"I want you to go back to the computer and finish it up so I can read the rest and see how you pull Elizabeth out of the water."

She smiled against the warmth of his chest. "No way, I'm on vacation. You'll just have to wait."

They made plans. In a couple of weeks it would be time for Trevor to go back to the island, but when the Beintemas were back in two months or so, Raine would go to St. Barlow. He would arrange to get a computer for her and have it installed in her very own writing room.

The idyllic week on the water ended, which was unfortunate. Raine wouldn't have minded it to go on longer, say another month or so, and forget about the book altogether. This sentiment arose only in the most tender and passionate of moments, and she knew that she needed to be strong and go back to work on her writing. Besides, Trevor had to go to Rome for a meeting and to generally oil the wheels of his consulting business, which meant wining and dining or being wined and dined. This would not be an altogether unpleasant interlude as Trevor was fond of Italian food, and especially fond of Italian food cooked in Italy. Since Raine was also fond of Italian food, she felt rather abandoned.

"I'll make do with bread and cheese," she said, sounding vaguely martyrish.

"I'll bring you back some cannoli," he said soothingly and kissed her.

Raine went back to her writing with renewed energy and much new inspiration, trying not to think of Trevor.

Trevor called the night he arrived back at the sailing school and Raine felt herself grow warm just hearing his voice.

"Did you bring me the cannoli?" she asked.

"Of course," he said. "I promised. Is this a good time to bring them over, or are you working?"

She was working, but anytime was a good time when it meant seeing him.

"It's teatime. The Dutch would deport me if I worked through teatime. I'll put the kettle on."

Half an hour later he arrived carrying a small white pastry box with Italian words she couldn't read and inside the much-longed-for cream-filled pastries.

They hugged and kissed. "God," he muttered, "it's only been two days and it seems like weeks."

"Yes," she whispered. *I love you,* she wanted to say, but didn't. "Let's forget the tea and go upstairs," she suggested boldly.

His arms tightened around her for a moment, then he drew away so he could look into her eyes.

"We need to talk, Raine," he said.

"Talk?" she said, surprised. Talking wasn't what she'd had in mind. Talking wasn't what she'd thought he'd had in mind, either. Apparently she was wrong. His face looked very serious and she felt a flare of alarm.

"There's something I need to tell you," he said.

Chapter Eleven

She swallowed hard. What was it he needed to tell her that was so serious? That gave him that look of apprehension?

"All right," she said, moving out of his arms. She picked up the tea tray and carried it into the living room and set it on the coffee table. Then she sat down next to him on the sofa and folded her hands in her lap. She felt like a frightened convent girl about to be told some tragic news.

"Go ahead and tell me."

"Pour the tea."

She poured the tea, feeling a sense of doom settle over her. *He's going to tell me he lied to me and is married after all, or that Suzanna changed her mind and is back on the scene. Maybe they met in Rome.*

She could imagine the scene, in some fancy restaurant. Trevor having dinner with some stuffy officials from the Food and Agricultural Organization, a tableful of luscious food and bottles of expensive wine. In sashayed the gor-

geous Suzanna in a black silk mini and glittering dia-
monds. Their eyes met. Passions flared instantly. She
stopped at his table. They hugged—after a lengthy affair
that had ended amiably, certainly they would hug. Her
companion, a tall, handsome Italian count, looked on with
nostrils flaring and eyes burning. Suzanna and Trevor made
plans to meet later that evening for a drink, after they'd
discreetly shed their present companions, to talk over old
times. After which they would end up in bed and make passionate love. Then they decided to get back together again,
Suzanna having realized that if she had her private twin-
engine plane, she could manage to live on the island after
all.

Oh, God, I can't take this.

She sat down again. "I'm not going to like this, am I?"
she asked, spooning sugar into her tea.

"No," he said, "you're not going to like it." He put his
arm around her and drew her closer. "But I hope you'll try
and understand. I want you to know that what I feel for you
is real and that I don't want to hurt you, even if I do."

That did not sound promising. She knew a setup when she
heard it. She felt her heart pounding in her chest. She stared
blindly at the tea in her cup, seeing it tremble in her hands.
She put it back on the table and faced him, trying to gather
the strength. "So tell me."

He took a deep breath. "I knew who you were before I
met you at the party at the sailing school. As a matter of
fact, it was not by chance that I was there, that I had rented
a boat from Max."

For a moment she stared at him wordlessly. "You mean
you searched me out?"

He nodded. "Yes."

She had a sinking feeling. She remembered his eyes that
night at the party, eyes looking at her, following her every-

where, looking as if he could see straight into her head. "How did you know who I was? What did you know about me?"

"I knew all the basic details. That you grew up in Chicago, lost your family in a car accident, lived with your aunt Wanda, where you went to college."

She came to her feet, her legs trembling, and moved away from him toward the window. She had to get away. All this time he had pretended he knew nothing about her. She felt light-headed with fury, remembering opening up to him, telling him about herself and all along he had already known.

"And all this time..." She closed her eyes briefly to compose herself. "All this time you pretended you didn't know me before."

"I did. And it wasn't right, so I decided to tell you. I couldn't let it go on any longer."

And no doubt she was supposed to be grateful for his manly courage owning up to it. Her body went rigid. "How did you know where I was?"

"Wanda told me."

"*Wanda* told you? You mean you know her?"

"Yes."

She felt her body grow icy cold and suddenly everything was clear, so very clear. "You know Wanda." She stared at him as if she were seeing a stranger. He came toward her, but she drew farther away.

"And why didn't you tell me who you were?" she said, her voice alien to her own ears. "Why didn't you tell me you knew about me?"

"Wanda suggested it would be better. She wouldn't tell me why. I should have insisted."

"So she sent you here?"

"I was in the country anyway. I thought I'd look you up."

"Another one of Wanda's schemes." Her voice broke. She felt tears burn behind her eyes.

He moved quickly, putting his hands on her arms. "Raine, please. Listen to me."

She shook her head wildly. "No, no." She pulled away from him and ran out of the house, her legs trembling violently. Wanda had sent him to find her. And he had.

He had deceived her, lied to her. She sat down by the pond and hugged her knees. Her stomach hurt. She felt a burning rage, which was easier to feel than the pain of disillusionment. She'd thought she loved him, she was beginning to believe that something wonderful was happening between them, something valuable that was worth nourishing.

He had betrayed her in the most despicable way, playing on her most intimate emotions. She felt manipulated, exposed, stupid.

Her hands lay in her lap, balled into fists. In the stillness she could hear her heart pounding.

There had never been any substance to her relationship with Trevor—no truth, no value. Nothing but sweet illusion. From the very beginning it had all been a farce.

She watched the play of shadow and light on the water, the glimmering reflection of a perfect sky, the swaying of the tall plumy reeds in the breeze. Small flying insects skimmed the water and all around the air was warm and still, so very still. So peaceful.

"Raine?" He was standing beside her.

"Go away," she said, her voice choking.

"I'm not going away, Raine. We need to talk. I want to explain to you—"

"I don't want to hear any of your lies."

"I haven't lied to you."

"You deceived me on purpose! You never let on you knew about me or my background. After all this time...you made me believe...and it's Wanda who's behind all this. Wanda—" Her voice broke. She turned her face and bit her lip, fighting tears. What did Wanda want now? It didn't make sense. She didn't understand anything anymore, but none of it really mattered, nothing except the fact that Trevor was tangled up in Wanda's schemes and that he wasn't the man she'd thought he was. All her hard-fought-for independence lay shattered at her feet.

"You and Wanda, what a team," she said, trying to sound caustic, but it didn't come out that way. It sounded more like a sob.

"You're wrong, Raine," he said, his voice low and rough.

She leapt to her feet and faced him. "I *was* wrong, you mean! Wrong about you!" She stormed back into the kitchen and locked the door behind her. Tears were running down her cheeks, tears of fury and humiliation. Oh, how could she have been so gullible? How could she have been taken in so easily? Her instincts had been right from the first moment. She'd felt in the depths of her being that something wasn't quite kosher about Trevor Lloyd, only she'd fallen in love and her good sense had flown out the window. The same old story. When women fell in love, they took leave of their senses. They found ways to excuse discrepancies, rationalize behavior. They became blind. *She'd* become blind.

He was at the door, rattling it. She walked into the living room so she wouldn't have to see him behind the glass. "Damn you," she whispered, dropping onto the couch and covering her face with her hands. Silence enveloped her, bleak and still. She didn't want to think, to feel.

"We'd better have a talk," he said, and she jerked up her head. He was standing in front of her, hands in his pockets. She looked at him furiously.

"Did you break down the door?"

"Nothing as dramatic as that," he said calmly. "Your office window is open."

"What do you want?"

"I want you to listen to me."

She steeled herself. "I've heard enough of your lies!"

"Perhaps you should hear the truth."

"It's a little late for that, isn't it?"

"I hope it isn't," he said, his voice rough.

"You can forget it! You deceived me, Trevor! And I trusted you!"

A voice called her name loudly and someone was knocking on the back door. Raine jumped to her feet, glad for the interruption.

It was Kim with an armful of books she'd promised to drop by. Raine had never felt more relieved to see her.

"Come on in." She stepped aside to let Kim in. "Tea's ready."

Tea and cannoli from Rome.

Kim dropped the books on the kitchen table and looked at Raine. "Good God," she whispered, "what's wrong?"

Trevor entered the kitchen before she could answer. He nodded at Kim in greeting and opened the back door. "I was just leaving," he said. "See you later."

The door closed behind him and a silence ensued. Kim looked at Raine. "Did I come at a bad time?"

Raine shook her head. "I'm glad you're here. I think I'm losing my mind."

They went into the living room. Two cups of cold tea sat on the table along with the unopened box of pastries. Kim took the cups back to the kitchen, tossed out the cold brew and poured some fresh.

"All right, tell me what's going on."

Raine told her.

Kim took a sip of her tea. "Do you think Wanda sent him to find you?" she offered.

"It was my first reaction, but no, I don't think so." She swallowed at the lump in her throat. "She told me I could never come back."

"Said in the heat of the moment. Maybe she's sorry. Maybe she changed her mind. Maybe she's worried."

"I don't know." Raine looked down at the tea in her cup. There was a sudden flickering of hope. Maybe Wanda *was* sorry. Maybe, as time had passed, she'd started thinking. Maybe she understood what had happened between them, understood about her wanting to live her own life. Yet it was difficult to imagine.

"It's hard to believe, you know," she said in a low voice. "I mean, her sending someone to find me."

"Trevor has never said anything about it?"

Raine shook her head. "No. He always pretended to know nothing about me or my background. He said Wanda told him not to tell, but he wasn't sure why."

"Maybe after what she said to you she's afraid you won't want to have anything to do with her. Maybe he's a middleman to smooth things over."

A middleman to smooth things over. She stared into the distance—green meadows, a blue, blue sky. Somewhere in the giant oak tree a bird began to sing—a musical chirping, crystal clear in the sunny afternoon.

No matter why, no matter what the reason, he had deceived her. A painful mixture of anger and despair churned inside her.

"He betrayed my trust," she said, and her voice shook. Her hands trembled in her lap. "I hate him," she whispered. *I feel I know you very well.* Trevor's words echoed in her mind, took on a whole new meaning. *Bastard!* she thought wildly. She wasn't sure if she wanted to cry or scream.

Kim gave her a stricken look. "Raine? Are you all right?"

Raine swallowed painfully. "I don't know what I'm going to do."

"Let me get you a drink." Kim jumped to her feet and crossed over to the bar, coming back a moment later with a bottle of brandy. She poured some in a glass and handed it over. "Damn," she said, looking worried. "I wish I didn't have to leave tonight."

"Of course you do. Who wouldn't want to go to Paris?" Menno had a week-long international convention in Paris, and Kim was going with him.

Raine lifted the glass and drank the brandy down in one go. Kim gave her a horrified look. "Are you nuts?"

"Yes," said Raine, feeling the drink burn as it moved down into her stomach, "but it's all right. I'm not going anywhere." She held out the glass. "I'll have another one."

"Not on your life." Kim put the bottle away, and Raine dropped her head on the table and burst into tears.

"I hate him!" She pounded the wooden table with her fists and the cups rattled on their saucers. "I hate him, I hate him, I hate him!"

In the end, she calmed down and they finished the pot of tea and finally opened the box with the cannoli and ate two each, finishing the lot.

"I don't have to go to Paris," Kim said. "I can stay here with you if you need me."

"I don't need you," said Raine. "Go to Paris. I'll be fine." She wasn't going to ruin Kim's trip. Kim had gone through a traumatic experience and she needed the diversion of a trip to Paris.

After Kim had reluctantly left, Raine dutifully took the tea things into the kitchen and put them in the dishwasher, working as if in a trance, moving automatically, trying not to feel. It seemed absurd to be doing this—cleaning up as if it mattered. Her universe had collapsed and she was stacking the dishwasher.

The house was too empty, too silent, and her emotions, temporarily repressed by the cognac and the determination not to distress Kim, returned full force. She stood in the middle of the kitchen and wept into a tea towel.

Then, with feet of lead, she climbed the stairs.

She had to get away. She could not stay any longer. It was the only thought in her head. In her bedroom she dragged out the suitcases and frantically began to tear her things out of drawers and closet, dumping them on the bed.

She didn't know where she was going. It didn't matter. Anywhere, anywhere away from Trevor.

She couldn't take all her stuff. She'd bought clothes and shoes in the eight months she'd been here and she'd need another suitcase to put it all in. She gazed blindly at all the stuff on the bed and on the floor.

The Beintemas. She'd have to tell them . . .

The animals. Who was going to take care of the animals if she left? Attila, Sheba, Caesar, Genghis, Matahari—helpless creatures all of them. She'd made a commitment and she had to honor it. She took in a shuddering breath. She couldn't leave. She couldn't just pack up and go. The house and the animals were her responsibility for at least another two months.

Her mind went around in frantic turmoil. Damn, damn, she was stuck. She couldn't leave. Defeated, she dropped herself down in the middle of the mess on the floor, crying and cursing her bad luck. Cursing Wanda for getting her into this, cursing Trevor for betraying her.

Her tears spent, she just sat there, numb with misery, unable to move, to get up and put everything away. It didn't matter, nothing mattered. All sense of time left her as if life simply had stopped, until the sound of a car jerked her out of her stupor. The sound of a door opening, footsteps moving through the rooms below, climbing up the stairs.

Trevor stood in the door, looking down at her sitting on the floor surrounded by shoes and sandals, tears streaming down her face.

"Leave me alone!" she said fiercely.

He dragged her to her feet, held her close and kissed her hard.

"Raine, will you please listen to me?"

"No!" She struggled to get away from him, but he was too strong.

"You don't believe me?"

"You've got it! From the moment you saw me at Max's party you set out to seduce me. Don't you dare talk about *love!* Love had nothing to do with it! Money is more like it. How much is Wanda going to pay you if you get me back to Chicago?"

"Pay me? Good Lord, Raine, what's got into you? She's not paying me anything and I don't give a damn if you ever go back to Chicago." He glanced around. "Are you planning a move?"

"Would you like the address and phone number?" Her voice dripped sarcasm.

"Somehow I don't think you'll be willing to supply them." His dark eyes met hers. "I'll find you, you know," he said softly. His voice held an odd tone.

"Sure," she said, giving him a withering look. "You love me so much, you'll search till the end of the earth."

He didn't answer. He turned away and gazed out the window. "Your aunt is a very lonely woman," he said quietly. "I felt sorry for her."

She couldn't believe her ears. Lonely wasn't what you thought of when you knew Wanda. Wanda was self-sufficient, competent and happy with her own company. People didn't feel sorry for Wanda. They admired her or despised her or envied her.

"Why were you feeling sorry for her?"

He shrugged. "I'm not sure why."

"Did she ever tell you what she said to me when I left?" she asked, wondering why she even asked the question. She'd bet her bank account on it that Wanda hadn't.

He turned to face her. "No."

"I didn't think so."

"So you tell me," he said and there was a tightness in his voice.

"Why? Why should I tell you?"

"Because I want to know the truth."

"I'm impressed! I didn't know you cared so much about the truth! You sure fooled me! Did it occur to you to tell me the truth about yourself when we met?"

His brows rose fractionally. "Oh, yes, it occurred to me, but it did not seem wise at the moment."

"I can see why you would think that."

"I wanted to wait for the right time. I thought yesterday would be the right time. I hoped..." He made an impatient gesture with his hand. "For heaven's sake, Raine, what is it between you and Wanda?"

She looked at him coolly, saying nothing.

"Tell me this," he said after a moment. "Why did you disappear like you did?"

"I didn't disappear. I didn't *mean* to disappear."

"Wanda had no idea where you were."

"She didn't know because…" A great lump formed in her throat. Tears were hot behind her eyes. "She didn't know because she . . . she didn't want to know."

"What do you mean, she didn't want to know?"

She felt suddenly very weary. "She was furious when I told her I couldn't work for her anymore and that I wanted to find my own apartment." She bit her lip hard. "She…told me that if I left I…I could never come back."

She saw the shock in his eyes, and then the compassion. "Don't feel sorry for me," she said coolly. "I'm doing fine." She met his eyes. "And I'll do fine without you, too."

There was a silence as he looked back into her eyes unblinkingly.

"I'm not leaving, Raine," he said at last, his voice calm and determined. He turned and walked out of the room.

Raine got up and looked out the window, seeing the bright green stretch of the meadows dotted with black-and-white cows grazing peacefully in the warm summer evening. The setting sun was streaking the sky peach and lavender and gold.

Add it all up, she said to herself. *It's not a pretty picture. You let yourself be swept away and sure enough, you ended up being manipulated again. If love is this painful I don't need it. I should have followed my instincts. I'm better off alone for a while until I learn to be a little wiser.*

After Michael, something had been destroyed inside her, an innocence lost. Loving would never be simple or easy again. There would always be too many doubts and questions—a protection against pain. That's why she'd never been serious in her other relationships. Maybe subconsciously she'd picked the losers she had, as Kim had suggested. No, not maybe. Of course she had.

But Trevor was not a loser and things had been different. She'd let her defenses crumble. She loved him and her need for his love had overcome her fears. "Oh, damn, damn," she muttered, pressing her forehead against the cool glass of the window.

She should not have gotten involved with Trevor. She should simply have followed her plan: write, no men. Well, she could still do that. She straightened and squared her shoulders. Glancing out the window, she saw Trevor's car parked near the barn. He said he wasn't leaving. She wondered what he thought he'd gain if he stayed around. She went downstairs, out the back door to give the animals their evening feed, but saw no sign of Trevor.

Back in the kitchen she quickly made herself a sandwich and took it upstairs with her. She surveyed the mess in her room. Then, methodically, she began to put everything back where it belonged. She wasn't going to run; it wouldn't change the truth, or her feelings.

It was almost dark now. Past ten, she saw on her clock. What had happened to the time? She got ready for bed, but sleep eluded her. She tried to read, but couldn't concentrate. Where was Trevor? She put on a robe and went down the stairs. Maybe a cup of tea would help.

She found him in the living room, sitting in the dark, drinking a glass of Scotch.

"Why are you still here?" she demanded.

"I'm not leaving." He did not sound friendly.

She made an expansive gesture with her arm. "Well, by all means, stay. Be my guest."

"I intend to."

She went into the kitchen and put the kettle on. She'd take in the night air while she waited for the water to boil. She reached to open the door. It was locked. The key was gone. Quietly she moved to the entryway to check the front door. It was always locked and the key was left in the door. But not now.

The heat of anger burned her cheeks. What did he think he was doing. Keeping her captive? Trying to keep her from leaving? If he thought that was going to work, he had another thing coming.

She marched into the living room and turned on the light. She stood in front of his chair and glared at him. "If you think that locking the doors is a good idea, I suggest you think again," she said coldly. "If you think manipulating me is going to get you what you want, you're sadly mistaken. I've been manipulated enough. I decided not to take it from Wanda, and I'm not going to take it from you." She paused significantly, looking straight into his eyes. Then slowly she held out her hand. "Give me the keys."

She could hear her heart thumping against her ribs, and for an endless moment it was the only sound in the room. He did not avert his eyes, he did not move, and the moment seemed to stretch endlessly. Then he slowly reached into his pocket, fished out the keys and dropped them into her outstretched hand.

"Thank you." She turned away, feeling dizzy with relief.

The kettle screeched for attention and she hurried to turn off the shrill sound of it. As in a daze she made the tea and climbed back up the stairs.

She sat up in bed, nursing the tea, wide-eyed. Sleep was not forthcoming; she was too worked up. Maybe what she needed was a shot of rum in her tea, just to help her relax.

Once more she went downstairs, into the living room, ignoring Trevor still sitting in the chair. She took the bottle of rum and made her way to the door.

"What do you think you're doing with that bottle?" His voice was like a shot in the silence.

"Drinking it."

"You don't drink hard liquor."

"Well, I do now." She walked out, back up the stairs, and she heard him leap out of the chair and follow her.

He grabbed her as she reached the landing.

"Don't be an idiot! Give me that bottle!"

"No." She twisted out of his grip and went into her room, but he was right behind her.

"What are you going to do with that bottle?" he asked again.

"Chugalug it down. Drown my sorrows. Drink myself into a stupor." She gave him a derisive look. "Don't flatter yourself. You're not worth it, darling. All I want is a shot in my tea so I can sleep." She opened the bottle and poured a measure into the cup, closed up the bottle and handed it to him. "Here you go."

He took the bottle, turned and left the room without a word. She locked the door behind him, knowing he'd hear the sound of the key turning.

Trevor went down to the living room, poured himself another Scotch and sat down again in the chair. He had the taste of ashes in his mouth. He had not liked the way she looked at him, with bitter contempt. He had not liked the tone of her voice. He hadn't liked the sound of the key turning in the lock, locking him out.

It had been too much to hope for. The last few weeks had been too good to be true. He'd been so careful, watching his every damned word, and now this. He had tried to do the right thing and it had turned out wrong. He took a long swallow of his Scotch. Maybe he should have kept his mouth shut until later, until she'd been safely settled in his villa on St. Barlow. Maybe then she would have felt more secure, more capable of understanding his motives. Now she didn't even want to listen to him.

Wearily he closed his eyes. He didn't know how he was going to salvage the situation now, how he could ever gain back her trust, her love.

Love. He groaned. He loved her with a deep, aching need. And he thought she loved him, too. But it had all been too young, too fragile. His confession had smashed it all to smithereens. How could he even blame her? After years of manipulation from Wanda, after what she had gone through with Michael, how could he ever blame her for feeling deceived? Her life had been a string of rejections—parents dying, Michael leaving, Wanda telling her never to come back. Love and support systems ripped away from her. Rational or not, it was no wonder she had reacted the way she had.

He closed his eyes, remembering her sitting, tear-streaked, amid her clothes and belongings, trying to pack. She'd looked so desolate, so utterly defeated, his heart had ached for her. He'd wanted to wrap her up in his arms and wipe away her pain, make everything all right. She did not deserve this. She deserved her share of loving and he wanted more than anything to give it to her. And for a while, a few precious weeks, she had accepted that love. Now she'd shut the door on him and he himself had caused it to happen.

He tossed back the last of his drink. Fear clutched at his heart. How was he ever going to make things right? Oh, God. He groaned again. Never in his life had he screwed up anything as badly as this.

Somehow, he had to make it right.

* * *

The next morning Raine dragged herself out of bed, feeling wretched. She'd barely slept, and when she had, nightmarish dreams had tormented her. She stared at her reflection in the mirror and winced. She looked like hell. Trevor was still in the house; she could smell the coffee all the way up here. Coffee, she longed for a cup of coffee, but she couldn't go down looking like she did, so she took a long shower, trying to fortify herself for the inevitable confrontation. She dressed in a pair of loose pants and a sleeveless black shirt and carefully made up her face. Taking a deep breath, she went down the stairs and into the kitchen.

The table was set for breakfast and Trevor was at the stove, making pancakes.

She wondered if he'd stayed in the chair all night or if he'd made up the bed upstairs and slept there. She hadn't heard him move around.

"Good morning," he said evenly.

"Good morning." She moved to the back door and opened it.

"I already fed the animals," he said.

"How efficient." She poured herself a cup of coffee and sat down. He put a plate of pancakes on the table between them. For a fleeting moment she was tempted to say she didn't want any, but doing that would be rather juvenile. Besides, he might think she was nursing an emotional hangover if not a physical one. The pancakes looked wonderful and she was hungry. Maybe the best way to fight him was simply to do nothing—no accusations, no anger. She was going to ignore him as much as possible and go about her way. The trusty computer would keep her plenty busy.

She ate in silence, and he didn't make an attempt at conversation. Having finished, she poured herself another cup

of coffee and carried it with her across the living room into
the office, wishing she had a door to close.

She heard the soft humming of the computer and
frowned. She'd turned it off yesterday, she was sure. But it
was not off. She advanced toward the desk and stared at the
writing in the middle of the screen.

TRUTH: I DIDN'T COME TO SEE YOU TO DO YOUR AUNT
WANDA'S BIDDING. I CAME TO SEE YOU FOR REASONS OF
MY OWN.

Chapter Twelve

She sat down in her chair. "Hah," she muttered. "You're finished conning *me,* mister." She cleared the screen and called up the file of the chapter of her book she was working on. She glanced quickly over the last few pages she'd completed the day before.

Hunger gnawed at her belly. She should have accepted the stew Rajko had offered her an hour ago. Tired and wet from the long trek they'd made that day, Elizabeth lay down on the makeshift bed in her wagon. She could hear the chickens squawking in the pen suspended underneath the cart.

She must have slept for a while, because it was dark when she opened her eyes. Music spilled through the night air, the men playing their violins, and people singing and dancing.

She peered out into the darkness. There was a fire and the rain had stopped. As she watched the cheerful scene, she felt a terrible loneliness engulf her. She was their captive, despised and mocked as a gorgio *and considered unclean. Not even marriage would give her status, as the old woman had explained to her with a malicious cackle. She'd be an outcast forever.*

Raine was startled out of her imaginary world an hour later when Trevor appeared at her side with a cup of coffee.

"Would you like some coffee?" he offered.

Her eyes glued to the screen, she waved her hand. "Sure, thanks." She was going to be civilized if it killed her. Her book's heroine had a more volcanic temperament and had thrown a bowl of wild rabbit stew into the Gypsy's face. *I'll starve before I'll eat your food ever again!* she'd said.

It had been a big mistake.

Trevor placed the cup next to her on the desk. "You can't escape into your work forever, Raine," he said.

She jerked her head up and looked at him. "And what am I escaping from, may I ask?"

"Reality. Me."

"I don't care to dwell on mistakes. I've made my share, and I'd like to salvage what can be salvaged and go on the best I can."

"You're making a big mistake now." He turned and left the room without waiting for a reply.

She stared blindly at her hands, which trembled in her lap, trying hard not to let her anger get the best of her. She wondered if he had expected her to react to the message he'd left on the screen. Well, he could forget it.

She took a sip of the hot coffee. The words danced in her head, taunting her.

I DIDN'T COME TO SEE YOU TO DO YOUR AUNT WANDA'S BIDDING. I CAME TO SEE YOU FOR REASONS OF MY OWN.

Reasons of his own? How stupid did he think she was? He hadn't even known her until he'd come here. She'd never seen the man in her life, so what could possibly have motivated him to find her? It was crazy. Another question loomed. *How* had Wanda found her? Wanda had never met Kim and certainly didn't know she lived in Europe. How had she figured out Raine was in the Netherlands?

She went back to work, but it took an effort to concentrate. The most important thing she could do now was to pick up the pieces and go on, not let herself be dragged down in anger and reflection and become immobilized.

At lunchtime she made herself a sandwich and took it back with her to the office. From outside came the hum of the lawn mower. At least Trevor was making himself useful. He seemed determined to hang around. She was equally determined to ignore him, or at least pretend she didn't care if he were there or not. Since she couldn't physically throw him out of the house, she had no other choice.

Chewing her ham-and-cheese sandwich, she stood in front of the window and watched him. His big body following the push mower with easy grace. He'd taken off his shirt and the dark skin of his broad back gleamed in the sunlight. He was a beautiful man, masculine and strong, his body well-proportioned with long muscular legs, narrow waist and wide, square shoulders. She watched the play of muscles, feeling the familiar knot in her stomach, the treacherous warmth stirring in her blood. "Damn him," she muttered, and turned away from the window. She sat down again at the desk, trying desperately to concentrate on her writing, on the captive Elizabeth and her passionate Gypsy lover.

He was telling her things she didn't want to know, his eyes full of anger. Lies, all lies. The Prince had never caused the Gypsies any harm. She would not believe it, ever.

Time and again Raine found herself staring blankly at the screen, her hands idle on the keys. In the middle of the afternoon she gave up. She hesitated before switching off the computer, then, before she could change her mind, she retrieved Trevor's file. He'd labeled the file Truth and she grimaced as she punched in the words. The message flashed back on the screen.

She took a deep breath and began to type.

SINCE YOU DIDN'T KNOW ME, WHAT POSSIBLE REASON
COULD YOU HAVE FOR WANTING TO FIND ME

She saved the file, shut off the computer and left the room.

He was outside, stretched out in a lawn chair, reading a book. He was an addicted reader; his cruiser was full of books of all kinds. She wondered how long he intended to stay around. If she weren't so utterly disillusioned by his betrayal, she could actually find it exciting. There was a challenge of wills and she intended to win.

She prowled around the kitchen, drinking the last of the orange juice. She was restless, her body needing some physical work. Cleaning house was physical work, so that's what she did. She dusted and vacuumed in a frenzy, then scrubbed the bathroom. It didn't help her mental state, but her body was getting tired.

Trevor was moving around getting ready to make dinner, lighting the grill outside and preparing a salad from the lettuce growing in the garden and the vegetables in the fridge. They liked cooking dinner together, but all she could think of was getting away from him, so she went out into the garden and began to weed with a vengeance, ungently yanking out the unwanted greenery.

She hadn't planted much, just some tomatoes and lettuce and cucumbers. She'd never had a chance to do any gardening of her own, but her mother had always grown tomatoes and lettuce in a small corner of their flower garden at home. She remembered working with her mother, talking about school or friends as they dead-headed the annuals or weeded the flower beds. So many memories. So much pain, still. Her father, a busy businessman, had enjoyed working in his workshop in the garage in his spare time. He had built a playhouse for her and her sister Amy in the huge old oak tree at the back of the garden. It had windows and a door and she had spent hours there with her friends planning and rehearsing their sketches and plays.

After ten years, she could still ache for her parents, her sister and brother. She wondered if the pain would ever totally go away, if she could ever think of them without that terrible sense of loss. She sat back on her heels and stared out over the green meadows, seeing their faces, their smiles, wishing with all her heart she had a family to go home to, a place to belong. For a moment the colors blurred before her eyes. Only days ago she'd had hopes and dreams of making a home with Trevor on his island. She should have known better. It was too romantic, too idealistic to think such a thing could ever come true. A wonderful, handsome man, an idyllic tropical island—it was fairy-tale stuff.

A sound startled her, and she looked away, seeing Trevor standing at the edge of the garden, watching her.

"Dinner's ready," he said.

She stiffened. "I'll be right there." Her voice sounded husky, and she swallowed at the constriction in her throat.

He didn't leave, but instead moved closer and reached out a hand to help her up. She took it almost automatically and came to her feet. He stood in front of her, studying her face, saying nothing. Then he let go of her hand and together they crossed the lawn to the cobbled terrace where he'd set the table for dinner.

It was amazing how tasteless a delicious dinner could be. She ate dutifully, swallowed her wine without pleasure and tried to avoid looking at Trevor.

There was a numbing coldness inside her, freezing out the pain. She didn't want to feel anything. She couldn't afford to. If she'd given into the anguish, she'd fall apart; she'd kick and scream and cry. And it wouldn't stop. She might cry for the rest of her life. It was better just to freeze it out, to feel nothing but emptiness. She'd done it once before. She could do it again.

"How's the writing going?" he asked casually.

"Fine," she lied.

"Not in the mood for conversation?" he asked.

"Not in the least."

"I thought you might have calmed down enough to talk this over."

"I'm perfectly calm and I have nothing to say to you."

His eyes bored into hers. "But I have something to say to you." His voice was full of calm determination. "I regret the circumstances under which we met more than you know and I understand how you feel. I understand that you feel manipulated by Wanda and me both, and you have reasons to feel this way. I am sorry."

She said nothing, staring stonily at her plate.

"I would like us to talk about this rationally and clear the air. I'd like you to think about this with an open mind. I'd like you to understand my point of view."

She put down her knife and fork and met his eyes. "As you may know, some women have an enormous capacity for rationalizing the undesirable behavior of their men, to find innocent excuses for the most outrageous trespasses. Well, I'm not one of them." She pushed back her chair and stood up. "Thank you for dinner. Leave the dishes and I'll do them later." She turned and went back to her weeding.

* * *

He watched her go, his heart heavy. Her long legs, smooth and tanned, carried her gracefully across the lawn. She walked with confidence and determination, her fiery hair swinging silkily around her shoulders. *Don't follow me,* her back said. *I don't want you. Just leave me alone.*

He had seen the tears in her eyes and it had cost him all his strength not to take her in his arms. It would not have been any use. She didn't want his comfort, or his love.

He turned away from the door and started clearing the dishes.

She thought he was in cahoots with Wanda. He gave a harsh little laugh. He probably liked Wanda about as much as she did, although...

He frowned and sighed, seeing again the elegant woman with that little cat in her lap, her ringed fingers, stroking it gently.

There was something strange about her, the cool, detached way she had talked about Raine. As if Raine had been a project to execute, a task to be completed, not a frightened girl who had lost everything and needed to be loved.

I think of her as my daughter, Trevor, she'd said. It had sounded strange in his ears, out of character for her to say. He had sensed in her no sentiment, no emotion. Yet there was that little alley cat, and those perfectly manicured hands stroking it so softly.

He'd wondered vaguely if the only thing she was capable of loving was that little feline. But love took many forms. And many people hid their feelings behind carefully constructed barricades. Wanda was a well-barricaded woman. He saw her in his mind's eye, sitting on the floor of her living room, surrounded by Raine's papers, the wild look in her eyes. The barricades had been down, if only temporarily.

Raine managed to avoid him for the rest of the evening. He made no attempt at approaching her, nor did he come to her room that night.

In the morning, she went into her office, finding the computer switched off, as she had left it. She felt a pang of disappointment, then realized that it didn't necessarily mean he hadn't added to the file. Since she knew it existed, there was no reason to leave the computer running with the file on the screen. If she was interested, she could retrieve it.

I'm not interested, she said to herself.

Of course, you are, the other self said. You're intrigued. You want to know.

"Oh, what the hell," she muttered and retrieved the Truth file. Annoyed, she realized she was holding her breath. There it was, an answer to her question. Her gaze flew across the lines.

FOR A FICTION WRITER YOU'RE SHOWING A DISAPPOINTING LACK OF IMAGINATION. HOW ABOUT THIS: YOU'RE AN HEIRESS TO A HEALTH FOOD EMPIRE. I WANT YOUR MONEY.

"Ha, ha," she muttered. Health food empire? Wanda's company was a good and profitable one. An empire it was not. Her fingers hit the keys, typing a reply.

WANDA IS 46 YEARS OLD. SHE'S GOING TO LIVE TO BE A HUNDRED AND TEN. YOU WANT TO WAIT THAT LONG?

She wasn't going to be an heiress, empire or no.

She didn't care about that. That wasn't the reason she had ever fallen in with Wanda's plans.

Wanda's plans.

Together we can make it a phenomenon in the business world, she'd said. *You and I, because we care, because it is ours. We'll have the best products, the most integrity in our research, the most scrupulously clean advertising. I'm sick and tired of the public being duped and deceived and misled. We won't do it. We will show how it can be done with total honesty.*

There had been talk about expansion, research, finding new products, marketing. Wanda talking and talking and Raine listening, sometimes asking a question, sometimes offering a suggestion. And always there had been that hard knot of despair in her stomach.

Raine pushed the keyboard out of the way and lowered her head on her arms. She had tried hard to make Wanda understand and she had failed.

So she should have done it earlier, much earlier, but it had all been confused. Feelings tended to confuse issues. Feelings distorted reality. Guilt, obligation, fear, oh boy, she'd had a mess of them.

"I tried," she muttered to herself. "I tried." She lifted her head and pulled the keyboard toward her.

Dear Wanda,
I have come to the understanding that I have made some mistakes, which led to the breakup of our relationship last year.

Taking the blame herself—another tactic. Well, it was partially true. Manipulation took two. Wanda couldn't have used her like a doormat if she hadn't lain down in front of her feet.

I should have told you years ago that I was unhappy about the plans you made for me. But I didn't. I kept quiet while you decided. I thought I owed you. And of course I do, in many ways, but I should have told you that I did not want to go into business and wanted another sort of life.

You are a very commanding person. People respect you for your business talents. You have made a success of your life and you wanted me to make a success of mine.

Raine's fingers were still for a moment. Of course Wanda had wanted to have her make a success of her life. And of course Wanda had done that the only way she knew how: the way she had done it herself, in business. And lucky Raine: There was a place ready-made and waiting for her in Wanda's company.

Only she hadn't wanted it.

Raine reread what she had written and sighed, unsure of how to go on. Maybe later. She saved the file and called up the file of the book chapter she was working on.

The day stretched. Her writing suffered because her mind was on other things. Trevor's presence hovered at the fringes of her consciousness. He did not show himself, but she could feel in every cell of her body he was near. In the afternoon he played the piano—classical, jazz, even some country tunes. He played well, and under any other circumstances she would have enjoyed listening to him, but now he was setting her nerves on edge with his romantic tunes. Was he doing it on purpose to wear her down?

At four in the afternoon, the phone rang. It was Kim calling from Paris.

"How are you?" she asked. "Have you spoken to Trevor yet?"

"Yes." Raine told her what had transpired. "I told him to leave, but he won't go."

"He must think he can change your mind about him."

"Well, he can't. I've had enough of people manipulating me, Kim. I'm done with it."

There was a silence.

"Why aren't you saying anything?" Raine asked.

"I'm not sure what to say. I mean, I do understand your feelings, but I keep thinking about why he did this. And the fact that he told you himself. It wasn't as if you found out by accident. He didn't try to hide it from you. He wanted you to know, Raine."

"That doesn't change the fact that he deceived me, Kim."

Kim sighed. "No, it doesn't."

"I didn't mean to depress you. I'm fine, don't worry. Tell me about Paris."

Kim did, but her heart wasn't in it. "What does Trevor do with himself all day?" she asked after a perfunctory description of her Parisian adventures.

Raine sighed and switched the receiver to her other ear. "So far he's mowed the lawn, fed the animals, cooked dinner, read two fat paperbacks and driven me crazy playing the 'Moonlight Sonata.' I hide in the office and pretend to write my book, but it's not going well." Raine tucked a strand of hair behind her ear. "Oh, yes, and he sends me messages on the computer."

"Messages? What kind of messages?"

Raine told her. Kim seemed to find it amusing.

"Maybe tomorrow he'll let you know his real reason," she said hopefully.

"I don't care."

"Yes, you do."

* * *

The next morning Raine awoke with the light. The window was open and the birds' cheerful chirping made it impossible to go back to sleep. She wondered if Trevor had put another message on the computer. Last night had been a trial and her nerves were beginning to wear thin. He'd cooked dinner again and she'd eaten it dutifully, saying nothing but the most necessary things. It was amazing how little needed to be said if you were determined enough not to talk. But all the time they were together she was aware of his eyes, aware of his hands, his body when he came close. The need to touch him and hold him seemed to have nothing to do with her angry thoughts. It was impossible to freeze out the need. It was too powerful and she knew Trevor was very much aware of it.

It was no use lying in bed any longer. She put on a robe and crept downstairs, into the office. She switched on the computer and called up the file.

SO, ALL RIGHT, FORGET THE HEALTH FOOD EMPIRE. HOW ABOUT THIS? I WANTED TO FIND YOU BECAUSE I WAS IN LOVE WITH YOU.

She groaned. He was in love with her. A reason even more preposterous than the first one. Yet she remembered the black eyes looking at her the first night she had met him. The intense look, the secrecy, as if he knew something she didn't, as if he could look straight into her soul. She wondered what he had been thinking, what had been in his mind when he saw her.

HOW COULD YOU BE IN LOVE WITH ME WHEN YOU DIDN'T EVEN KNOW ME?

The day dragged. Tension mounted. Every time she was near him, the electricity sparked between them. Whatever she thought she'd worked out, this wasn't it.

"How long are you going to keep this up?" he asked again. There was tension in his voice, and the tight features of his face spoke volumes.

"I've no idea what you're talking about," she said coolly, getting up from the dinner table and noisily stacking the dishes.

"I'm not leaving here until we've talked."

She shrugged. "If that's what it takes." She sat back down, crossed her arms in front of her chest and leaned back in her chair.

"So talk."

"I don't want to lose what we have, Raine."

"I'm not sure what it was we had, but I am sure that I don't want to put up with deceit and manipulation. I've had enough of it."

"I understand that, and you have no idea how much I regret all this. In the beginning I didn't know the nature of your relationship with Wanda. I didn't understand your... reluctance to let me close. I understand it better now."

"Oh, you do? And what do you understand?"

"You're afraid of being manipulated again, of losing control of your own life. But I never had any intention of doing that, Raine. You must know that."

She wasn't so sure. "What's your connection with Wanda?" It was the question that had haunted her, and she had to admit that she was not altogether sorry they were talking.

His mouth curved. "She's my aunt, or ex-aunt, I should say. She used to be married to an English uncle of mine, a half brother of my mother's."

Raine only vaguely remembered Wanda's husband, her uncle, a tall, thin Englishman who spoke with a funny accent, or so she'd thought as a child. She'd been just a girl when they had been divorced and at any rate, she'd seen little of her aunt and uncle.

"Why didn't you tell me who you were?"

He rubbed his neck. "Wanda asked me to look you up, not to say anything. I had reasons to think mentioning her would not be a good thing. Something happened between you two, but I have no idea what. She was quite distraught."

"Distraught?" Raine didn't believe it. All she could hear was the echo of Wanda's parting words. Her stomach churned and involuntarily her hands clenched, as if she needed to defend herself. "Wanda doesn't get distraught," she said tonelessly. "Wanda gets mad. She's mad as hell with me."

"Why is she mad with you?"

"She's made quite an investment in me and she doesn't like losing." Raine tried to sound calm; it wasn't easy. The words sounded cynical, yet she didn't mean them to be. It was the truth. The truth as she saw it.

"Is that why she has a photo of you on her desk?"

For a moment Raine was speechless. "She has a picture of me on her desk?"

"Is that strange?"

Raine nodded. "Yes, that's strange. She's not the sentimental type. She has no photos of anybody anywhere, not even in her apartment." She studied his face. "What were you doing in her office? You said she didn't hire you to find me, so what were you doing there?"

He sat down and began to butter his toast. "Business. We'd just opened a small factory on St. Barlow and I'd contacted her to see if she was interested in a new line of tropical fruit juices. Since I was in the states on other business I decided I'd meet with her and work out the details of the deal in person." He spread honey on his toast and took a bite. "Besides, I was curious to see her again. It had been a long time."

"What did any of that have to do with coming to look for me?"

"Nothing. Except that I saw your photo on her desk."

He got up to pour himself another cup of coffee. "You want one?"

"No." She didn't understand and her curiosity was getting the better of her, which was, she knew, exactly what he had intended. "So, you saw my picture. What does that mean?"

He leaned back in his chair and studied her face. "Something happened to me when I looked at that photo of you." He shrugged his broad shoulders and his dark brows drew together in a frown. "I can't explain it. It was the oddest thing that ever happened to me."

She swallowed uneasily. "What happened to you?"

His mouth tilted in a faint smile. "You seemed so familiar, so real, as if I knew who you were, as if somewhere inside of me I knew you very well, except of course, I didn't." He paused. "We met once, you know, when you'd just moved in with her. It was at a party."

"We met?" She couldn't believe her ears. "I don't remember any of it."

"I'm not surprised. You were physically present, and that was about it. You looked totally lost and very frightened."

She didn't have any recollection of the specific party, or of seeing him. She had recollections in general about Wanda's parties. How she was fussed over beforehand, taken to find a dress, taken to have her hair done. How she was coached into eating with knife and fork, like the Europeans did. Wanda liked European manners. *Don't switch your knife and fork. It's so awkward. And for Pete's sake, don't plow your fork into your meat vertically. It's not a hayfork!* She was taught what to do and say when being introduced. *For heaven's sake, don't stand there with your hands by your side like a ninny. Hold out your hand and smile. Say something.*

Trevor drained his coffee cup and put it down. "I didn't remember that party, either, until I saw your photo. It brought it all back to me. So I asked about you."

"And what did Wanda say?" She couldn't believe Wanda had a photo of her on her desk. It didn't make sense.

"She said you had vanished." His half smile was vaguely amused. "She invited me to stay at her apartment. She showed me some of your pictures and some of the college newspapers with your articles in it. We had dinner together and talked about you."

They'd talked about her. It was not a comforting thought. "Oh, great," she said. "That makes me feel even better. Then what?"

"I went back home, to St. Barlow, back to work." He met her eyes. "I couldn't get you out of my head." His voice was low and his features softened. "I kept seeing your picture in my mind, I kept thinking about you, wondering where you were, what had happened to you."

"That's crazy!"

He gave a crooked smile. "I told myself that, yes. But it didn't seem to help. The human mind works in strange and unpredictable ways."

"Yours does, at any rate," she said dryly.

"And yours is a straightforward computer—*Don't confuse me with the facts, I'm already programmed.*"

She deserved that one, she had to admit. She let it pass. "Does Wanda want me to come back to Chicago?"

"She wanted to find you, so I assume so, yes."

She didn't know if she was relieved or afraid, or both. Relieved because there was a possibility to clear things up between them. Afraid because she wasn't sure of Wanda's motives. She would not go back to work for her. The only relationship possible was one that was based on her being independent, living her own life. If Wanda could not accept that, there was no hope.

"I can't go back to work for her," she said.

"I know, and you shouldn't. Guilt is a terrible motivation. Besides, you should be writing." He paused. "I didn't come here to do Wanda's bidding, Raine. I told you that. I felt sorry for her, yes, and I was somewhat intrigued by the whole situation, and I thought it wouldn't hurt to set her mind at ease. But the real reason I came to see you," he said slowly, "was because I couldn't get you out of my mind." His dark eyes held hers, not wavering.

She wished she could believe what was in those eyes, wished she could believe that it was true that this big, dark, sexy man had fallen in love with her picture.

But she didn't have it in her to believe in such romantic nonsense. She couldn't possibly afford to believe it.

His gaze lingered on her face. "Maybe we should call Wanda. She's quite distraught about your disappearing. She thinks of you as a daughter. That's what she told me."

Daughter. Raine closed her eyes against a wave of regret. "She had a strange way of showing it," she said huskily

He held her gaze and for a moment it was very still in the room. "Not all women are earth mothers," he said softly, "baking cookies with their girls, making Christmas ornaments, sewing frilly dresses for them."

He had seen her childhood pictures. He knew about her, things she had never even told him. Visions, memories floated through her mind, mingling in a kaleidoscope of color and joy and warmth. Her mother, the large kitchen, the fragrance of cookies in the oven, a glittering Christmas tree with homemade ornaments, the pretty dresses her mother had sewn for her and her sister Amy. She could feel her mother's hands, braiding her hair; her hand, cool on her forehead when she had a fever.

"You saw my pictures," she said, her voice shaking.

"Yes." He didn't smile. "Wanda showed them to me. You were a beautiful little girl."

"Where did Wanda find these pictures?"

"They were in a box she'd found in your room. There were college papers in there, newsletters with your articles in them. I sat up hours that night reading them. You're a good writer, Raine."

She remembered the box. And then she remembered something else, and fear ran cold down her spine.

"My diary was in that box," she said, her voice barely audible. She'd remembered the diary too late; she'd forgotten to bring it.

He nodded. "Yes."

Chapter Thirteen

Her life had been in that diary. For five years, all through her first year of college, she'd poured her soul into it. All the anguish of losing her family, all the pain and sadness of those first few years had been committed to the pale blue pages—all those painful emotions she'd not been able to share with Wanda, who'd been so competent and efficient and not given to sentiment. Trevor had given her the freesias because he had known her mother had grown them in her flower garden and they'd been her favorites.

"You had no right," she whispered, seeing in her mind an image of Wanda and Trevor sitting in Wanda's sterile apartment, looking at her pictures, reading her diary, discussing her. It was more than she could bear and she felt something snapping inside her.

She rushed up to him, shaking. "How did you dare!" she cried. "How did you dare!" She pounded his chest with all her might, as if somehow it would alleviate the anger and embarrassment. She felt naked, exposed to the very depths of her soul.

He grabbed her hands. "Stop it!" he said. "Raine, stop it! I didn't read your diary! Listen to me!"

"No!" she cried wildly, fighting him, hearing words but not their meaning, wanting to hear nothing from him ever again. "You had no right, no right!"

She was crying. Tears of helpless fury and despair. He had known everything about her from the very beginning. He had looked at her at the party and he had known. He had known her name and her situation and everything about her life.

He held her tight and she was sobbing against his shirt and the fury inside her was a terrible thing, alive and violent like a wild animal. She fought against him with every ounce of her strength and she heard him curse under his breath when she yanked at his hair.

He picked her up off the floor, carried her out the door across the lawn. She kicked and struggled in his iron grip, her eyes blinded by the sun. Stars in her head, fire and heat. Suddenly he let go of her and for a moment she felt suspended in space. Then there was wet, cool darkness as water engulfed her. Her body found no more resistance and her arms and legs flailed aimlessly in the water.

He'd dumped her into the pond. Instinct took over and there was no time for thought. She raised her head above water and swam to the side, gasping and sputtering. She waded out through the long reeds, her feet sinking in the soft mud. With solid ground under her hands and knees, she collapsed on the grass like a wet rag doll, all her strength seeping out of her. Tears ran down her face, coming of their own accord, silent and without rage. She felt utterly empty and utterly defeated.

He was there, taking her in his arms, holding her, wiping the hair away from her face.

"I didn't read your diary, Raine! Aren't you listening to me? I didn't read it!"

She closed her eyes, hearing nothing, feeling nothing, the words dripping off her like the water. He lifted her up, carried her into the house, up the stairs into the bathroom and deposited her straight into the tub. He took the hand-shower off its hook and turned on the water, adjusting the temperature, and began to spray the mud off her.

The tears had stopped and she sat limply in the tub, feeling the warm water going through her shorts and shirt. She had no fight left in her. Nothing mattered. She didn't want to think about it anymore. Then he was in the tub with her, hanging the shower on its hook and lifting her to stand. Her knees buckled and he held her, standing in the water spray with her, getting drenched.

"I'm sorry I had to throw you in the pond."

She said nothing and he lifted her chin and kissed her mouth. She turned her face away.

He began to take off her shirt, unbuttoning it, sliding it off and throwing it on the floor. He unhooked her bra, and tossed it on top of the shirt, all with seemingly clinical detachment.

"Please talk to me, Raine."

She said nothing. There was nothing to say; her mind was blank. He stripped off her sodden shorts and panties and it took her an effort to step out of them.

He took a towel and began to rub her dry, quickly, efficiently. He wrapped another towel around her and took her hand, taking her to her bedroom. She sat on the bed, looking down at her hands in her lap.

"Please, Raine, say something."

She looked at him. "Go away," she said thickly. She couldn't bear to be with him. All she could see in her mind was Wanda and Trevor, going through her papers, eating dinner, discussing her. "Please, just go away."

Raine sat up. She was alone. The sun was streaking across the room. She wasn't sure how long she'd lain on the bed, curled up, eyes closed. An hour, maybe longer, but she had managed to calm herself down. Slowly she sat up, wiping the damp hair out of her face. The towel had come loose and lay on the bed. She got up, found some clothes and put them on. Glancing in the mirror, she hardly recognized herself. She looked like a witch with her still half-wet hair standing out in all directions. Brushing it out, she tied it into a ponytail and left it at that.

I am calm, she told her reflection. *I am completely in control. I feel exposed and manipulated, but I'll live. I'll get over it. There are worse things in the world. I'm in control; it's not going to happen anymore, never. Now I am going down and not lose my composure.*

In the kitchen she poured herself a glass of iced tea and squeezed some lemon in it. Trevor was outside on the terrace, reading. He wore only shorts and his chest was bare and brown. She walked out and stood in front of him. He lowered the book and took off his sunglasses. He didn't say anything, just sat there looking at her as if he were waiting for something. His face was tense and he looked suddenly much older.

She did not sit down. She stood straight and faced him, anchored her feet to the ground and prayed for composure.

"I've had my tantrum and now it's over. I apologize for losing my cool. I've contemplated the situation and our relationship and I've come to the conclusion that what I want is for you to leave. I'm sure you understand why."

"Yes, I do." His voice was calm and businesslike.

There was a silence. She had expected him to say more, try in some way to dissuade her, tell her he loved her, say he wanted her to reconsider.

He did none of these.

Had he already resigned himself to the inevitable? She scrutinized him in the silence. He did not look resigned. No hunched shoulders, no defeat in his eyes. He looked as calm and determined and in control as ever, his dark eyes settled unwaveringly on her face. For a moment she was confused, then she turned abruptly and walked back into the house.

The story wasn't working. As the clouds darkened the sky and the air grew still and heavy, Raine struggled with her hero, who had a mind of his own and wasn't obeying her orders. She struggled with the unsinkable Elizabeth whose spirited stubbornness was drifting her way off course. Something was wrong, only she couldn't figure out what.

Raine pressed her hands against her eyes and sighed. Damn, damn. She wasn't getting anywhere. The air was thick and oppressive and it seemed hard to breathe. She stood up and looked out the window. Ominous clouds hung in the sky. A thunderstorm in the making, no doubt.

She called up her plot outline and scrutinized it. She'd had it all figured out in the beginning, so why didn't it work anymore? She sighed. The story had taken on a life of its own and hadn't followed her outline very closely. Now she was stuck in the worst way. She reread the last chapter, hoping to find some clue. A sound made her look up. What was it? Thunder? No, a car.

She got up and glanced out the window. Trevor's car was going down the long, uneven drive, bumping up and down as if doing a cheerful dance. Her heart leapt into her throat.

Was he leaving? She'd heard him move around in his room earlier.

She ran up the stairs, into his room. It was empty. His duffel bag and clothes were gone. She rushed down the stairs again, through the living room and the kitchen, out onto the terrace. She wasn't sure why she was running. She peered across the meadows, her heart racing. Trevor's car crawled along the narrow country road, disappearing into the cloud-darkened distance.

She felt the first heavy drops of rain on her arm. Then a streak of lightening split the sky. More drops came down, bigger, faster, until they turned into a torrent of water. Raine didn't move. She just stood there, listening to the thunder, getting drenched.

Finally she turned, wiping her hair from her face, wiping her eyes.

She wasn't crying. It was just the rain.

It was a relief to have the house to herself again, to be free to move around and not have to think about where he was or see those dark unreadable eyes observing her. She closed the kitchen door and locked it. She wouldn't have to worry anymore about what he was thinking, what he was remembering about the things he had found out about her in Chicago, the things Wanda had told him over a cozy dinner.

It was over.

He was gone.

Time to celebrate. She shivered suddenly, aware now of the cold, wet T-shirt sticking to her skin. Water was dripping from her hair down her face and neck. With a kitchen towel she dried her face. She sat down at the table and stared out the window. There was nothing to see but a gray-green sea of water.

Trevor had betrayed her and she wanted nothing more to do with him. Those few brief weeks of love were nothing but a beautiful dream that had ended in a nightmare. It hadn't been love—it had been a game of deceit. She should have listened to her instincts and not given in, not fallen for Trevor Lloyd. She closed her eyes, seeing him behind her closed lids, his stark male appeal, the seductive glints of humor in his dark eyes. She shouldn't fool herself. She'd been helpless. She'd had no defenses against him.

But now it was over. She was free of him now.

Thunder rumbled through the sky and rain lashed the windows. Raine sat in the darkened kitchen, head on her arms, her heart breaking.

The next day she worked like a woman possessed, blocking out thoughts of Trevor, forcing herself to write. It didn't work. Maybe she should just give it a rest for a few days, let it all settle. Maybe her subconscious mind would come up with the answer in her sleep, or while she was weeding the garden some sunny morning.

There were no miracles. She weeded the garden, but no answer materialized mysteriously. Trevor's words kept echoing in her head. *Your heroine is on a road to self-destruction. She's either going to have to give up her pride or lose her man.*

She dreamed strange, mixed-up dreams, and she was always lost. Lost in a boat on the water looking for Trevor. Lost on a plane looking for an island that wasn't there. Lost in a rain forest looking for Trevor.

It rained in the rain forest, a driving, drenching rain. It was dark and eerie and she could see nothing but wet, dripping leaves and insects crawling up her bare legs. Sodden, hungry and terrified, she was searching for Trevor, but she could not move because of thick lianas curling themselves around her arms and legs and neck. She screamed, but her voice made no sound. Trevor was somewhere in the forest, she knew, but he eluded her. She was being tested to see if she was strong enough. Strong enough for what?

She woke up crying and wet with perspiration. The sheets were tangled around her legs. Outside she heard the rain pelting on the roof.

She moved through the days in a trance. Kim, back from Paris, dropped by a couple of times, but Raine didn't feel like talking. She didn't feel like doing much of anything—eating, writing. She was beginning to feel disgusted with herself. There were worse things in the world than a broken heart. People were starving to death, people were losing their homes in hurricanes and tornadoes, people were dying in mud slides and earthquakes. The BBC from London kept her well-informed. How dare she feel sorry for herself?

"You need a break," Kim decided. "Let's go to the beach, or spend a day in Amsterdam."

Raine shook her head. "I've got to get this book finished. I haven't done a thing for days."

But Kim persuaded her in the end, and they went shopping in Amsterdam. It was a gorgeous sunny day and the old city center was alive with activity—tourists from all over the world crowded the streets, the markets and the shops. They walked around the narrow ancient streets, across picturesque bridges and past centuries-old patrician houses facing the canals.

The cheerful, festive ambience of the place made it difficult to stay depressed and Raine enjoyed browsing through the numerous little shops carrying exotic merchandise from Africa, the Far East, South America. There was a world out there, a whole world full of excitement and new adventures and she had a life to live. As the day wore on, she began to smile and feel better.

But home on the farm again that evening, Raine's spirits sank with a crash. There was no avoiding her personal reality, was there? It could be ignored or denied, but it would always be there.

And the reality was that she was in love with Trevor and that somehow she would have to get over it. He had manipulated her, just like Wanda had manipulated her. She wasn't going to take it—not from Wanda, not from Trevor, not from anybody.

If there wasn't honesty, how could there possibly be love?

Trevor stood in line for passport check, waiting impatiently for his turn. He didn't like lines. He didn't like waiting. But then, there is was, whether you liked it or not. He sighed and moved his weight onto his other foot. There were a lot of imponderables that happened whether you liked it or not. Raine's reaction to hearing the truth being a case in point.

It hadn't been strictly necessary to come back to Geneva, but it was just as well to be gone for a couple of days, if not for his own sake, for Raine's. There wasn't anything he could do right now and the situation only seemed to get worse.

There was only the weekend left. On Monday his time was up and he couldn't postpone going home to St. Barlow any longer. He had a new contract starting on Wednesday for which it was rather essential he go to St. Lucia.

If Raine really loved him, she'd eventually come around. If she really loved him she'd eventually forgive him, understand him. Maybe what she needed was time simply to get things into perspective without him around to stir up her anger. He probably shouldn't even try to see her on the weekend. He should just leave and let her fight her own battle.

She's better off without me for a while. It was not a joyous thought. Maybe she'd never want him back again. Another thought not very joyous. He pushed it away.

He handed over his passport, got it stamped and moved on to find his luggage. Customs was fast and efficient and he was out of the building in an amazingly short time. He took a taxi to his hotel, settled in, ordered coffee from room service and began to prepare for his meetings the next day.

It was difficult to concentrate. He kept seeing Raine's face, the anguished look in her eyes.

He could not reach her. Barricades of fear and walls of anger separated them. His words and reassurances were useless. She was not ready for them. She didn't want to hear them. She was so damned stubborn, so full of angry pride. In spite of himself, he smiled.

He remembered that first night in Wanda's apartment reading Raine's articles and essays in the university paper. Articles on finding a place in the world, loyalty, education and government, friendship—articles that had given him an insight into her reasoning, her values and ethics. And all of it, the things Wanda had told him, the writing of the college student, had added up to something fascinating: a woman of depth and passion, a woman he was in love with before he'd ever met her. He'd known in the depths of his being that he wanted to be with her, the flesh-and-blood woman that was the reality behind the words on paper. He knew without a doubt that he could share with her his life and ambitions like he had never been able to do with Suzanna. Suzanna had accepted his work; she hadn't really understood the driving force behind it—the need to make a difference in the world—at least in the lives of a few people. The need to share his knowledge and good fortune with others. He knew no greater satisfaction than to see his work pay off and see a family break the vicious circle of poverty and become self-sufficient.

He ran his hand through his hair and sighed. Raine. He wanted her. He needed her.

And she needed him. He wanted her to need him. Despite all her courage in taking charge of her own life, fighting for a future and independence, she was still so vulnerable. She'd suffered a terrible loss, stood up to a domineering, manipulating aunt, and now he, too, had added to it all. He had hurt her to the depths of her soul, and the look in her eyes would haunt him for the rest of his days. He wanted to hold her and wipe away the pain, tell her he loved her.

Dammit, he wasn't going to give up on her.

Chapter Fourteen

Raine took the towels from the dryer and folded them. The blue one had been Trevor's. Closing her eyes, she saw him standing in the shower, water dripping down his brown torso, his grin as he invited her to come in with him. Her throat closed and her eyes flooded with tears. She put the towel to her face, but nothing of him was there. The towel smelled like all the rest of them, baby clean and soapy.

I'm not going to stand here and weep into his towel like some theatrical movie star, she said to herself. There was life after Trevor, like there had been life after all the other crises and misadventures of her life.

She had let Trevor into her life, and he had become part of her universe, so carefully constructed out of her new freedom, self-sufficiency and control. Now it had collapsed. She had to pick up the pieces and start over and reconstruct her world; there was no choice. She gathered up the towels and moved to the stairs. No matter how bravely she talked to herself, the misery inside her did not subside. An entire day of talking bravely had made no difference.

She stood still and looked at the painting of the dolls. The forlorn look of the two dolls touched her again as it had before—the gentleness of the larger doll's arm around the shoulder of the smaller one in pathetic comfort. The hair of the larger doll lay in disarray, the face was cracked and there was a split seam in the cloth chest. Raine looked at the bandaged leg, the inward curving toes. Some child had once loved these dolls. Now they were discarded junk. Yet the painter had made something beautiful out of it, something that touched her heart. He had rearranged the discarded past and returned it to life.

A thought flitted briefly through her mind, then faded, as if afraid to hang on, as if perhaps she was not yet ready to recognize it. She stood very still, holding her breath, feeling a sudden urgent need to hang on to the thought, to not let it escape. She closed her eyes in concentration, willing the thought to come back and reveal itself. It was suddenly very important to know.

And then it was there. Clear, precise.

She had fallen in love with Trevor and she'd woven a pretty dream of sweet perfection. It had been wonderful to love him, to be with him, her universe more perfect with him in it.

And then something had happened and the shiny surface of her universe—so new, so fragile—had cracked, like the face of the dolls. Mistakes had been made and feelings had been hurt and she was blinded by disillusionment and pride.

She was throwing out Trevor's love because she was too proud to see beyond the pain of imperfection, beyond her own hurt feelings, beyond her own fear—too proud to reach beyond it all and see the truth.

She lowered herself on the stairs, clutching the towels to her chest, hearing, somewhere in her head, Trevor's voice. *Your Elizabeth is on a path to self-destruction, you realize that? She's going to have to give up her pride or lose the man.*

She lowered her face against the towels, feeling tears burn behind her eyes.

She called the sailing school, her hands trembling as she punched in the number. Please, she prayed, let him be there.

"Max, it's Raine. Is Trevor there?"

"No, he left yesterday." His voice was muffled as if he was chewing something.

She felt her heart sink. "On the boat? I mean, is he gone with the cruiser?"

"No." There was a pause as he swallowed. "His lease ran out. Another client had it reserved, a German podiatrist and his three girlfriends."

Her heart sank. "Oh, no," she muttered.

Max laughed. "Does that offend your American sensibilities?" he asked.

It took a moment to make sense out of his question. She was not in the mood to joke around with Max, who had many colorful stories about the eccentricities of his clients. "Oh, for God's sake, Max!" she snapped. "What do I care to whom you rent your boats? I'm trying to find out where Trevor is, and you talk about a lecherous podiatrist. Give me a break. I've heard a whole lot worse. Did he say where he was going?"

"Who?" asked Max. "The podiatrist?"

Raine closed her eyes and let out an exasperated sigh. She heard Max chuckle at the other end of the line.

"Sorry," he said, "I couldn't let that pass."

"So you don't know where Trevor is?"

"I didn't say that."

She was ready to scream. She gritted her teeth, then took a deep breath. "Would you please tell me where he is?"

"Of course. Why not?"

"I'd like to know that, too. Where is he?"

Max laughed. "He's in Geneva. He said he'd be back for the weekend to pack up his stuff. He'll be staying with us for a couple of nights and then he's off to his island paradise again on Monday. He was in a rotten mood when he left." He paused meaningfully. "Anything to do with you, perhaps?"

"Thank you, Max," she said sweetly, and hung up.

All the tension seemed to flow out of her body and she felt giddy with relief. He hadn't left the country yet.

There was still time.

She glanced at her watch. It was seven hours earlier in Chicago. Wanda would be at her desk, dressed to kill, getting ready for some high-powered meeting.

Maybe she should call her. After all, she was part of her old, discarded life. Maybe there was something yet to be salvaged. *She considers you her daughter, you know,* Trevor had said. Could that possibly be true?

If you don't try, you'll never know.

She'd made many efforts at writing a letter. The last one still languished unfinished somewhere in the computer.

Once you walk out of this door, don't expect to come back.

She cringed, remembering the words. But she had taken Wanda by surprise. She'd never told Wanda how she felt, had hidden it all behind a carefully cultivated mask. She'd thought she'd owed Wanda and she'd been willing to pay her debt until the burden became unbearable and she'd turned on Wanda, who'd been unsuspecting.

It was partially my fault, too. It was not a new revelation. It had grown slowly over the last months.

She closed her eyes and took a deep breath, then went into the living room and dialed Wanda's direct line, her heart racing.

A secretary answered on the second ring, wishing her a cheerful good morning. She did not recognize the voice; she must be new.

Raine's hand trembled. "Good morning. Trevor Lloyd calling long-distance from the Netherlands," she said, pretending to be a secretary herself. "Ms. Strickland, please." Wanda would accept a call from Trevor, but maybe not from her.

"One moment, please."

"Trevor, how are you?" Wanda's voice was crisp and businesslike, the line crystal clear and static free.

"It's not Trevor, Wanda. It's me."

There was a silence, a void stretching across the ocean.

"Wanda?"

"Raine? Raine, where are you?" The business voice was gone. It was a voice Raine had never heard—husky, unsteady. She couldn't believe it, not from Wanda, who was always under control. Her heart began to beat even faster.

"I'm still in Holland." *Wrong,* she thought, *but never mind; no Friesians here to hear me.*

"How are you?"

"Oh, I am fine. I like it here."

There was an awkward silence. "Are you coming home?" Wanda asked at last. It was not a demand. There were no accusations, no recriminations. It was a question, nothing more.

Are you coming home? It was not a question Raine had ever expected to hear from Wanda, not after what she had said the day Raine had left. There was a sudden lump in Raine's throat and she couldn't speak.

"I shouldn't have said what I said," Wanda went on. "I was very... distraught at your leaving, but that was no excuse."

"I should not have dumped the news on you the way I did."

"I never knew how you felt. You never told me."

"I know." *I was a coward. I didn't dare.* "I'm sorry how it all worked out, Wanda."

Wanda cleared her throat. "We need to talk, Raine."

Raine swallowed hard. "Yes."

"I've not handled things well where you are concerned." Wanda coughed to cover up a break in her voice. "I'd like you to come home so we can talk about it. Please."

It was the closest Wanda had ever come to begging.

Raine closed her eyes and leaned back in the chair. "I don't know when I'll be back. In a few months maybe." The conversation was stilted and awkward.

"What are you doing over there? Are you working?"

"Yes. I'm writing a book, a novel. It's almost finished."

"A *book?*" Wanda's voice was full of amazement.

"That's what I've always wanted to do. Write books, be a writer."

There was another silence.

Raine bit her lip. "I can't come back and work for you again, Wanda. I want you to understand that."

"I do, I do. It's not important. I just..." Again the catch in her voice. Raine wondered if emotion was getting the better of her, but it was hard to imagine it. Wanda wasn't given to sentimentality and tears. Yet one thing was clear: Hearing from her had shaken Wanda considerably.

Raine rubbed her forehead. *She considers you her daughter, you know.* Could it possibly be true that in her own strange, convoluted way, Wanda did?

"I'd just like to see you again," Wanda said, in control again. "To talk things over."

"Yes. I'll call you when I know more."

Wanda did not ask for her phone number. Maybe she already had it. Raine replaced the receiver and let out a deep sigh. Her hand was shaking. Then she came slowly to her feet and went back to the office and turned on the computer.

She reread the last couple of chapters and everything was clear, so clear. Pride, Trevor had said, pride is going to ruin your heroine.

Pride had made her heroine blind to the truth.

It was easy after that. She began to write. She wrote and forgot all time, lost in the magical world of her own creation, the joys and fears, the triumph of love in the end. She worked for the next two days, barely noticing the world around her, barely eating, sleeping only when she couldn't keep her eyes open any longer. She could not leave it now. She had to finish it.

When she finally typed *The End,* she felt the most glorious satisfaction she'd ever felt. She'd done it! She'd actually done it! And it was good. She *knew* it was good. She printed out the last chapter and as the machine rattled away, she sat back and sighed, feeling the tension slowly seep away. What was left to be done now was the editing, smoothing the rough edges and checking the details. She looked in shock at her watch. It was ten after three in the morning.

It was Saturday. Trevor was back.

Chapter Fifteen

She didn't awaken until after nine that morning, having slept in complete exhaustion. After she'd taken care of the animals she called Jannie, who told her that Trevor had come back from Geneva late the night before and was out now with Max at the school.

Raine drove to the sailing school, wondering how she should approach him, what to say. Would he even be willing to listen to her? Maybe he'd had enough of the whole situation and all he wanted was to get away.

She parked the car, feeling tense. Walking around to the back of the building, she saw Trevor standing by the water's edge, a big, quiet man, staring out over the lake, hands in his pockets. Her heart lurched and for a moment she just looked at him, feeling an aching need to just run up to him and throw herself into his arms, feel his strength, the beating of his heart.

Max was nowhere in sight. Taking a deep breath, Raine crossed the grass and walked in his direction. He must have heard her coming because he turned around and watched her approach him.

"Hello, Raine," he said evenly. His face registered no reaction. His dark eyes were calm as they surveyed her face.

"Hi." She glanced away, out over the lake. The choppy water glittered in the morning sunshine and white clouds drifted through a bright blue sky. A stiff breeze blew her hair around her face and she pushed it back over her shoulders to no avail. "It's great weather for sailing and windsurfing," she said for something to say.

"Yes." He gestured at a wooden bench facing the lake. "Have a seat."

She sat down and he took a seat next to her. She stared at the brightly colored sails of the boats on the lake.

"Did your meetings in Geneva go all right?"

He nodded, stretching his long legs and crossing them at the ankles. "Yes, very well, actually."

"I hear you're leaving on Monday."

"Yes." He chewed on a blade of grass. "I have to be on St. Lucia on Wednesday to start a new contract."

"Small-livestock development," she said. "You told me."

He tossed the blade of grass away. "Right." He put his hands behind his head and looked up at the sky, squinting against the bright light.

She waited, but he said nothing more. She wasn't sure what she had expected, but his silence unnerved her. He wasn't asking her to come with him. He wasn't even asking her about her plans. Had she not come here, would he have come to the farm to say goodbye or would he have left without a word? It looked like it. Her heart contracted.

"I finished my book," she said at last.

He looked down to meet her eyes. "You did? Great. We should celebrate. I'd offer you champagne, but I am homeless and bar-less at the moment."

"It doesn't matter." She looked away and watched a sparrow struggling to extract a worm from the soil.

"Did you resolve your heroine's problem?"

She bit her lip. "Yes, I did."

Two strangers making polite conversation. Her chest felt tight, as if some heavy weight was pressing down on her ribs.

"Did you get all the pieces to fit?"

"Yes." She swallowed. "You were right, you know."

"About what?"

He knew about what, but he wasn't making it easy for her. The weight on her chest seemed to get heavier. It was increasingly difficult to breathe.

"About the heroine's pride," she said.

"So what did you do?"

"I made her see the light and give it up. I made her grovel."

For a moment amusement flashed in his eyes. "You made her grovel?"

She gave a casual shrug and looked at him challengingly. "Yeah."

"It must have been very hard."

She bent down and picked a purple clover blossom. "Oh, it was," she said lightly, "but the alternative was unthinkable."

He frowned, feigning concentrated thought. "What was the alternative again?" As if he didn't know.

"She'd self-destruct and lose the hero."

He nodded. "Oh, yes, I remember now, the sexy Gypsy man." He looked around contentedly, surveying the lake, the lawn, the colorful flower beds surrounding the building. "It's a beautiful day, isn't it?"

Her heart sank. He was purposely being obtuse, making it hard on her.

"Yes, it's gorgeous," she said, twisting the flower between her fingers. "Would you like to read it? The last few chapters, I mean? You might as well, since you read the rest of it."

"I'd like to, but I'm out of here the day after tomorrow."

Anger burned in her throat. She swallowed hard. "Why are you doing this?"

He raised a brow. "Doing what?"

"You *know* what! You're making it difficult for me on purpose." Her heart was beating wildly. She felt like slugging him. She jumped to her feet a little too fast and almost lost her balance. He grabbed her arm just in time. His eyes bored into hers, dark and unsmiling. "Tell me, Raine," he said slowly, "why did you come here?"

"To tell you about my book!" Pride was not easy to relinquish. She wasn't happy with her own weakness. Why couldn't she just come out and say she'd come because she wanted to talk to him, to see if things between them were still salvageable? She herself had sent him away. It was up to her. Please, she prayed, please don't let it be too late.

"Well, you did. So why are you mad?"

"Because you're stupid and ignorant and you pretend not to understand what I've been saying!" To her horror, tears welled up in her eyes. She blinked furiously.

He'd taken hold of both her upper arms. "You told me the heroine in your book saw the light and gave up her pride, isn't that right?"

"Yes! No! Oh, dammit, let me go!" She struggled against his hold. He relaxed his grip slightly and she wrenched herself free and ran off, back to her car. He didn't follow her.

Her hands shook so much, she had trouble putting the key in the ignition. Taking a deep breath, she forced herself to calm down. The last thing she needed was to run off the road and turn over into a ditch.

Carefully, slowly, she drove back to the farm.

She had tried, she really had, and he had played with her, refusing to understand what she was trying to say.

Maybe he didn't want to understand. Maybe he had enough of her and didn't want her anymore.

She parked the car and went into the barn and got out the hedge trimmers. Sitting still was not what she needed now. She had to do something, anything. Her body felt restless with rampant aggression, ready to do battle with something or someone.

She started snipping away at the hedge that separated the front lawn from the drive. It was way out of control, even a city girl could see that. Snip, snip, snip. In a short time an impressive pile of trimmings lay at her feet and the hedge was looking rather bald and sheared.

Snip, snip, snip. *Damn, damn, damn,* her mind echoed. I don't care anymore, she said to herself. He can play all the damned games he wants, but not with me anymore. No more. Finished, *finito, schluss.* Snip, snip.

A car was coming down the drive. Automatically she narrowed her eyes and peered to see. Trevor's car. Her body tensed, her fingers tightened around the clippers. So now what?

She went on clipping, pretending not to know he had arrived, and moments later he came striding around the house in search of her.

"You're doing quite a job on that hedge," he said. "Did it offend you?"

She did not turn around and did not answer him. Her jaws clamped together, she went on clipping.

"Let's talk," he said after a moment of silence.

"Don't make me laugh."

He was suddenly right next to her, taking the trimmers from her hands. "Stop it," he said quietly. "There's going to be nothing left of that hedge. Take your aggressions out on me. It's more constructive."

She glared at him. "I came to see you this morning to talk. You weren't very receptive to what I was trying to tell you."

"You weren't talking about the heroine in your book, I take it."

"You know I wasn't."

"Yes, I did. Of course I did. You said your heroine was giving up her pride and you made her grovel, but you weren't quite prepared to go to that length yourself, were you? You thought you could take the easy way out and let me guess by inference."

"So what's wrong with that?"

"Why don't you tell me the real reason you came to see me this morning? I think I'd like to hear it straight. No game playing."

"Do you even care?" she asked bitterly.

His eyes held hers. "I care, Raine," he said, his voice soft and low. "I care very much. That's why I'm here." He closed his eyes briefly, and his face looked pained and weary. "Do you think, Raine, that all this has been easy for me? From the very beginning I've felt like a rat for what I had done. I tried to make it right. I did the best I could and I hoped you'd understand."

The anger was gone. She felt suddenly oddly weary, broken. She wiped the windblown hair out of her face. "Let's go inside."

In the kitchen she washed her hands and sat down at the table. He sat down across from her.

"I know we didn't start out our relationship in the most ideal of circumstances," he said. "But I didn't have a choice."

"I felt manipulated and deceived by you," she said slowly. "You must understand that."

"Yes, I do."

"It was a terrible feeling." She swallowed hard. "First Wanda, then Michael, then you." One night on the boat she had told him about Michael, how she hadn't known he'd had a wife and son in California, how betrayed she had felt. "I don't like being manipulated," she went on. "It makes me feel extremely...demeaned, humiliated. To say the least."

"I didn't mean to humiliate you." He got up impatiently and stood in the open door, looking outside. She stared at his broad back. Then suddenly he turned around and stood in front of her, his eyes holding hers, dark and tormented.

"So it was crazy," he said tightly. "Crazy to fall in love with a photograph and a bunch of articles and essays and some stories someone told me. But I did, and there was nothing I could do to convince myself I wasn't feeling what I was." He straightened and closed his eyes briefly. "I wanted to meet you. And when I did it only confirmed my feelings. All I wanted was to love you and for you to love me back. And I hoped that you would understand that. I hoped you would understand that it was never my intention to deceive you."

She swallowed at the constriction in her throat. Tears burned behind her eyes. "I'm trying," she said, her voice thick with tears. "I'm having a hard time coming to grips with the fact that you came here pretending not to know about me, and that Wanda was involved in it."

"I know, Raine." He voice sounded anguished. "I know. I wish to God there was something I could say to make it right, but there isn't." He rested his hands on the table and leaned forward, his eyes probing hers. "Tell me, Raine, why did you come to see me this morning?"

She felt as if she were falling into a deep black hole. She didn't know if he still loved her, if he still wanted her. But she had to take that risk. She felt herself begin to shake.

"Because I love you. Because I don't want to lose you." Tears ran down her cheeks.

He drew her up out of the chair, against the solid wall of his chest. "And I love you," he said huskily. "I was beginning to think you didn't care, that my love wasn't enough to overcome the problems." He kissed her hard and deep, a desperate, hungry kiss that sent her senses reeling.

She trembled against him, feeling his hands roam over her, touching, caressing.

Everything's all right, she thought, dizzy with relief and joy. And suddenly none of what had happened seemed to matter anymore. He loved her. He wanted her. Everything else could be forgotten and forgiven. And all the lovely visions and dreams were back in her mind—she and Trevor on the island, hiking in the rain forest, swimming in aquamarine waters, making love under the stars on his private beach. Writing. Her own office with a view of the Caribbean and the cool trade wind breezes wafting in through the open windows.

Trevor released her, his eyes smoky and barely focused. He took her hand. "Come on," he said, leading her out of the kitchen and around the pond. Behind the barn he began to take off her clothes, kissing her throat, her breasts, her stomach—hot fiery kisses that made her body tremble. "You're beautiful," he said huskily. "I like seeing you like this, in the sunlight, out in the open." He trailed his fingers through her hair, lifting the strands and letting them slide back into place. "It's like fire," he said.

There was no way to still the storm that spun and swirled inside her, sweeping away all thought and reason. She loved this man and nothing could ever change it. She stirred restlessly in the grass, reaching out to touch him, wanting him closer. "Make love to me," she whispered.

A bee droned nearby, buzzing around the blooming clover. It was a hypnotizing sound, and Raine listened, her body heavy with sleepy languor.

Something tickled her nose and she wiped it away. She opened her eyes, seeing Trevor's grinning face, a small daisy in his hand.

"Don't tease me," she muttered lazily.

"You were going to sleep on me."

"No, I wasn't. I was just dozing."

He bent over and kissed her mouth, his lips firm and tender. "I have a question," he said softly.

"What?"

"What made you change your mind? What was it that made you decide to come to me?"

She met his eyes and gave him a half smile. "The painting of the dolls."

One dark brow quirked upward. "The painting of the dolls? How?"

"It made me think that I should take all that was old and broken in my life and make it new again."

"I love you," he said. "Under all that toughness there really is that soft romantic green-eyed girl I saw on the picture." He traced her mouth with his finger. "I knew I loved you when I saw it," he said softly, leaning over her, kissing her again. "Remember the roses I gave you the day after the party?"

She nodded. "Yes. There were fourteen of them."

"So you noticed." He gave a crooked smile. "I wanted so much to tell you how I felt, and I couldn't. I saw the roses, remembering how Michael had once given you thirteen and I wanted to buy all the roses in the world for you and make you happy."

She swallowed, touched by the tender passion in his voice. "How did you know?"

"Wanda told me. She said you were a very romantic, sentimental girl, and that when Michael sent you thirteen roses, you were very upset. She was there when they were delivered to the apartment."

"Yes, I remember. She thought I was quite silly to let it bother me."

"Well, I didn't think it was so silly," he said and smiled. "So I bought thirteen roses plus one, some obscure symbolic gesture I didn't understand myself. I wasn't sure you'd notice, and even then you'd probably not have any idea what it was supposed to mean."

"I noticed, but I didn't understand it." She smiled at him, feeling love swell inside her. She reached out and touched his sun-warmed chest. He was beautiful, inside and out, and he was hers—a prince, a pirate, a dark-eyed Gypsy rolled into one.

They dressed slowly, feeling lazy in the afternoon sun.

"I called Wanda," she said, as she tied back her hair.

"You did? How did she react?"

"She sounded quite shaken when she heard my voice. I couldn't believe it."

"What did she say?"

"She said she didn't handle things well and she asked me to please come home and talk about it. I said I would but I didn't know when yet."

"Why don't we ask her to come here?"

"Here, why?"

"So she can be at the wedding."

Her heart stopped for a moment. "Wedding?" she asked weakly.

He grinned, drawing her back into his arms. "Yes, wedding—the ceremony people have when they get married. Of course, if you don't want to—"

"I want to."

He laughed out loud. "All right, what are we waiting for? Let's go talk to Mrs. Boersma." He took her hand and began striding down the path back to the house.

"Mrs. Boersma? Oh, yes. But you're leaving on Monday!"

"I'll come back. We just want something simple, don't we?" He stopped. "Sorry, I'm making assumptions here. What kind of wedding do you want?"

"I don't care. I mean, simple is fine. Simple is good."

"Then simple it is."

The next two weeks slipped by in a haze of unreality. After the posting of the banns, Trevor left for the Caribbean to start up the new contract, and the fact that he wasn't even around made everything even more unreal. Kim took charge of the arrangements, making reservations and organizing the dinner-dance party for after the ceremony. Raine and Trevor would spend their wedding night in the romantic bridal suite of an historic hotel in Sneek, then two days on the water in one of Max's cabin cruisers.

"Two days?" Kim asked, horrified. "What kind of honeymoon is that?"

"He's in the middle of a contract," Raine said. "He can't get away for more."

Kim shook her head. "You two are nuts. Why not wait to get married when you go to St. Barlow in another six weeks?"

"We don't want to wait."

Kim rolled her eyes and grinned. "Ah, young love," she said, as if she were eighty years old herself. "So no real honeymoon?"

"We'll have one when I come to the island. He'll be able to have some time off then." Six more weeks until the Beintemas would return and she could leave for St. Barlow. It would give her time to finish editing her manuscript, but how she was going to live without Trevor for that length of time, she had no idea. What a way to start a marriage, she thought. Well, their relationship had been strange from the beginning—an omen for an interesting life. She smiled at the thought.

Kim drove her into Amsterdam to find a wedding dress. In an exclusive little boutique Raine found just what she wanted: a short white silk dress, simple but utterly elegant. They celebrated with tea and hazelnut torte, sitting on a small terrace, watching the people go by. But once she was back at the farm, alone, without Kim's chatter to keep her distracted, Raine looked at the dress and panic assailed her. Her throat closed.

What if Trevor didn't come back?

She sat down on the bed and took in a deep gulp of air. What if history repeated itself and for the second time the man she loved disappeared from her life?

Don't be an idiot, she told herself. He loves you. After all he's gone through to get you, why would he not come back?

She could think of plenty of reasons.

Stop it! she said.

She came to her feet and hung the dress in the closet, out of sight. Maybe he'll call, she thought, as she took a quick shower and got ready for bed.

But he didn't call and she lay awake for a long time.

* * *

The day before the wedding, Raine drove to Schiphol to pick him up. She arrived at the airport much too early and walked around nervously, hyped up with coffee and anxiety. The plane was delayed and she drank some more coffee and had visions of Trevor not being on the plane. What if he wasn't? What if the wedding had to be called off? It was a simple one, yet numerous arrangements had been made. His parents were flying in this afternoon. Wanda had arrived yesterday. What if Trevor didn't make it? Just thinking of it made her break out in a cold sweat.

Her meeting with Wanda had not been a comfortable one. For the first time even Wanda had listened to Raine without interrupting her saying things like "Nonsense," "You're not seeing this right," "You should have more sense than that," and other such comments. Somehow, she and Raine had managed to come to grips with the past. Wanda had accepted the fact that Raine would not come back to work for her now or ever. Raine had learned that somewhere under all the cool control of Wanda's life, she was afraid of emotion, afraid it would make her vulnerable. It wasn't something that was likely to change much, but understanding it made it easier to accept. It made it easier to accept that Wanda had done the best she could raising her, that she had had the best of intentions, even though her methods of manipulation and control had been very destructive.

So, the two of them, their hearts and minds willing, had made peace. So much peace in fact that Wanda had offered to take over the care of the animals, after the wedding, while Raine and Trevor could spend two days on the water in one of Max's cabin cruisers.

"You're kidding!" Raine had said, practically gaping at elegant Wanda in her designer clothes.

"Why not? If you can do it, I can."

There was a certain logic to that. Besides, Wanda was a very competent person. She could change car tires in a rain storm. So Raine had initiated her in the art of feeding and watering the goats, sheep, geese and chickens.

"Do I have to milk these goats?" asked Wanda and Raine laughed.

"No. But make sure you don't let them escape or they eat the flowers and bushes."

"Goat's milk is very nutritious. I wonder if we could do anything with it in powdered form or start a cheesery on Trevor's island. Lots of goats there, he told me. I'll ask him to look into it."

Back to business. Raine smiled. She handed Wanda a piece of paper with phone numbers. "If there's any trouble with these beasts, here are the numbers to call." She was not altogether sure this was actually happening: Wanda, alone at the farm, feeding the livestock. It was incredible.

Raine glanced at the arrivals monitor, searching for Trevor's flight. The time had not changed. An Arab in flowing robes bumped into her. "Excuse me," he said politely, and moved on.

She thought of Kim's mother-in-law who was to marry them. When they'd called her, she'd asked them over for tea that same afternoon and for an hour they'd talked about their work and plans for the future while she'd taken pages of notes.

"I use these to make my speech, you see," she'd said. "I like to make my wedding speeches personal." She was more than willing to perform the ceremony in English.

Raine stared at the arrival times for the hundredth time, afraid another delay was forthcoming, but it was not. Twenty minutes later Trevor walked off the plane, dark eyes searching the crowd. Raine felt her heart leap into her throat. Running up to him, she threw her arms around him and hugged him hard.

He laughed. "Did you miss me, by any chance?"

She straightened her face. "I was too busy to miss you."

"Hah," he said softly, covering her mouth with a kiss. "Everything all right?"

She smiled, feeling her heart run over with relief. "Everything's just perfect."

They were married in the historic city hall building in Sneek, with its high-ceilinged rooms, its antique clock and coat of arms. There weren't many people in the large Council Chambers where the ceremony took place, but it was a happy gathering. Wanda was resplendent in a gorgeous designer creation. Trevor's parents were there, a tall handsome couple. Despite the short notice, they had managed to make arrangements to come over to attend the wedding. Raine had been a little concerned about their reaction to the sudden news of their son's wedding, and the fact they hadn't even met their future daughter-in-law.

They did not seem to hold it against him.

"He's never done anything the normal way," his father said to Raine with a laugh. His mother smiled warmly and patted Raine's hand. "Don't worry about it," she said reassuringly, "we're used to it." Raine loved them on the spot.

It was a beautiful ceremony. Mrs. Boersma, in her formal justice of the peace robe, had a special word for Trevor's parents and Wanda, thanking them for coming all the way from America, and how much it must mean for the happy couple to have them there. She had crafted a wonderful wedding speech, very personal and with warm touches of humor.

It couldn't have been better.

After the ceremony, the party moved to the restaurant by the lake for drinks, dinner and dancing. It was late when Raine and Trevor finally arrived at the hotel in Sneek, but Raine was too exhilarated to feel tired. She couldn't keep her eyes off Trevor who looked quite devastating in his dark suit. It was hard to believe this was really happening, that the two of them were actually married. She wrapped her arms around him and held him tight. "I can't believe it's true," she whispered.

"It's true." He smiled into her eyes. "I have a present for you." Moving out of her embrace, he took a flat package out of the closet and handed it to her. She knew what it was as soon as her hands closed over it. Hastily she began to take off the paper and the protective coverings.

It was a framed reproduction of the painting of the two dolls, identical to the one hanging in the Beintemas' house.

"Oh, Trevor," she whispered. "Thank you."

"Look on the back," he said.

She turned it over. There was a card taped to the cardboard backing, a few lines scrawled on it in Trevor's bold handwriting.

Our love will change over the years, but to me it will always be new and you will never be too old to cherish.

Trevor

The words blurred before her eyes. Gently she put the painting down and wrapped her arms around him once more. He was hers, this big, dark stranger from a faraway island.

"I'll love you always," she whispered.

* * * * *